I0760970

Neanderthal Seeks Duchess

LONDON LADIES EMBROIDERY BOOK 1

LANEY HATCHER

WWW.SMARTYPANTSROMANCE.COM

Print Edition
ISBN: 978-1-959097-47-1

Developmental Edits: Emerald Edits
Editing: Write On Editing

Dedication

To anyone who has ever felt like the supporting role in their own life story

One

"Bollocks."

I gazed down the length of my pale green bodice and noticed the unfortunate three-inch tear in the fabric. Twisting my head and peering over my shoulder did nothing to improve my situation. My gown was still torn. I suddenly wished I had my friend Fiona's skill with a needle. The duchess had embroidery talent unmatched in our circle.

I closed my eyes and tried to think of a solution to this problem, but only succeeded in reminding myself that my luck, as of late, had taken a turn. The decision to attend Lord Sullivan's social gathering of the season only served to further the gossips of the ton. I had hoped to continue on, business as usual, but the rend in my garment, if discovered, would only add new fodder for the things whispered about me in ballrooms. Particularly this ballroom.

This luxurious home in the heart of Mayfair was the site of the most sought-after invitation this season. I was still unsure why I was included among the guest list. I had not been introduced to the old duke nor his socializing son, Lord Quinton Jameson. He held the courtesy title of the Earl Sullivan while his father retained the dukedom. Although gossips indicated father and son were quite estranged in their relationship and had not been seen together in an age. The Duke and Duchess of Benton had remained in the country following their eldest son's death years prior. I was told, despite never having inquired, Lord Sullivan himself had been absent from society for many years. It all seemed very mysterious. This gathering at the family's impressive London home, one of the many Benton estates, was said to be Lord Sullivan's reintroduction to the *ton*. Nevertheless, I was unacquainted with the entire family. I couldn't pick Quinton Jameson out of a lineup of lords if pressed.

My friend, Lady Eliza, merely hoped showing my face and my fortitude at the Earl's ball would put gossipmongers in their place. But with the latest development involving my gown and my exposed… Well, posterior, that might no longer be possible.

As the peculiar bluestocking daughter of a marquess, I was already regarded as an oddity associated with scandal. But my recent broken courtship with Lord John Holesome, the Earl Fairbanks and son of the Duke of Archford, intensified the chin-wagging among my peers.

My father took the news of our broken courtship and subsequent non-engagement rather badly. While I remained the aging middle daughter of a marquess, the title was all we had. Through debt and family scandal, we were woefully low on funds and reputation. John had promised to cover my father's debts and turn a blind eye to my sisters' scandals in making me his countess in the future.

Apparently my father couldn't abide my decision to end my relationship with the Earl Fairbanks. He'd demanded that I return to our country home in Hampshire to avoid further gossip if I couldn't find it within myself to resume the courtship. Father deemed the remainder of my London season wholly unnecessary since I had made the decision to insult an earl and future duke with my scruples.

Alas, I had no plans to return to the country and be swept under the rug the way my sister was. I had my own business to see to in London. In this instance, my father's complete and total disinterest in me came quite in handy. He only needed me when I could be of use. As I was no longer courting a wealthy and reputable earl, I was pleasantly out of sight and out of mind. I was however, blessed by a close circle of friends, several of which offered to sponsor me for the remainder of the season. Ultimately, I decided to remain with my dearest friend, Lady Eliza Morgan. And thus, how I'd landed myself in my current predicament.

"Damnation," I murmur again, looking down.

If possible, the gaping seam between my bodice and skirt had grown. Only moments ago, the heel of my slipper had caught the back edge of my dress when I stood. Deciding the ladies' retiring room would be the best place to assess the damage, I made my escape.

With the quartet playing a lovely tune and the attendees enjoying the dance floor—Eliza included—I tried to unobtrusively maneuver around the edges of the ballroom until I spotted the entrance to the retiring room. In my first lucky stroke of the evening, the room was blessedly empty. Not even a servant in sight. I paused, listening intently as the sound of footfalls met my ears. I peeked my head out into the corridor on the blind hope Lady Eliza was making her way toward me. No Eliza in the hallway. However, there was a gentleman. And a dapper looking gentleman at that. What a strange thought to have at a time like this. But I supposed he was universally handsome, and even in this disastrous situation, I could appreciate his form. Tall and rather dashing, the gentleman had dark hair and very light blue eyes. A black topcoat, dove gray waistcoat, and a snowy cravat completed the overall impression of an attractive male. A general sense of intimidating beauty was all I could really discern before I retreated into my hiding place once again.

Leaving thoughts of the elegant gentleman in the hallway where they belonged, I considered my options. Perhaps a maid would come through shortly. I could then have a servant deliver a message to Eliza. Huzzah!

No longer hearing the footsteps of the passing gentleman, I again inched into the hallway to try my luck.

I immediately stumbled back, once again catching my hem.

He was *right there*. Standing directly outside the door to the ladies' retiring room, was the dashing gentleman.

My abrupt and indelicate retreat was punctuated by the sound of tearing fabric.

My eyes went wide as did the gentlemen's.

The ensuing silence was suffocating. Finally, the unknown man spoke.

"I beg your pardon, my lady. Are you quite well?" His deep voice rasped quizzically, eyes narrowed as he searched my face. He seemed to be cataloguing my features and his expectant gaze momentarily stunned me.

"Yes. Quite," I forced out, unable to believe my rotten luck as a warm flush began to crawl up my neck. I attempted to straighten back from the doorway but could feel my heel still snagged on the back of my dress.

Riiiip. I paused immediately and one eyebrow rose on the gentleman's stern face.

"Quite," he confirmed in a disbelieving tone.

I risked a small shake of my foot in an attempt to dislodge my slipper while nodding most assuredly. "Indeed. Quite. Wel—"

Riiiiip. I stopped abruptly, eyes widening. Another black brow rose to join the first.

"Are you sure?" he remarked uncertainly, eyes sparkling.

Riiiiiiiiiiiiiiip. Sigh.

"Yes. I was merely attempting to gain the attention of my friend so we could be on our way," I said brightly, ignoring the sound of ripping fabric and the true meaning behind his inquisition. I was likewise distracted from my predicament by his handsomeness. The brief glimpse in the hallway hadn't done justice to his lovely form. And he was that… Very well formed.

"It's a bit early to be leaving, is it not?" he said, looking discretely behind himself toward the sounds of merriment coming from the main ballroom. Without giving me a chance to answer, he continued, "Are you not enjoying yourself?"

"It's a lovely ball," I countered. "I've merely had a trying day. I think it best if I take my leave… Especially in my… um, current situation." I ended the statement on a near whisper, mostly to myself. But I realized he must have heard my hushed admission as his mouth quirked up just a bit at the corner.

And then the gentleman slowly leaned to the side as if to see around me. Despite knowing I was alone in the doorway and room beyond, I turned in tandem with him. I realized too late he was investigating "my current situation" and the initial ripping sound that punctuated our meeting in the hallway… and the subsequent audible fabric destruction as I attempted to regain my posture. I gasped, clutching my skirt to my bodice above my ample buttocks and whirled back to face him.

My abrupt spin elicited one final *riiiiiip*, and I could feel my heel's newfound freedom. *Finally.*

"Ah, yes. Your current situation. I see," he choked out even as a faint pink tinged the tips of his ears.

Was I detecting mirth in his tone? Well, I never...

"Yes, um—" I cleared my throat delicately while also hoping the ground would open up and swallow me whole. "As you can see, it is of utmost importance I make a hasty exit. Lovely ball or not," I said, eyes moving over the hallway beyond.

I found suddenly I could not maintain eye contact with this beautiful creature. I would wager he never associated with women like me. Tall and awkward, prone to saying all manner of oddities. He seemed every inch the polished lord, and there were a multitude of lovely inches to gaze upon.

"Perhaps I can be of assistance," he offered, bringing my attention back to his handsome face. He continued before I could object, "I'm happy to lend the use of my carriage. Come, I'll escort you through the kitchens to the servants' entrance. We'll attract less attention, and you can be on your way out of... your current situation."

And without waiting for my response, he placed my hand on his arm and we made our way down the corridor away from the sounds of music and frivolity. And away from Eliza.

The more I thought about dragging Eliza and her lovely father away from Lord Sullivan's ball, the more I regretted my own clumsy nature. They shouldn't have to suffer by mere association with me. And they would be disappointed to miss the social event of the season.

I didn't know this man leading me through hallways. But I did know he was a gentleman and his offer of escape was well-timed. One does not look a gift lord in the mouth.

However, I did finally manage to voice an immediate concern, "My lord, I beg your pardon, but we have not been introduced. You cannot simply escort me from the ball."

His steps, and subsequently mine, slowed as the gentleman considered my objection. "Of course, my lady. But please understand, I'll do what I can to see you safely on your way," he murmured as his gaze found mine.

"That's… kind of you, seeing as we are unacquainted. I'm Jane, by the way. Lady Jane Morrison," I said in an attempt to learn his identity in turn. If my subconscious had its way, I would be calling him Lord Dashingham of the Hallway Encounter. Lord Dashing, indeed.

Before he could return my introduction, the newly appointed Lord Dashing halted abruptly. All at once, the reason for his stillness became clear. Voices. And footsteps approaching. Reacting to the threat of sudden discovery, the gentleman calmly directed us through a nearby entryway and quickly pushed the door closed with a quiet snick.

We appeared to be in a darkened study or library. The moonlight filtering in the far window provided little light, as did the fire banked in the fireplace. I knew well enough to remain quiet as the sounds of voices grew nearer. Being discovered in this secluded room with an unnamed gentleman and no chaperone would only succeed in further ruination of my reputation. From the noises in the hallway, I could deduce two young men were conversing. The lord at my side stiffened while I maintained my silence and clutched my ruined skirt.

I waited nervously for the danger to abate. My eyes vacillated between the unknown gentleman and my surroundings. So many books! Yet, no matter how intrigued I was by the room beyond, my attention occasionally alighted on this stranger's large form. He was tall with dark hair made even darker by what little light seeped in through the window. His bladelike nose and sharp cheekbones culminated in an intensely masculine face.

Despite my obliviousness at times, even I could appreciate the symmetry of his features. Lord Dashing was attractive. He would be sought-after by the marriage-minded mamas and their daughters.

I wonder who he is…

My musings were interrupted as my roving gaze caught sight of the bookcase to my right and snagged on a familiar book spine. I smiled involuntarily. *The Count of Monte Cristo*. It was one of my favorites. Vengeance and justice, action and adventure. What's not to love?

Eventually the footsteps and discussion outside the door receded. The relief I felt at avoiding discovery and subsequent ruination was profound. The only sounds now were from our deep breaths filling the space. Realizing the nearness and heat from the man at my side, I unthinkingly blurted in an exaggerated whisper, "Have you read Dumas?"

I fixed my eyes on the book's spine as I continued quietly and quickly, giving Lord Dashing no opportunity to respond to my unplanned inquiry. Anything to distract myself from this lord's glorious face. "It is a fairly ruthless story filled with vigilante justice. I do not have personal experience with that sort of thing myself, but it makes for a very entertaining novel." Absurdity and handsomeness made my words run all over each other.

The nameless gentleman followed my line of sight and narrowed his eyes in response to my unprompted ramblings. "Is that so?" he ventured.

"Yes. I like to think if someone wronged me so grievously, I, too, would dedicate my life and fortune to enacting justice in all its forms."

He paused, perhaps in confusion, but eventually marshalled his thoughts. "I suppose there is a certain entertainment, as you say, in witnessing vengeance performed on the deserving. But perhaps a life dedicated to enacting justice is not as fulfilling as Monsieur Dumas makes it out to be."

His voice had gained confidence as he spoke. I wasn't sure if we were referring to Edmond Dantès any longer, and my gaze turned speculative in response.

I should have probably chosen a more appropriate topic of conversation. Nevertheless, my words spilled forth. "I suppose that is true. But how often do people outside of grand novels get to dedicate their lives to revenge?" I managed with a curious smile.

"More often than one would think," came his unexpectedly soft-spoken reply.

My smile fell with a growing awareness.

What was happening here?

We were gazing oddly at each other, this stranger and I. Assessing and reassessing. Eyes narrowing and gears turning. Seconds passed that felt like an eternity steeped in intensity.

A momentary glance at the closed door and then, "I think it's safe to venture out." Lord Dashing motioned silently, breaking our connection.

Fine by me. I was eager to put the awkwardness of our interaction behind me. My skin felt itchy and tight. Further proof I was completely incapable of having a normal conversation with a handsome stranger.

Focus more on the weather, Jane.

Don't speak aloud every random thought in your head.

Make passing conversation about... gowns and... horses.

Alas.

My companion carefully opened the door and reemerged in the passageway with me at his side, occasionally sending questioning glances my way. I could tell the ridiculousness of the situation was even affecting him. I had the strangest urge to laugh aloud. But I bit down on my wavering bottom lip until I felt quite sure of its good behavior.

Despite my giddy relief at our near discovery, levity deserted me entirely as we encountered witnesses. Following in the gentleman's wake through the kitchens, surprised servants quickly averted their gazes and went about their business.

Who was this man?

I wondered inwardly if the staff would gossip about the handsome lord and the tall, auburn-haired lady in their midst, but one glance at Lord Dashing's expression made me think otherwise. He either commanded loyalty or fear. I couldn't determine which. But somehow, I didn't think Lord Sullivan's servants would be recounting the tale of misplaced guests trespassing through the kitchens.

Once the damp night air was upon my skin, I breathed a small sigh of relief. Perhaps I would make it home in my ruined dress with none the wiser. Well, none the wiser aside from this mysterious gentleman. My cheeks heated at the thought. Luckily the cover of darkness shielded my embarrassment. Of course my private shame would be witnessed by the most handsome man I'd ever seen.

Of course.

Without noticing my renewed humiliation, my savior for the evening led me past the mews to a waiting carriage. It was dark in color and looked like all the other carriages parked along the drive waiting for their passengers to spill from the merriment within… at a much later hour.

“I trust Vincent here to see you home safely,” he said earnestly, indicating the driver of the carriage.

Some commotion near the house drew the lord’s attention, and he hastily turned back to me with a quietly uttered curse.

In a low rasp, he said, “I’ll send word to Lady Eliza of your absence. Wait for me inside the carriage. I have another matter I wish discuss with you. Just—” He again looked behind us toward the house. Voices had risen and I could make out several men moving in our direction. “Just wait for me inside,” he finished on a rush.

Despite my confusion at his request, I needed to express my gratitude. “Thank you, my lord… for everything,” my quiet statement died in the growing space between us as he darted away. Finally the shadows of the house swallowed him as he intercepted the men I’d spotted earlier.

With a confused and regretful sigh, I boarded the carriage with Vincent’s assistance. He offered me a friendly smile and pointedly ignored the fact I was keeping my dress together in my other hand. Despite Lord Dashing’s command to wait for him in the carriage, I found I simply could not. The humiliation of the last few days, the interminable gossip, and my current situation did not allow for clandestine meetings in the backs of carriages. No matter how dashing the gentleman. I was tempting fate as it was by accepting a stranger’s assistance in exiting the ball. He had done enough. And I couldn’t afford to do any more.

I would accept the gift of a loaned carriage. I would return to Eliza’s home and attempt to figure out the rest of my life.

I kindly directed Vincent to my desired location. As I gazed out the window of the carriage, my eyes searched the darkness behind Benton House. Brows wrinkling in sudden confusion, I couldn’t help but wonder belatedly, how did Lord Dashing know to inform Lady Eliza of my particular whereabouts? I didn’t recall having mentioned our association.

The lurch of the horses jolted my thoughts. And as the carriage bounced along the drive, another thought rose above all the others.

I still didn’t know his name.

Two

"Well, if you ask me, Lord Fairbanks had some nerve assuming you would retain his suit after placing his exceedingly large nose where it did not belong," Cassandra proclaimed from her position on the settee.

Murmurs of agreement rose from the assembled ladies around the drawing room. Our weekly ladies' salon was currently taking place at Fiona's stately manor near Hyde Park.

"Is his nose quite large?" I asked quizzically.

"Quite."

"Lord, yes."

"Unequivocally."

"Like a bird of prey landed on his wee face." This last observation was from Miss Ashleigh Winstead, often brutal in her straightforward Scottish honesty. The majority of the gathered ladies joined in her laughter.

"Well, I suppose I never noticed," I added weakly.

"Jane, I imagine there is a lot about Lord Fairbanks you never noticed," Fiona began.

"But—"

"I am not saying it is a deficiency on your part," Fiona quickly added. "I just meant perhaps you do not know Lord Fairbanks as well as you had hoped. I never got the impression you cared a great deal for him. Am I wrong, Jane?"

"I…" Drifting and unsure of my feelings, I considered Fiona's gentle insinuation. Did I still care about John? Had we been a love match? My mouth felt a bit dry and I forced a swallow.

As was Fiona's way, she was encouraging me to think for myself while also providing support in the loving nature of friendship. I had known the duchess for some time. I would be forever grateful for her gentle guidance in society. She had discovered me, and Eliza as well, hovering on the edge of a ballroom several years earlier. As the middle daughter of a marquess out in society with a scandalous dead mother and two scandalous sisters, my ability to hide away at social events had become a necessity. Fiona was exceedingly generous to take me under her wing. No one would dare question her alliances, and taking me on helped ease my way into drawing rooms, musicales, and ladies' afternoon tea. I knew what Fiona was saying regarding my feelings for John had merit, and I valued her honesty.

I did not love John. I was at ease with him and had grown quite complacent in his attentions. We danced. We went riding together. We had picnics in the park. But I rarely thought of John beyond his role in my life. A convenience. A means to a decidedly uneventful end. I was a woman. I had no dowry and a ruined family reputation. I needed a husband whether I wanted one or not. John had fit the role. And I had let him.

Considering Fiona's assertion, perhaps I just *thought* I was exceedingly happy with the match I had made. John… John was a friend, someone with whom I felt I could be entirely myself. He didn't seem to mind my oddities, often calling me endearing and unique. And my preference for books over people regularly amused him. I thought John was happy with me, and I thought we could be happy together. Our courtship should have led to an engagement, a happy union between our families.

However, John's recent identification in a dreadful scandal sheet, *The Ton Tattler*, caused me to reevaluate our relationship. He was caught in a compromising position at a society function with an unidentified and unwed lady. My relationship with John came under scrutiny in the article. I'd been made a fool of by the very gossip I so despised. When confronted, John didn't deny the claim. He called it a momentary weakness and begged my forgiveness.

Many ladies in my position would simply look the other way when suffering a public indiscretion from their intended. According to the rumors, I should have been thanking my lucky stars the son of a duke still craved my companionship or any association with my family. Despite public opinion on the subject of my future, I disagreed with John's actions and couldn't abide his unfaithfulness. So I ended our courtship.

Perhaps my perceived oddities made me incapable of tolerating his disloyalty. It no longer mattered. He was now free to pursue his mystery lady from the rumored report. And I was equally unattached, mourning the loss of… something. Future and friendship? Perhaps merely complacency?

Fiona was right. There were indeed a great number of details I never bothered with. John's nose being the smallest of them. Figuratively. Not literally.

"It is understandable to want to reflect on your feelings, Jane. We're not trying to overwhelm you," Lady Mary Harris confessed as her eyes rose from her embroidery to meet mine in encouragement.

"No, you are quite right, Fi," I said to the duchess but returned Mary's sympathetic smile. "I think I was using John to serve a purpose. I don't know him nearly as well as I should. And I'm not nearly as disturbed as I should be over his apparent deception. It's time I reevaluate my future."

"That's the spirit." Cassandra raised her teacup in an encouraging toast from across the table.

"Well, you can plan and plot as long as you need," Lady Eliza reassured me.

Fellow former wallflower Eliza and I had met on the outskirts of the *ton*. We made quite the pair—the tall, awkward one and the sharp, sad widow—but she was my dearest friend. Her Grace, Fiona Bowen, the Duchess of Compton, rescued us both with her kind attentions. Invitations here, introductions there, and we were now elegant acquaintances of a duchess and accepted in any circle in London.

Our own inner circle had grown and expanded over the years, and we all had the duchess to thank for such genuine friendships. In a society where gossip and information are prized above all else, honest and sincere affection is not commonplace. Marriageable ladies and their matchmaking mamas are competitive and cruel. I felt irrationally lucky to be surrounded by women who supported me no matter what. Even steeped in scandal and near ruination, Fiona, Eliza, Cassandra, Mary, Ashleigh, and Kathleen offered me endless encouragement and kindness. And laughter and joy. Above all others, they were the most entertaining ladies of my acquaintance.

"Thank you, Eliza. You are a true friend." Allowing me to remain in her London house, Eliza had afforded me the opportunity to claim my future as my own. She smiled back sweetly while adjusting a blond curl near her ear.

"So, are you going to tell everyone about your exit from the Benton ball?" Eliza asked mischievously while taking a nonchalant sip from her dish of tea.

Curious glances emerged from behind embroidery hoops to assess my response and, no doubt, the heat quickly climbing up my cheeks.

"I take it back. You are not a true friend. You are a scheming schemer." Flaring my nostrils, I met her blinding smile. Her blue eyes sparkled, and truthfully I could not intentionally dim her light. Despite my jesting, she *was* a true friend. And these bouts of humor and joviality were very rare for my serious friend.

"Do tell, dear Janie. The ladies are waiting." I feared a tooth might crack under the intensity of Eliza's glee.

"I was at the Earl Sullivan's ball. I don't recall seeing you in attendance, Jane. I remember Eliza making a hasty exit and excusing herself from our circle however," Cassandra supplied helpfully. "Do you have something to share with the sitting room, my dear?" Tossing her embroidery aside with a flourish, Cassandra leaned forward in her seat and gave me her full attention.

"Might as well." Sighing in defeat, I took a fortifying bite of biscuit and chucked my useless embroidery hoop aside as well. "I ripped my dress and was smuggled from the ball by a mysterious gentleman in an effort to avoid gossip." My pronouncement was met with silence and a great deal of blinking.

"Aye, of course. That is how I exit all society events," Ashleigh intoned from her seat by the fire. "When yelling 'fire' does not do the trick."

"Ha!" I belatedly murmured, "I did not think of that." Meeting her smirk, I continued my tale of the disastrous dress debacle. When I recounted the events in the hallway with Lord Dashing and the subsequent fleeing in the carriage, no one was smiling any longer. Wide-eyed stares regarded me as I concluded my report of the evening.

"Jane! You went with him… a … a stranger! Who is he?" Fiona inquired urgently amid her sputtering. Fiona never sputtered. She was utterly unflappable. I must have truly shocked her.

Beyond the urgency of my escape from the ball, I had surprised myself as well. Survival was paramount and I could not envision enduring the scandal of the *ton* had I remained at the ball one second longer. It was fight or flight, and my wings had unfurled without second thought. Lord Dashing had provided the means and my instincts took over.

I can guiltily admit it was nice to have had an accomplice in my efforts of escape. Typically I do all my running on my own. Lord Dashing made me feel supported and in just this one instance, I was grateful for the rescue. Was that so wrong? But Fiona was, as usual, correct. He was a stranger with origins, honesty, and integrity unknown.

"Who cares who he is? It matters not. He was obviously a kind-hearted gentleman in attendance. Describe his eyes again, Jane," Cassandra helpfully added with a ridiculous wiggle of her eyebrows.

"Fiona, I must confess, he never provided his name. But Cassandra is right. He was obviously a gentleman, dressed in attendance for the Earl Sullivan's ball," I reassured my friend in an effort to assuage her obvious worry. "And, Cassandra, they were an icy blue unseen in nature," I concluded on a sigh.

She gave me a little wink and shifted on her seat in excitement. "He sounds quite handsome. I wish you had a likeness of him to share."

"Aye, Cassandra. If only there was a way to stealthily draw someone's likeness without their knowledge in order to show one's friends. So we can all delight in his *icy blue eyes* and handsome smile. That is important to note in this situation. Only ye, my little lamb," Ashleigh remarked dryly with an indulgent smile and shake of her head. Cassandra cackled devilishly from her position and patted a bright red tendril back into place.

"Well, he didn't really smile," I interjected abruptly. I didn't want them to think this lord was all flirtation and charm. "He was quite forthright and stoic. Reserved, if I had to put a finger on it."

"But he obviously took an interest in you, my lady." I was surprised to hear this softly spoken statement from Kathleen. She had remained quiet and observant thus far during our afternoon discussions.

"Why do you say that, Kathleen? He was simply being a gentleman. I'm sure he would have behaved similarly with any lady in the same situation," I insisted.

"Ha! As if just any young lady could find herself in such a situation, Jane," chortled Cassandra.

"Shush, Cassandra," Fiona admonished with an eye roll. "What makes you think he was interested, Kat?" the duchess asked gently. Our sweet Kathleen was still a bit skittish with the large personalities in our circle.

"I think the gentleman must have wanted to spend time with you, perhaps get to know you a bit. He could have summoned a servant to escort you to the mews or simply alerted Lady Eliza to your distress," Kat said quietly. Her voice trailed off at the end, perhaps regretting her decision to draw attention to herself in the first place.

Miss Kathleen Tannen was our newest addition and, at times, seemed very uncomfortable during our Tuesday gatherings in the company of society ladies who spoke their minds with little regard to propriety. Kat had arrived rather unexpectedly to the duchess's household. After a fortuitous meeting and subsequent introduction from a common acquaintance, Kat came to be employed by the Bowens. Her past was a bit murky and unclear, but that was a story for another day. She was currently the beloved governess of Fiona's adorable children, Master Jack and little Grace. The duchess insisted on Kat joining our group on our Tuesday afternoons together. Like a lovely shy turtle, she was slowly but surely coming out of her shell.

While we all pondered this intelligent observation that, yes, Lord Dashing could have simply avoided further interaction with me by simply passing along a message to Eliza, Kathleen's gaze remained on the teacup in her hand without further comment. She seemed to want to dissolve into the lavish carpets of the sitting room.

"Hmm." Fiona cleared her throat delicately and narrowed her brown eyes in my direction. "Yes, well, Kathleen, that is a very good point. Perhaps he did take an interest in our lovely Jane."

I snorted inelegantly. "Yes. I'm sure he was drawn to my femininity and utter gracefulness, what with towering over all the other ladies in attendance, hiding from said ladies, and *oh*, ripping my blasted dress right in front of him."

"Some gentlemen like tall, statuesque ladies, Jane. Everything lines up a bit better," an amused Cassandra quickly interjected.

"Cassandra!" came a chorus from our assembly. Their scandalized outrage failed to hide their smiles at our delightful friend.

Lady Cassandra Fields was the brightest and brashest among us. A diamond of the first water, Cassandra had her pick of suitors and numerous proposals. With flame red hair and a luminous personality to match, the dowry from her father, the Earl of Crait, was wholly unnecessary. Cassandra was the belle of any ball and our most outlandish and entertaining friend. It was indeed a mystery as to why she had yet married.

"Truthfully, Jane. You are gorgeous inside and out. I've seen many gentlemen admiring your, um, physical attributes," Eliza cut in with a glance in the general direction of my décolletage.

With a quick sip of tea and an eyeroll, I acquiesced, "Yes, meandering gazes of men do make their way in my direction. But my looks and my mannerisms are not fashionable, and you well know it. Gentlemen, and Lord Dashing undoubtedly included, do not desire large ladies with wild auburn hair, no dowry, and a preference for books."

But a small voice in the far reaches of my consciousness was whispering *what if*? What if my mystery gentleman desired my company? What if he admired my figure, or more importantly, my mind?

"Well, perhaps ye should not lump yer Lord Dashing in with these English lordlings of dubious taste. He did, in fact, wish to remain in yer company. Jane, why did ye leave? He told ye to stay in the carriage and wait for him. Now we will never know what he wanted with ye," Ashleigh reminded me.

"She did the right thing. The *safe* thing, Ash. Her reputation was at risk simply by being in his presence unchaperoned. Jane is exceedingly lucky she went unobserved by members of society," said Lady Mary Harris.

If anyone understood the pressures and constraints on unmarried ladies of the *ton*, it was Mary. Betrothed since birth, Mary played by all the rules expected of her. I have never understood how she, lovely and beloved, could meet the demands of her family by remaining true to an engagement while her betrothed gallivanted across the continent doing as he pleased. I should value Mary's praise of how I handled the situation and conclusion of the evening. If there was ever a lady to imitate, it would be my beautiful friend. Gorgeous blond ringlets, wide blue eyes, and a slender figure, she was loveliness personified. Adored by one and all. A sought-after conversationalist, brilliant dinner companion, unmatched on the dance floor, and well regarded by nearly everyone, Mary's loveliness was wasted on a fiancé who did not value her or even recognize her. But she was accepting of her situation and would not hear Lord David's name besmirched. I had learned to tighten the reins on my wayward lips when the subject arose.

I acknowledged Mary's assessment with a nod. "Of course. I had taken enough liberties earlier in the evening. I knew waiting for Lord Dashing to return would tempt fate." I was no longer giving fate the opportunity to manage my affairs. I had no suitor. That meant no offer of marriage and no husband to repair my family's reputation. Yet I still had my plans and my own discreet business to attend to in London. I was taking my future in my own capable hands.

I did not, however, feel the need to relay this internal commitment to my friends. They would just worry. Especially Mary and Fiona.

Kathleen excused herself to check on the children despite Fiona's urging for her to remain. And we resumed our blasted embroidery but continued the afternoon with laughter and light.

Our teatime conversation turned away from my disastrous evening at Benton House. But my thoughts kept returning to Lord Dashing and our strange time together. Even if he found me as interesting or intriguing as I found him, it mattered not. It wasn't as if we would see each other again. He would remain a beautiful mystery and an entertaining story for Tuesday afternoon tea.

Despite my recent bad luck, the ladies surrounding me had provided a helpful reminder of the many blessings in my life. A life I was determined to claim as my own from this point forward.

"Apologies, Lady Morrison, but Her Grace is not accepting callers at this time."

"But we have an appointment, Jennings. Every Friday morning at half past eleven," I protested. I sounded desperate even to my own ears. Jennings must have heard it too because he gave a sympathetic wince.

"Yes, my lady. However, at *this* time, the Duchess of Archford is no longer accepting visitors," Jennings asserted.

"Yes, well. I will be on my way then." I gathered my parasol, tightened my hold on my reticule, and hurried down the rain-slick stairs in front of Archford House. Of course I felt awkward attempting to meet with the Duchess of Archford. Breaking my courtship with her son did not mean I would evade my responsibility to the duchess and her estate, however. I was honor-bound to maintain our appointment… Or so I thought.

My frustrations had only grown as the morning progressed, and the murky gray drizzle did nothing to improve upon my mood. After being rejected at three separate standing appointments this morning, I finally admitted to myself something was afoot in Mayfair.

Having never relied upon my family name to open doors among the *ton* (that would have been an utter waste of time), it seemed the latest scandal involving myself and John had created another divide among myself and my peers. My plans to control my own future in my own way were already falling apart.

When one is a lady in London, one does not have many options beyond landing a titled and moneyed lord. With that option seemingly behind me, I had hoped to continue managing my own affairs. And yet it seemed fate had once again attempted to thwart all my good intentions.

My father was a gambler, and a poor one at that. The loss and embarrassment of my mother had loosened his less than tenuous hold on reality and provided him ample opportunity to gamble away our fortune, my dowry included. In consequence, I have never looked to my father for pin money or any other substantial means or allowance. I had lived in his modest home in London until recently. But I have always known I could not approach my father for anything even remotely frivolous. A new dress? *Wasteful, Jane.* New books? *We have a library full already.*

Therefore, I knew from an early age I would need to take care of myself. My odd profession of sorts had been thrust upon me for the most part.

In my early acquaintance with Her Grace Fiona Bowen, the Duchess of Compton, I often remarked on her extreme competence. She seemed so proficient and wise. Fiona was responsible for a large household in London with several other holdings in the country as well. Her husband was often away managing businesses, investments, and agricultural affairs for the dukedom, so much of the accounting was left to Fiona. She had two small children and an active social and philanthropic life. During one of my early visits to her home, I offered my assistance. I was so grateful for her friendship; I wanted to be able to return it in some tangible way. She assured me that was not how friendship worked, and yet it was a concept I struggled with. How could I earn my place? What was she possibly gaining by my presence in her life? Our friendship seemed terribly one-sided and I simply wanted to even things up a bit, balance the scales of friendship. So, I offered to help manage her household accounts.

With my propensity for mathematics and affinity for the language of numbers, I had managed our own family's household affairs for some time. As a young adolescent, my mother realized my usefulness and utilized my abilities. And once she died, my father did not concern himself with trivial affairs such as the running of the estate and payment of the staff. Truthfully, my father did not concern himself with much of anything. He rarely left his London home and would spend all his days confined to his own misery. I continued my role as lady of the house and manager of affairs with no one the wiser. I was going to have to continue my duties from afar if the remaining servants were to be paid. There was not much money left for anything else. My thoughtless father had spent it all. I reminded myself to get in touch with our solicitor to ensure the estate was functioning.

Once I assured Fiona I could easily handle this aspect of her demanding life, she seemed grateful to have one less item on her to-do list. Something about her husband, Gregory, not trusting solicitors. Alas, I was happy to contribute to our friendship in a way that was quantifiable. So we continued thusly. And then Fiona had introduced me to a friend who needed similar assistance. And then another acquaintance requiring regular aid with their accounts and holdings. After several years of utilizing my mathematical talents, I had twelve households I regularly advised in all financial matters unbeknownst to the male aristocrats of those same households. I felt needed and useful. I also felt secretive and well-versed in secrets of the *ton.*

I was paid handsomely for my services and my savings would fund my uncertain future if I could continue on the path before me. But perhaps most importantly, the compensation I received rewarded my discretion. In return, the duchesses, countesses, viscountesses, widows, and proper ladies were quick with an invitation and a recommendation. My patronage was spread by word-of-mouth in drawing rooms all across Mayfair, whispered behind fans, and bragged upon by the same ladies who would have once turned up their noses at me.

I, Lady Jane Morrison, daughter of a cuckold and a scandalous adulteress, was a sought-after commodity in London. Or at least I was… Until today when I had been summarily dismissed by two countesses and finally a duchess. At least Jennings had the courtesy to flash me a sympathetic look before booting me from the property.

I feared the events of the morning would prove the new standard for my services. If the ladies of the peerage decided the gossip surrounding John made me untouchable, then a professional pariah I would be. I had savings and could support myself for a time, but plans would need to be made. I needed a solution for the near future. More than my financial circumstances would be impacted by the change in my status. John's mother was one of my first clients, for lack of a better term, and it seemed as if she was not in agreement with my decision to end my courtship with her son.

My involvement with the Duchess of Archford was how John and I met initially. A monthly meeting ran long and John's unexpected appearance in the old duke's study provided an interesting encounter. Instead of being met with rage and offense, John was bemused and curious. I was initially confused by his interest in me, but after a time, I believed him to be sincere in his suit. John paid me compliments and sought my attention. And his mother was kind and encouraged our attachment. John never revealed the secret of my involvement in the household accounts to his father, the duke. And he supported my efforts to better my situation with what he referred to as my "little hobby." He seemed to understand my determination to distance myself from my father. John did not want me to have to rely on the man. But upon further reflection, I saw now that perhaps John wanted my reliance all for himself.

I had allowed these wayward thoughts long enough. I would put forth every effort with my remaining clients and if I continued to be turned away… Well, I would just figure something else out. I had savings. I would be okay. Obviously I could not remain in Eliza's household forever. And I refused to be carted off to the country as my father intended.

"Damn," I muttered under my breath as I bustled the short distance to the home Eliza shared with her father, Dr. Finley.

However, upon encountering the butler at Eliza's house, I actually *wanted* to turn around and leave instead of being admitted into the foyer.

"Apologies, my lady, but Lord Fairbanks insisted upon waiting for your arrival. Lady Eliza sent Meg in with some refreshments, and he is awaiting your return in the blue drawing room," Eliza's butler, Botstein, quietly explained. He gathered my cloak, parasol, and other sodden items before ushering me down the hall.

I entered the open doorway of the drawing room and encountered a tense face-off between my former suitor John Holesome, the Earl Fairbanks, the future Duke of Archford, and Lady Eliza Morgan, my formidable friend. Meg, Eliza's lady's maid, was pouring tea into lovely blue dishes and seemed undaunted by the tension nearly choking everyone else in the room.

"Thank you, Meg," Eliza spit out through gritted teeth as her maid turned and fled. Perhaps she had noted the palpable hostility radiating from her mistress after all.

My soggy arrival finally registered and Lord Fairbanks hopped to attention. "Jane, dearest, you have returned! I was hopeful we could speak in private."

"That would be highly improper as you well know, my lord." Eliza relished delivering this lesson on propriety. "I should be delighted to remain as chaperone and support of my dearest friend." Her blue eyes were narrowed in challenge and alight with daring. It seemed Eliza was not inclined to forgive John his transgressions. Which I found odd, because I had. Forgiven perhaps, but not forgotten.

"Well, I do not feel that is necessary, my lady," John sputtered in return.

"Hello, John," I cut in before Eliza could slay him with her next verbal barb. "And good day to you also, Eliza. Feel free to remain. John and I will just move over by the fire for our conversation. It was rather damp outside and I should like to warm myself." I shot a pointed look at Eliza. "And I should like to hear what he has to say."

Eliza frowned and aggressively grabbed a biscuit from the tray. "As you wish, Jane."

Moving swiftly across the floor, I deposited myself in my favorite armchair arranged by the fireplace. John dropped into the armchair across the way. He made to reach for my gloved hands, but Eliza cleared her throat pointedly. John cast a wary glance in Eliza's direction before leaning back in his chair instead.

"Jane, I was hoping we could discuss this silly matter and put it all behind us. I shall speak to your father and we can be married within the month. Gossip will surely change course when they hear of our impending nuptials. I know Mother will be thrilled to welcome you to our family." John rushed to deliver his brilliant plan and apparent proposal. Considering his mother was disinclined to welcome me on her front porch this morning, I had my doubts about being welcomed into the family.

"John," I began earnestly while holding his gaze with some difficulty, "we have already discussed the silly matter, as you call it. I no longer wish to seek a future with you when your interests lie with someone else. I will not be made a fool of, nor will I provide gossip for the people of this town—"

"But—" he made to interrupt me.

"I value your friendship, but that is all it shall ever be. I will not be your betrothed or your wife or whatever it is you are offering." Relieved at having delivered my speech, my eyes finally skittered away. I sighed deeply as John resumed his position.

"This is not settled, Jane. We are not finished. It was a mistake. I let myself be tempted, and it will not happen again. I want to take care of you," he rushed to reassure me. My eyes had grown soft during his pronouncement, but only because I felt saddened by the loss of his role in my life. Encouraged by my wistful expression, John continued, "You need me."

And that was a very wrong thing to say.

My face must have reflected my offense and inner ire because his eyes widened and he attempted to backtrack. "Just… just think about it. Consider my proposal. We can meet again to discuss it."

Did I really need more time to consider his proposal? Did I want to marry John? I didn't think further consideration would change my instincts where he was concerned. But then again, I didn't know if these sudden doubts were linked to the very eye-opening failure of my morning business pursuits. I did not *want* to need John, but was he right? I knew we had a hypothetical future together. We were compatible. I was quirky and odd, and John found me interesting and endearing. He'd told me on numerous occasions that he found my intelligence refreshing. John made it sound like being a rational female was a good thing, and I was desirable as a result. However, I could now imagine the allure of some irrational behavior.

I had never before considered the possibility of having more than a comfortable friendship with my future husband. I was not aware there was something else until recently. Something instinctual… Something essential… Something warm right in my center. *Icy blue eyes unseen in nature*. Could I be happy with a life of complacency, a life with John? Could I turn my back on the idea of *more*? And if John was wayward in his attentions even now, so early in our courtship, would his affairs become commonplace in the scandal sheets? I refused to let my marriage and future be reduced to regular appearances in *The Ton Tattler*.

John took my silent wonderings as consent, or maybe as the opportunity he needed, and quickly excused himself with promises to call again to discuss matters once more.

I finally emerged from my inner turmoil and met Eliza's eyes across the room. Mine unsure and worried and hers full of fire. A rare occurrence in the time I had known her. Since the death of her husband at such an early age, Eliza's vitality had always simmered at a low burn—a tiny flame in a snowstorm, one gust away from extinguishing.

"We have plans this evening," Eliza reminded me, her smile growing by the second.

"I don't know, Eliza. I do not feel up to dancing or mingling or even speaking."

"Well, tonight you are not required to do any of those things. Tonight, the presence of Lady Jane Morrison is not necessary. You can be whomever you wish," she remarked while rising from her position by the tray of biscuits which by now had been significantly diminished.

"What ever do you mean?" I demanded.

"Tonight is Lady Foxworth's masquerade ball," Eliza answered with a flourish… and a cascade of biscuit crumbs from her skirts. "And it's sure to be an outrageous time."

After dressing and being attended by Meg, Eliza's lady's maid, we were on our way to Lady Foxworth's masquerade. Honestly my head was a bit sore from Meg's ministrations on my auburn curls. From Eliza's wincing and tentative probing of her scalp, I imagined she was feeling similarly.

"Why do you keep Meg employed, Eliza? You and she clearly do not get on. She doesn't even attempt to hide her jealousy and disdain," I ventured as we jostled around a turn.

Eliza gave a dramatic sigh. "Despite Meg's approach, I know she needs employment in our household. I wouldn't turn her out in such a manner. She does perform the tasks I require of her… Just with an unfortunate attitude."

"I see," I murmured quietly, marveling at my friend's generosity.

"That said, my scalp bloody hurts. She needs to control herself with the curling tongs," Eliza ended on a strangled laugh.

I joined her in amusement. "It does smart! Perhaps your butler can attend us next time."

"Ha! Botstein would *love* that."

Our smiles met across her father's carriage. Our journey up the Foxworth drive caused the carriage to bounce on the cobblestones rather forcefully and I remembered my unease as my décolletage caught the edge of my vision and I glanced down.

Eliza must have noticed my attention stray to the top of my elaborately beaded bodice because she admonished me preemptively, "Don't even think it. You look lovely. You know how outlandish ladies dress for Lady Foxworth's social events. You should celebrate your assets, I should think. Besides, we will all be wearing masks. Despite knowing who nearly everyone is, we shall all carry on as if we do not."

Eliza was right. I knew the standard for these affairs. It was as if the addition of a half mask suddenly removed twice the natural inhibitions these ladies possessed. And the men were made bolder in their attentions.

Eliza was obviously attempting to improve my mood after John's unwelcome visit earlier in the day. I realized she meant well. The distraction Lady Foxworth's masquerade provided *would*, in fact, be more than beneficial. I planned to test out my theory regarding my shunning among ladies of the *ton*. If they no longer required my discreet accounting services then I would surely find out this evening. Being turned away at their front door would be nothing compared to being given the cut direct at a society event. The possibility made me uneasy. If nothing else, I would have my answer very shortly.

Eliza was aware of my profession of sorts. She supported me. Of course she did. As a woman trying desperately to be respected in her study of medicine, Eliza understood the importance of independence. And as a widow, her attempt to carve out a place for herself in our society was a necessity. With Eliza's refusal of support from her late husband's family, she was doubly determined to follow in her father's very successful footsteps. Dr. Finley was well respected and well regarded among the peerage. Eliza was slowly building her reputation as well with the unwavering support of her father, but she was still a woman in a field occupied almost exclusively by men. Despite the challenges we faced, I truly believed we would both find our place and be successful in our pursuits.

And tonight would be an important step in that endeavor. I would know the truth of my peers and just how deep the well of potential ruin would run.

~

Early autumn in London had seen the aristocracy return to town and the first events of the season brought the gossip to the forefront. And after Lady Foxworth's masquerade, they would have plenty to discuss.

"It is magical."

"How delightful!"

"Can you imagine the cost?"

"Gads, that bird is real!"

As Lady Eliza and I finally emerged through the congested archway, we overheard many exclamations from revelers already within. The gardens had been transformed. I could no longer discern if I was on the outskirts of Mayfair or in the jungles of India. Foliage unseen in England had obviously been imported at great cost to make this affair the talk of the *ton*. Exotic birds and flora were warring for attention. Guests openly gawked and musicians played to the sounds of our enchantment. I noticed a sitar among them. *How lovely*. Torches burned and the heavy scent of incense caught the breeze. Footmen and other servants passed trays of refreshment. Hired costumed dancers twirled and drew the eye of nearly everyone in their orbit. I moved with wonder throughout the lush outdoor space. The grandiose display was unequivocally outrageous. Eliza had been correct on that account.

Speaking of my friend, I turned to find her sparkling gaze behind her delicately jeweled, navy-blue half mask. I was sure my own black, beaded mask was unable to completely hide how marvelous and magical I found this whole affair.

We finally settled ourselves along the periphery to better admire our lovely surroundings. However, it was impossible to avoid the reactions of our peers. They gathered in small groups and attempted to control their initial shock. Appearing unaffected by the grandeur of the gardens now appeared to be the aim of the evening. I felt sad and disappointed for them. How very pretentious must one be to refuse to acknowledge the obvious splendor in one's midst? Lord forbid a guest compliment their hosts by appearing delighted by the spectacle they labored to create. I rolled my eyes unabashedly at the displays of my peers.

Lady Eliza must have detected my inner displeasure. "Jane, are you well? Are you not enjoying yourself?"

"Actually," I began, "I find myself rather enchanted. This is perfectly distracting."

"Oh good. I was worried you were still upset regarding John's visit." Eliza adjusted her mask, I assumed so she could better see my reaction to her statement.

"No. I am not dwelling on John or our conversation. I did not tell you earlier upon my arrival at your father's home, what with John's intrusion and then preparing for the ball, but my regular appointments this morning"—lowering my voice to a near whisper, I continued—"turned me away."

Eliza appeared thoughtful. "Do you believe this is in support of Lord Fairbanks? Repercussions from the scandal of your broken courtship?" My clever friend had already reached the same conclusion I had.

"Precisely. His mother was one of the households who pretended ignorance at my arrival for a standing arrangement. I had hoped to investigate further this evening. Perhaps deduce their intentions by their reaction to my presence tonight." I made sure to keep my voice low as I explained my plan for the evening. Though they were masked, prying eyes and wondering ears were everywhere in this magical garden.

Fidgeting with my reticule and refusing to meet Eliza's worried gaze, I heard her equally quiet reply, "Janie, we can go." Adding a staying hand to my attempted protest, she continued, "Coming here with the intent to prove yourself and your place among these people is not required for your future or your happiness. You do not need their approval or their acceptance, at masquerade balls nor in their drawing rooms. You should enjoy yourself for yourself. My intent was not to force you into a carriage with the express purpose of conducting an experiment and testing a social hypothesis. I merely wanted you, my friend, to be happy."

"I see your point. I do. But I cannot stop considering my future for a moment. I am happy to be here with you, but I cannot remain in your household forever. If my business in London is compromised, I need to know. I have savings and could move, if necessary. There are positions I might be suitable for. A companion or governess. I'm not sure, but I need to figure this out. The sooner the better. And I must give due consideration to John's proposal," I finished with heat burning my cheeks.

"You do not!" Eliza's raised voice drew the attention of a nearby footman. She quickly lowered her voice. "We will figure this out. You can stay with me as long as you need to. There is no end date on our friendship. Perhaps we can talk to Fiona. The duchess knows everyone. We shall find you more clients to conduct your business and you shall support yourself. Marriage should never be a last resort." Her voice cracked near the end of her plea, and emotion burned beneath her mask. My poor friend.

In response to her obvious emotions, I gentled my voice considerably. "I cannot rely on you or Fiona or anyone else to fix my problems for me. I adore you. You are my dearest friend. But my future is my own and I must be responsible for myself. At least a marriage to John would be my choice." I noticed a footman was approaching with a tray, so I hastened to finish. "You know as well as anyone, love is not required for marriage." Giving her hand an affectionate squeeze, I said, "I could be content with John, and more importantly… I could be myself."

The footman approached confidently with his tray of refreshment. "My ladies, would you care for some lemonade?" With a flourish, he presented our drinks and offered a brilliant smile. Blond hair and amused brown eyes met our undeniably surprised expressions. Servants were typically less flamboyant and obvious in their attentions. I noticed Lady Foxworth's charming footman was dressed to reflect the extravagance of the ball as well. He seemed to be playing a role to accompany the theme of the evening and indulging us at the same time.

"Why, thank you. We would be delighted to accept," Eliza finally managed while offering a shy smile. I thanked him in turn and off he went to further support his mistress in her outrageous affair. I was both grateful for the refreshment on this mild evening but also the respite from the seriousness of my interrupted conversation with Eliza. However, she seemed determined to pick up where we left off. But before she could open her mouth to question my intentions further, I looked over her shoulder beyond the closest palm frond and spotted something, nay, *someone* that caused me to suck in a large breath. Unfortunately, my mouth was full of lemonade at the time and I began choking quite fitfully.

Alarmed, Eliza took my glass and patted me gamely on the back. "Are you all right? You looked like something startled you." She started to turn to examine the gardens for the source of my alarm, but I quickly grabbed her arm and recovered my wits.

Eyes watering, I cleared my throat and whispered furiously, "Do not turn. He is behind you."

As one does, she completely ignored me and made to turn again while questioning, "Who is behind me?"

I made to stop her again and finally met her confused stare. "Him. The mysterious gentleman. Lord Dashing," I hissed. I risked a peek over her shoulder and squeaked. "Bollocks, he's coming over here. Just… Don't… *Ugh*. Stop looking, Eliza!"

"What? I can't help it. I'm sorry."

She did not look sorry. At all.

Lord Dashing, or whatever his name was because I still did not know, *bah*, approached with a quick bow. But before he could address us or offer any kind of greeting, I blurted, "It's you." Wincing internally, I took in the man before me. Dressed all in black with a plain domino half mask, he was stunning. His eyes shone behind his mask. *Icy blue eyes unseen in nature*. I openly admired his face and belatedly noticed the silence after my graceless pronouncement had gone on quite some time.

Eliza slowly leaned over to stare between us. I perceived her face entering my field of vision with some effort. "Good evening, My Lord," she began in an effort to draw our attention.

My mystery gentleman—I needed to stop thinking of him as mine—the mystery gentleman of my brief acquaintance (that's better) inclined his head and offered a polite, "my lady" in Eliza's general direction. His gaze returned to my person after the momentary departure. He absorbed me with his eyes, taking me in in pieces and parts. Lord Dashing's perusal warmed my cheeks, but a very small feminine part of me cheered internally at his appreciative once-over. Eyes strayed to my shoulders, neckline, before finally sweeping down the length of my deep violet gown. He returned my admiring stare as his gaze found my mask-covered one.

"Yes, my lady. It's me. Would you care to dance?"

All well-bred ladies could dance. We were trained and schooled in all manner of formal artful movement. And thank the good Lord for that particular demand on women of my station because if my feet had not remembered how to move of their own volition, I would likely have remained rooted to the spot, or worse, wound up face down on the dance floor.

Lord Dashing and I moved elegantly in time with the other lords and ladies. Hopefully none the wiser to the riotous thoughts and feelings happening within me. I could hear the violins and pick out the distinct and unusual sound of the sitar accompanying them, but all my other senses were overwhelmed by the man before me. His large frame filled my field of vision. As an absurdly tall woman, this was unusual for me. This enigmatic gentleman likely stood over six feet, and I enjoyed his considerable presence as we danced. He smelled familiar, like books or paper, ink and something more earthy. Cedar, perhaps. And the feel of his hand in mine, the strength in his arms, and his confident guidance as we moved… I was having trouble concentrating.

His touch would be my downfall.

"What are we doing?" I finally managed. They were the first words spoken since I had been led away from a mirthful Eliza onto the stone patio.

A small smile touched the corner of his lips as he replied succinctly, "We are dancing."

"Yes, but why? Who are you? Why are you here? Why are you dancing *with me*?" My rapid questions did nothing to diminish the amusement I saw shining in his icy blue eyes.

"So many questions," he tsked. "This is a masquerade. We are anonymous revelers enjoying a garden transformed. Let's just enjoy ourselves, shall we? That was my only motivation when asking you to dance. The pleasure of your company."

I did not know what to make of his statement. My face must have shown my bewilderment.

"Well, I am enjoying myself. If you prefer to leave—"

"I do not prefer to leave," I cut him off. Unsure how to explain, I finally settled on, "I suppose I am just confused." My mind and body were warring with one another. I was desperate to know his name and his intentions, but I was equally overcome by his nearness. Did he wish to discuss the events of Benton House—our mad escape and his sudden rescue? His motive in seeking me out tonight couldn't actually be rooted in the enjoyment of my company, could it?

What did this handsome devil want with me?

The song ended and my disappointment was multifaceted. I still didn't know who he was and his hands were no longer on my body. Would this be the end of our acquaintance or were we destined to have confusing run-ins in ballrooms throughout the season?

"Take a turn with me about the garden?" came the deep voice at my side. He made it sound like a question, but I somehow knew this invitation would lead to more. I hoped he was prepared for more questions. I could be quite relentless when fixated on a subject. And I was most definitely fixated on him.

In answer, I placed my hand on his arm and we began a measured stroll.

With a subtle glance around the garden, I noticed the other attendees seemed unconcerned with our promenade. They seemed enthralled in their own amusements. I was grateful for the perceived anonymity provided by the mask and the various entertainments and distractions of the masquerade.

If I was going to get to the bottom of this mystery, I would likely be required to speak. Therefore, I began, "Are you enjoying the masquerade? The gardens… They're unique, wouldn't you agree?"

"I am quite enjoying myself. More so now," accompanied his sly glance in my direction. "The gardens are eye-catching and extravagant to be sure. Seems a waste though, what with the assembled masses doing their utmost to avoid any sort of reaction."

I was surprised his observation had aligned so perfectly with my earlier annoyance at my peers. "I agree. This entire affair is excessive and outrageous, but I'm enchanted, nonetheless. It seems my reaction to the magic of the evening makes me vulgar and unrefined," I concluded.

"On the contrary, you are honest. There is a freedom in that. It's a quality I hold in the highest regard." His eyes held a challenge of their own.

I hadn't even realized we had stopped walking. Still in the gardens and visible to those around us, Lord Dashing had led us to a somewhat private bench where we were unlikely to be overheard. But with so many other guests filling the garden space, I wasn't concerned by our relative seclusion.

I removed my hand from his arm and missed the warmth of his body beneath his jacket. I had no idea why this thought had formed. It was completely out of character. I didn't touch men. I didn't think about touching men. At least, I hadn't. But taking in this mysterious gentleman… His masculine face, those insanely beautiful eyes, his pitch-dark hair reflecting the torchlight… I was feeling something I had never experienced before. My head finally acknowledged what my body had been fairly shouting. This was attraction. This was a drumbeat in my blood—pounding throughout my body but not originating from my heart. No, somewhere lower, deeper. Somewhere hidden and desperate.

I couldn't stop looking at him. And if that was strange, he didn't comment; he just returned my obvious scrutiny.

"Can I ask you a question?" he finally put forth. At my nod, he continued, "Why did you come here tonight?"

"Beyond being invited by Lady Foxworth?" I asked with rising confusion.

"Yes. Beyond that. As we discovered, you are honest. And you seem too practical for this sort of event," Lord Dashing stated, despite having not actually been introduced to me. He didn't know me.

But he was right.

"My friend, you met her, Lady Eliza Morgan. She thought it would distract me. Raise my spirits." My response was stilted, embarrassed. I didn't want to acknowledge my recent scandal with John. And it wasn't like Lord Dashing knew of my enterprise and subsequent plan to see if I was still accepted among the ladies here tonight.

"And what did you need distracting from?" he boldly inquired.

I shifted in my seat and smoothed the shimmering silk in my lap. I felt him move on the bench to face me more fully. "You really don't know?" I finally returned.

His eyes narrowed a bit, searching, but he finally said, "No."

That deep voice felt almost like a command and pulled the answer from me. "I ended my courtship with the Earl Fairbanks recently. There has been a bit of a stir. I had hoped to ignore the gossips and move on with my life, but that is proving more difficult than I anticipated."

Lord Dashing seemed thoughtful. He broke eye contact and looked around the gardens. I followed his gaze and saw the collected masses. Ladies and gentlemen in tight circles, whispering behind fans, unaffected by their extravagant surroundings.

He finally looked back to me and when he had my full attention, he began, "This may sound odd and unprompted, but just consider this for a moment. These people, your peers. You concern yourself with their regard. It's a fruitless effort. You'll find yourself trapped by their expectations. Society has created imprisonment for everyone in this garden. The servants are helpless and must perform for their masters. The lords do what they've always done—use their perceived power to oppress everyone in their orbit. And the ladies are ensnared. Trapped in golden cages, supplying heirs, perpetuating the deceit, and reliant on the perceived power of men. And all of them are lying. Lying to each other, and more importantly, lying to themselves."

I listened with blatant astonishment. I had never heard a man speak this way about the aristocracy. Our society ran on the unvarnished illusion of propriety and wealth, lessers and betters, and a hierarchy of means. But with rising emotion and strength in his voice, he continued his speech, "But, you. You know the truth and you are honest. I was quite serious before when I said there was freedom in that. You do not belong here among these liars in their gilded cages. Once you realize that, you can make your own path."

My shock must have shown on my face because he gentled his voice and his eyes softened as he went on, "Pay no mind to these gossips. Your future is your own."

I opened my mouth to speak but my heart was beating so powerfully in my chest that my voice would not steady. He presumed too much. This… this man—hell, I still didn't know his name. He spoke as if he could see into my mind, to all my worries and fears. And then he poured them out onto the bench between us. I felt irrationally exposed.

As if he could sense his misstep and my retreat, he regarded me carefully and made to speak again. But before he uttered a word, Eliza approached abruptly.

"Apologies for the interruption. But I must go, Jane." Eliza's rapidly spoken statement had me looking away from Lord Dashing to the concerned face of my friend. "Word came from Lady Ramsey's household that my father was unavailable and they require a doctor right away."

I knew how important this moment was for Eliza. She was needed and would finally be able to prove herself, standing on her own merit. Of course she had to go.

Lord Dashing had risen from the bench at her sudden appearance. I stood now as well and did my best to leave behind the effects of our strange conversation. I was unsteady on my feet and reeling from Lord Dashing's passionate speech. He reached a hand to steady me, and the warmth under my skin threatened to draw my attention away from Eliza.

Stepping hastily away from his touch, I turned to the man at my side and said, "Thank you for the dance and the conversation. It was… enlightening. Good evening to you."

I did not wait for a reply. I hurried with Eliza to the archway and we emerged from the gardens on a torch-lit path leading to the stables and beyond that the waiting carriages along the drive.

"I did not mean for you to leave as well. I apologize for interrupting your..." Eliza hesitated and finally settled on, "dance with Lord Dashing. You should stay. I'll send the carriage back for you."

I nodded without meeting her inquisitive gaze.

Continuing our walk to the carriages, Eliza removed her mask and began straightening the curls near her temples. "Janie, are you well? Your time with your mystery gentleman looked quite intense. Did he do something? Or say something to make you look so exceedingly nauseous?"

Regaining myself a bit as we put distance between ourselves and Lady Foxworth's gardens, I answered woodenly, "We had an odd conversation to be sure. But yes, I am well. All is well."

Eliza seemed unconvinced but pulled me into a tight hug as we reached her father's conveyance. "Stay. Have more lemonade. Enjoy the lovely distraction of the masquerade," she advised. And then seemed to feel the need to add, "Just be safe and don't go anywhere alone with Lord Dashing. No more scandals from here on out, yes?" She offered a bright smile and consulted the driver briefly before hopping in the carriage and making her way toward her own future.

I stood there on the cobblestones feeling unmoored, untethered. Sensing the heat and color in my cheeks, I reached up to touch my face, surprised to find the mask securely fastened.

How strange that I was still wearing a mask when I was suddenly quite sure I had finally been seen.

Six

When an animal is startled, they may halt in place instinctively. I'd seen deer do this in the country. They'd remain motionless to better assess their surroundings but then bolt away from the perceived threat.

I had remained frozen on Lady Foxworth's drive momentarily, and then like a frightened animal, I fled.

I thought about Lord Dashing's words—the lunacy he'd spouted regarding the *ton*. I couldn't forget his intensity and his honesty. No man of my acquaintance had ever spoken to me thus.

I thought about my future and how I desired to plot my own course. *You do not belong here among these liars in their gilded cages. Once you realize that, you can make your own path.* Was he right? Did I truly not belong? Did I agree with this stranger with whom I seemed to have an unsettling connection?

I thought of John and his desire to make all my problems go away. His influence and standing in society. His ability to course-correct my acceptance among the ladies of the *ton. The lords do what they've always done—use their perceived power to oppress everyone in their orbit.*

I thought of my sisters. Swept under the rug by my father. Ruined. My elder sister June and her inability to accept her place in society. Her refusal to marry and her overwhelming desire for some intangible *more*. June's decision to escape from our household and cut off all contact with us had made me angry at the time. I'd thought her selfish. But now I did not know what to think about June. And Gem. *Sigh.* My younger sister Gemini and her scandalous discovery in the stables with a young lordling who had no intention of marrying her was a blight on our family's reputation as well. But why should Gem be relegated to the country and her lordling obliged to carry on with his life? *And the ladies are ensnared. Trapped in golden cages, supplying heirs, perpetuating the deceit, and reliant on the perceived power of men.*

I thought about how much Lord Dashing's words made sense, and how they echoed my own feelings on the nobility. It is an odd thing to have your thoughts tumbling out of someone else's lips. Their very fine lips.

However, not once during my sudden flight from the masquerade did I think about where I was going. The direction of my thoughts mimicked the direction of my feet, aimless and unconscious. I was ignorant of my surroundings, led by my confusion and discontent. Escape was my resolve. It wasn't until I nearly collided with a large form suddenly blocking my path that my brain reengaged to the present and self-preservation kicked in.

But it was too late for that.

"Well, wot 'ave we 'ere, Billy Boy?"

I started at the discovery of a large man in front of me. The shape that emerged from the darkness and disturbed both my internal ramblings and my progress along the walk was a man. Wide and tall, with a barrel chest and a rather large forehead. His face was bloated and skin blemished. He looked like a man who was frequently in his cups. And he smelled like that was the case currently.

My eyes darted to my surroundings as much to avoid the man in my path as to attempt to ascertain my location in Mayfair. But I was no longer in Mayfair. The darkness was oppressive. There were no lamps lit to mark the street. Carriages and hacks were nowhere to be found. How far did I walk when I fled the masquerade?

Another man stepped out of the adjacent alleyway and joined his companion. "Looks to me like a lost little lamb, Charlie. Well, not so little in some areas." This apparent Billy person, gestured to his chest in an obscene imitation of a lady's bosom. I could feel my heartbeat in my throat, nearly choking me. In my absentminded escape from the ball, I had navigated myself into very real danger.

I attempted to school my features and apply rational thought to the situation. Praying my voice was steady enough to carry, I addressed the men in my path. "Good evening, gentlemen. I believe I have gotten turned round. I shall be on my way and you can continue your… your… nighttime stroll."

"Our nighttime stroll, is it?" the newcomer questioned mockingly. He was as tall as his friend, but leaner. His face looked hard in the low light from the moon, all shadows and angles. Clothing hung on his lanky frame. "Did you hear that, Charlie? This lost lamb is going to apologize for interrupting our evening and just be on her way." Both men laughed unkindly.

I began slowly backing away, but they met my retreat step for step. I wished I could wake up from this awful moment as if it were a terrible dream. How could I have been so careless? I recognized the insanity of blaming myself instead of being appalled that it simply wasn't safe for a woman alone. And yet that pervasive guilt landed squarely on my shoulders and stayed there. In all likelihood, I would die at the hands of these men while blaming myself for being a woman.

Blood rushed in my ears and terror was at the forefront of all my thoughts. That is likely why I didn't hear the approach of rushing feet. But my would-be attackers heard and turned away from me just as a masked Lord Dashing pushed me roughly behind him and faced the two cutthroats.

The men stepped back with surprised laughs. "Is this a masked hero? A vigilante come to exact justice on us?" questioned the leaner man.

"Nothing as noble as that I'm afraid," came Lord Dashing's smooth reply, his voice edged with menace and impending violence. "But you should leave now while you have the ability."

I peeked around the shoulder blocking my view to see the assailants exchange an amused glance. "And yet there are two of us and just one of you. Do you feel scared, Charlie? I don't feel very threatened meself."

"So be it," Lord Dashing replied.

And then he attacked.

I quickly stumbled back to avoid any wayward battling bodies as my mystery gentleman engaged the gangly cutthroat with a quick and brutal punch to the face. He was obviously caught off guard and went down in a heap. The second villain lunged for the lord and made a grab for the back of his coat. Lord

Dashing slipped from it easily as if the man were simply his valet helping him undress for the evening. Lord Dashing spun while grabbing the outstretched arms of the jacket and jerked them forward. The larger attacker, still holding the coat sleeves, stumbled toward my rescuer and found himself on the receiving end of a vicious head-butt.

I covered my mouth as my heart beat nearly out of control. I then realized the intensity of the pounding was due in part to the arrival of a carriage and team of four. Reacting quickly, I leapt away from the road and pressed my back flat to the cold stones of the nearby building.

My attention was trained on the carriage and its abrupt appearance as a man fairly jumped from the back and landed soundly on the cobblestones as the driver drew the horses to a stop directly in front of me.

The carriage acrobat made his way to Lord Dashing only to realize that both cutthroats had been dispatched. No longer a threat to my safety, they lay like motionless heaps on the ground.

"Christ, Q. Ye could have left one for me. Ye know I have a fight coming up. I could have used the training." The man who had bounded from the carriage had a significant Irish brogue. *Q? Was that even a name?*

"Sorry to disappoint, Daniel. Next time I'll ask them to simply wait until you arrive to engage in violence," Lord Dashing, or Q, I suppose, replied to the newcomer. Daniel looked to be Q's age, no more than one and thirty, surely. But that was where the similarities ended. Despite the darkness, I could see enough by the light of the moon to differentiate the men easily. I observed as they went about tying the hands of the unconscious scoundrels with rope that had been inexplicably produced. Daniel appeared shorter than Lord Dashing, and thicker, stockier. His hair was shorter and not as dark as the midnight locks on my mystery gentlemen's head. And this Daniel didn't move with Lord Dashing's natural grace. If Q was a panther, then Daniel was a bull. If this man was participating in a fight in the near future, I could see he would be a formidable pugilist. His form lent itself to the sport. A man who could land a vicious punch and excel at violence.

Who were these men?

While I felt an odd and alarming connection to Q, he was still a relative stranger. And after seeing him exact such swift violence, I didn't know what to think. Yet despite my worry and confusion, my brain still wanted to describe what had transpired in the alley as *justice* and not *violence*.

In my renewed panic at being once again in the company of men I did not now, I must have made a sound alerting them to my presence.

Lord Dashing paused in his attentions and glanced at me for a long moment before turning to his friend and saying quietly, "Finish this up, will you? And get Stanley to help drop them where the constables will find them on their route."

Daniel gave me his attention, scanning me from head to toe. Not in a scandalous manner but in obvious appraisal. "What are ye doing here, Q?" he questioned quite openly, voice low and disapproving.

Surprise lanced through me and offered a distraction to the mounting stress in my body. Daniel was obviously in the employ of Lord Dashing. Judging by his attire and acquiescence to his master, I assumed this Daniel was a footman perhaps, or a bodyguard based on his professional interest in fighting. However, I had never heard a servant speak to his lord in such a manner. No title, no address, no obvious deference. What a curious relationship these two shared. I supposed I shouldn't be too surprised. Lord Dashing did speak very progressive and sensational ideas regarding the *ton*. He had shocked me into silence at the masquerade.

"Danny, just mind yourself. I'll see you later," Q responded with narrowed eyes and finality in his tone.

Daniel countered with an obvious eye roll behind his employer's back, and a muttered, "Yes, Your Grace. Fine, Your Grace."

Q cut him a look over his shoulder but he didn't slow his progress as he made his way over. Still pressed against the building, he approached me cautiously. "Jane, are you hurt? Did they…" He paused with clenched teeth and a ragged inhale. "Did they touch you?"

I shook my head in response. A small movement that required my full attention. I couldn't seem to meet his eyes.

I noticed in the periphery, he reached for my hand but seemed to think better of it at the last moment and instead took a handkerchief out of his waistcoat pocket. He passed it to me with a concerned frown marring his striking face.

"Can you talk to me? What can I do?" he asked, trying to catch my eye.

"I don't know." With a shaky breath, I finally raised my chin and met his steely gaze. "I think I need to sit down."

"I know a place."

WITH PARTING instructions to the driver, we set off on foot for a short walk to a nearby pub. I wasn't concerned about crossing paths with any more footpads. We seemed to be leaving the filth and squalor behind with every step we took. Perhaps I hadn't wandered as far from the masquerade as I'd initially thought.

I kept glancing at this mysterious gentleman, mask removed and in jacketless dishabille. My surprising savior this evening. *How had he found me? Why had he come?* He remained unreadable. His eyes were intent and focused as we moved quickly down the path. I never strayed from his side, my hand wrapped securely around his arm.

Lord Dashing delivered us to a rough wooden door with a sign hanging overhead. I didn't spot the name of the establishment before I was ushered inside, but by that point I was too distracted to care.

I'd never been in a pub before. Daughters of marquesses did not frequent pubs. They also didn't accompany strange men whose names they still did not know. *Gah!*

Alas. The pub presented the perfect distraction in my present state. A new environment would engage my interest and push the violent events of the evening to the trunk of bad memories in my mind. I'd tuck them away and refuse to let them resurface.

In blatant curiosity, I gawked at the interior. My eyes scoured the large space greedily. How strange that the mere thought of this place as forbidden made it so much more intriguing. It was essentially just a large room with tables and chairs and a stone fireplace. Men gathered and held mugs. I spotted a long L-shaped counter near the back with an open doorway to what I assumed was a kitchen beyond. All mundane objects and occurrences when taken separately, but reassemble them in an illicit venue not fit for my patronage… And well, my interest knew no bounds.

Lord Dashing escorted me to a small worn table near the fire. I gave him a grateful glance as I sat. "I thought you could do with some warming up," he ventured.

"You thought correctly, my lord," I agreed with a small nod of thanks.

He took the seat across from me but due to the size of the table (small) and the combined measure of our limbs (not small), our knees instantly brushed and our feet tucked right up against one another. "I beg your pardon," I murmured awkwardly, heat rising to my pale cheeks.

Q met my gaze with a small smile. "That's better. You were quite pale in the alley back there."

My eyes dropped immediately.

"Jane…" He hesitated until I returned his attention. "Are you hurt? Frightened?"

"No. I've found I'm quite adept at avoiding painful circumstances for the most part. I take whatever bad thing and lock it away in a trunk inside my mind, and then I'm able to compartmentalize the hurt or trauma easily enough."

His questioning stare was searching. Lord Dashing seemed unconvinced by my assurances. "Jane, what happened? When I found you, you were halfway to Seven Dials. Why were you alone in the street? Why did you run from the masquerade?"

Panic held my response captive. I couldn't very well admit it was my conversation with him that had left me feeling so raw and exposed. Forcing a measure of calm I didn't feel, I attempted a reply. "I made a foolish mistake and ventured where I should not have."

Perhaps Q could read the contrition on my features, or he assumed he was unlikely to receive further explanation. His gaze traveled over my face, down my arms covered by my cloak, to my gloved hands that were fairly strangling his handkerchief. I didn't even realize I still had it. "I gave you that out of reflex. I assumed you'd be upset and might be in need of something for your tears. Yet you've remained dry-eyed and apparently well-versed in handling difficult situations."

I immediately tried to pass the wrinkled linen square back to him. Q gave his head a small shake and said, "Keep it." I fisted the handkerchief once again and tucked my hands into my lap just as a harried barmaid approached. She had brown hair and eyes and seemed mistress of her domain.

How I envied that.

"Q, love, what can I get you? It's late but I can rustle up some supper for you if need be."

"No, Miss Victoria, that won't be necessary. Just two pints and some—" He paused here and looked over at me. "And some biscuits if you have any. Or cakes? Something sweet, if we may."

"Right, then. I'll get you and your lady friend here fixed up in a jiff," Victoria replied, casting me a curious but friendly look before bustling away behind the counter and through the far doorway. I should have been worried about her misguided assumption, but felt rather flattered at the notion. Men like Q did not have lady friends like me. Gentlemen had mistresses and wives—sometimes both. And I looked the role of neither.

"That's not necessary, you know. I've never had ale and I'm not hungry," I murmured as I took in his features. A small red mark marred his otherwise unlined forehead, likely from the headbutt. I was shocked it hadn't drawn blood. His gloves were still on and while there was no obvious sign of distress to his knuckles, I couldn't be sure. In any case, the barmaid hadn't noticed anything amiss.

Noticing the direction of my gaze, he lowered his hands from their resting place on the table and tucked them below the surface in an obvious imitation of my own action. "I keep thinking you shall pass out from shock any moment. Perhaps eating a bit of something will keep you upright."

I arched a brow at his highhandedness. "Afraid you'll have to carry me back to Mayfair?"

He ignored my taunt. "Indulge me, won't you. I know you say you're experienced in dealing with unpleasantness, but I can't help but think that tonight's event will catch up with you eventually. Let us sit a while."

I briefly scanned the room and noted the pub was sparsely occupied. Just a few men scattered about, no one overly loud or obnoxious or obviously inebriated.

"I assure you, Lady Jane, you are quite anonymous here. Your reputation is safe. *You are safe*." The end of his statement was made with quiet intensity.

I shifted a bit in my seat before returning my full attention to Lord Dashing, our legs tangling a bit in the process. I ignored them and spoke through my complete and utter awareness of his body in close contact with mine. "All right. We can stay for a bit."

If my begrudging agreement gave him relief, he didn't show it. That striking face remained passive and unreadable. In his icy blue stare however, I could read glittering intensity and victory.

Victoria returned with two mugs, nearly sloshing over the side as she placed them on the scarred wood of the table. She also delivered a small tin of biscuits. After a quickly muttered thank-you, she hurried off. Despite the lack of patrons, she still seemed to be quite in a rush. Perhaps she was so accustomed to the faster pace of busier evenings that she has only one speed of service.

I sat quietly nibbling on a biscuit, curious about the ale. I glanced nervously at Lord Dashing several times. He didn't seem to mind my curiosity or inability to look away from his magnificent face. He simply remained quiet and let me look. I imagined he assumed I was gathering my wits. If he only knew what he did to my wits.

There were so many things I wanted to say, so much I wanted to know. How often did he patronize this establishment? He and the proprietress seemed well acquainted. Did he prefer ale to scotch or brandy? He seemed like a whiskey drinker for some reason. My thoughts were a jumbled mess. I noticed his missing jacket and remembered abruptly how he lost it. It was likely still in the street some blocks away.

Realizing my thoughts were about to take a turn toward the violent events of the evening, and in an effort to derail that impending unpleasantness, I blurted without thought, "Ale and beer have been brewed for hundreds of years. Judging by the color and quality of our pints, I'd say this is an India pale ale which has grown in popularity in the last thirty years or so. Prior to that, porters and stouts were most often seen in taverns and pubs such as this. Pale *ale* is a misnomer actually. Any time hops are added in the fermentation process, an ale then becomes… a… beer." My speech trailed off a bit at the end.

Why couldn't I let silences speak for themselves? What did that even mean? Silence. Yes, I should be silent. In an effort to distract myself from my apparent inability to embrace intentional quiet, I gathered my fortitude and took a healthy swallow from my glass. *Gads, that is not pleasant at all.*

With some effort, I endeavored to school my beer-induced frown and glanced at Lord Dashing if for no other reason than to assess the damage done by my pointless lecture on alcoholic beverages. I half expected his seat to be vacated, but alas. There he remained, eyes bright and inquisitive.

"Is that so?" came his dry reply.

"Indeed," I miraculously managed through my awkwardness.

Leaning forward as if to hear me better, he said, "Tell me more."

I blinked at his soft-spoken demand. Typically, my peers looked at me as if they wished I had stopped speaking sooner. I could not recall a single instance when I'd been asked to expound upon a subject. My friends were very patient and interested in my random facts and odd research, but outside my tight-knit circle, that was not the case. I knew my propensity to talk *at* people rather than fully engage them in conversation. Generally, I was just a poor conversationalist. My mind would wander or become triggered by a statement and then set forth on a haphazard tangent. I often ended up blurting random information seemingly at odds with the topic at hand. It made sense to me. I could often track the route my thoughts traversed to reach my conversational malfunction, yet I remained odd and peculiar among my peers. At least that's what was whispered about me in ballrooms.

"Tell you more about beer?" I inquired apprehensively.

"Only if you have more beer wisdom to impart," he offered, his mouth softened in the barest hint of a smile. But it was his eyes that decided for me. Q looked at me, *really* looked at me. His eyes were intense and focused, not glazed over with boredom. Neither were they indulgent and kind. With the reassurance of his steady gaze, I began again. I spoke of the history of ale in England, imports and exports, preferences among the classes, and through it all, his focus never wavered. He wasn't scanning the room for a way out of our conversation or distracted by anything below my neck. He engaged me with questions and shared his opinions as well. There was something intoxicating about being the center of Lord Dashing's attention. His sole focus. More than being the face his eyes were drawn to, my words—my thoughts—held his favor.

Again, he considered me in ways my peers, especially the male aristocracy, did not. Men and women of the *ton* did not engage in discussions beyond the trivial, much less did men ask women to educate them on topics outside their realm of knowledge. He didn't seem inclined to push me to discuss the events of the evening, and for this I was grateful. I did not wish to recount what happened, nor my reasons for running away as I had. I imagined his curiosity would win out, but for now, we continued our aimless conversations.

A throat clearing brought my attention back to Q.

"I must say, my preference is for whiskey." He timed his statement with a swig of his beer and a glower at the offending tankard.

"I knew it!"

His brow raised at my enthusiastic admission. That singular eyebrow was quite accusatory. I stammered quite soundly, "I-I mean, I assumed that—about you. It seemed a foregone conclusion actually."

"Is that so?" he returned. This time with both brows high on his masculine forehead, amusement heavy in his tone.

"Indeed," I attempted distraction. "My good friend Miss Ashleigh Winstead makes whiskey."

"Winstead. Interesting." And he actually did sound interested.

I continued, "Well, not Ashleigh specifically, but her family business in Scotland is whiskey distillery and production."

"And what is it your family does, Lady Jane?" Lord Dashing eyed me with quiet intensity, awaiting my answer rather obviously.

I snorted in a very unladylike manner. "Instigates scandal mostly."

Having realized my unbidden candor, I shifted again beneath the tiny table. Honestly, was it shrinking? Our legs brushed again. Even through my layers of skirts I could feel the heat from his body, the strength of his form. Is this how it would be to share a bed with someone, simply for sleep? Limbs tangling, resettling yourself against someone else just to feel their weight, their presence, their comfort.

There came that feeling again, low in my center—warmth and light and a sudden change in elevation. Those icy blue eyes met mine and damn my complexion for enhancing every impure thought, making it readable in the heat of my cheeks and the flush on my chest.

Somehow, I don't think it was kindness that led Lord Dashing to ignore the obvious turn my thoughts had taken. He probably felt sorry for me. Inexperienced bluestocking feels the brush of a man's leg and nearly swoons. For the record, I would never swoon. It's undignified. I was merely entertaining a fantasy that led to unladylike thoughts. Nevertheless, Q ignored my visible discomfiture and returned to our conversation. "But you are trying very hard to avoid scandal, are you not?"

"I'm doing my best to rise above the gossip and whispers, but it is…" I trailed off, trying to pluck the right word from the wood grain of the table. *Impossible. Pointless. Utter bollocks*. "Challenging," I settled on.

Victoria returned just then and inquired if she could be of any further assistance. Q responded in the negative and pulled out a small coin purse from an inner pocket of his waistcoat. In doing so, a small notebook fell out and landed on the table. Leaves fluttered and the book landed open to a well-used section, judging by how flat the pages lay. Q paid the book no mind as he counted out payment for our nearly untouched biscuits and ale.

However, I took note of the pages, and more specifically the numbers therein. Neat and tidy columns showed obvious transactions: deficits, profits, dates, monies owed. The column farthest to the left side of the page was numerical but seemed like a code or an assignation. Perhaps the numbers stood in place of a name. It almost seemed like the mysterious Q carried around a miniature ledger filled with secret debtors.

"There is an inaccuracy in the twelfth row, fourth column. The total after the previous deduction should be six thousand eight hundred pounds," I said once Victoria bid us good evening and returned to her remaining patrons.

Lord Dashing did his best to remain unmoved, but even I could see the surprise in his features. He quickly scanned the entries in his little notebook, and finally met my eyes with an inscrutable expression.

I declare, I did my best not to appear smug but imagine I failed spectacularly. My smile was wide as I confidently met his gaze. I shrugged in an attempt to appear humble, and confirmed, "I'm good with numbers."

"Is that so?" he murmured for the third time this evening, expression unreadable.

"Indeed," came my rote reply, this time allowing a smile to sneak through at our exchange.

"And do you *do* anything with this propensity for numbers?"

"Why? What have you heard?" I realized belatedly how alarmed I suddenly sounded. *Tone it down, Jane. You're being suspicious.*

"Why? What have you done?" Lord Dashing countered immediately with narrowed eyes.

"Well, until recently—" I stopped abruptly. "I would appreciate if this remains between us." He nodded once in agreement to my request. "Until recently, I was an accounts manager of sorts… In secret… For ladies of the *ton.* I aided them in successfully managing their household accounts and paying their staff across multiple estates."

"Do their husbands not have solicitors and stewards of their own?" He seemed surprised but also genuinely curious. I don't know how I could tell, but I got the sense he was respectful of the profession I had carved out for myself.

"Some do. Some are so often wasting precious income on drink, brothels, and gaming hells that their wives manage their accounts in secret to keep their households running. And some are so oblivious to the care their wives take in running their households, they wouldn't know how to manage an estate if their life was dependent upon it. For the most part, these husbands don't care who keeps their money balanced as long as it's abundant and available. That makes me valuable in my position. I know the margins. I know how to make a household efficient and profitable. And until recently, I had regular clients who I assisted for a handsome return on my part."

His face was passive, but Lord Dashing's eyes were quite entertained. "And you, what, made house calls with these clients?"

"Yes. We had standing meetings once a month to review their books and make decisions," I answered warily.

"Why do you say 'until recently'?"

"Because my latest brush with the scandal sheets has made me a risky commodity. My services are no longer required for these ladies. I'm worthless to my family without an imminent betrothal. And it seems I'm equally useless to the women I once called clients for the very same reason," I finished hotly.

"What if I required your services, my lady?"

Why oh why did those words sound so utterly salacious? Perhaps because they were delivered with that mouth.

I cleared my throat and replied, "What does that mean?"

Q was unfazed by my suspicion. "It means I need your big brain to untangle some accounts for me. I recently acquired a business and we've been having a hard time deciphering the methods used by the previous owner."

"Why not just ask the previous owner?" I fidgeted a bit in my seat but ultimately sat up straighter. I sensed an opportunity here.

"Unfortunately, that's not possible," he assured me, finality in his tone.

I said nothing. I knew waiting was a successful negotiating tactic. I didn't really know what we were negotiating, but I did know I wanted the upper hand.

After a moment, Lord Dashing offered, "You could work with my solicitor, Mr. Stevens. There would be a chaperone on premises. And, of course, your employment would be very discreet. It would be a help to me, my lady. And who knows, perhaps your clients are just temporarily withdrawing until they have another scandal to feast upon." He paused for a moment, before finally concluding, "Or perhaps you needn't depend upon their unreliable support at all."

Your future is your own.

"I'll require my usual fees."

"Done." No sense of victory in his tone whatsoever. *Hmm*. "We should take our leave, it's quite late. I'll escort you home."

"To Lady Eliza's if you please. Dr. Finley's, rather," I corrected. Eliza Morgan's actual home stood empty and forgotten.

He made to stand and held out his hand to assist me as we made our exit from the tavern. I caught sight of the sign on my way out. It simply read JOHN'S in a hard-carved block print.

I was unsurprised to find Lord Dashing's carriage waiting for us on the deserted street. Daniel was up in the driver's box. He gave me a wink and greeted me rather enthusiastically. I caught Lord Dashing in the middle of a tremendous eye roll as he opened the carriage door and helped me inside.

Once we were seated and the horses were away, I faced my mystery gentleman. "So, are you going to finally introduce yourself after helping me escape not one, but two disastrous evenings?"

His lips twitched. I know because I was having a hard time not noticing them. "My friends call me Q."

Sigh.

As we came to stop in front of Dr. Finley's residence a short, quiet ride later, Q helped me alight from the carriage and passed me a calling card. Finally, something with his actual name on it. It was honestly rather embarrassing that I had gone so very long without knowing his name or who he was.

"There is an address on the back of this card. Come there Monday at eleven in the morning. Our work will begin. Until then, my lady." With a kiss to my gloved hand, he was off. Back in the carriage and down the drive.

I made my way around to the rear entrance and quietly entered through the kitchens. I hastened over to the banked fire, coals still burning and putting off a scant bit of light. Flipping the calling card over in my hand, I saw no name at all. Nothing that started with a Q. No Qs whatsoever. *Blast.*

I did however see the address to a well-known business and there at the top, in blood-red script, was the name of the most notorious gaming hell in London.

Piker House.

Seven

The following morning, Eliza still had not returned from the emergency that drew her to Lady Ramsey's household. I imagined it was a difficult birthing which kept my friend occupied. It was common knowledge among the *ton* that Lady Ramsey was spending her confinement at her Mayfair home. The countess was quite young, just nineteen, and the second wife to the Earl Ramsey. In need of an heir, the old earl had taken a rather young bride after the death of his first wife in an effort to see the continuation of his line. I supposed that was the way of nobility, to enter into marriage contracts to ensure the production of heirs, but it all felt so artificial and disingenuous. My opinions were my own of course, but I couldn't ignore Q's echoing sentiments from the Foxworth masquerade. *Trapped in golden cages, supplying heirs, perpetuating the deceit, and reliant on the perceived power of men.*

I was distracted from my musings by a throat clearing on the opposite side of the table. Dr. Finley took a sip of tea and turned the page of his morning paper. We made eye contact as he paused.

"I'm sure Eliza will arrive shortly. Lady Ramsey's pregnancy was progressing well and she is quite healthy. Don't look so troubled, my dear. Eliza is indeed capable," Dr. Finley said with a reassuring smile.

I wasn't sure what expression I was wearing for Eliza's father to feel the need to comfort me. I knew Eliza was quite skilled and a suitable physician for anyone in need of medical assistance. My thoughts had been in a tangle since I'd left Q in the carriage the previous night. I'd slept poorly, hounded by thoughts that had tried valiantly to escape the locked trunk in my mind.

Attempting to focus my wandering thoughts, I replied, "Of course. I'm sure all is well."

After a rustle of newsprint, I ventured again, "Eliza was eager to attend to Lady Ramsey when the messenger sent for her at the ball. Are you quite well, Dr. Finley? They were unable to locate you to assist."

"Yes, well… I wasn't available last night, and the Ramsey servants knew to seek Eliza in my absence." He gave me a quick glance and then went back to his paper. Dr. Finley seemed cagey. *Hmm*. If the servants had exhausted their efforts to locate the good doctor at his clinic, his home, and his club, I cannot think where he would have been.

My speculation was interrupted as Eliza entered the room with a muttered, "Good morning." Disheveled and exhausted, wearing her formal gown from the prior evening, she made her way to the table. Both Dr. Finley and I looked over to her expectantly as she poured a dish of tea and made to grab a scone from the platter. Once she had settled herself, Eliza finally looked up and seeing our expectant faces, declared, "A healthy baby boy!"

"Congratulations, darling." Dr. Finley offered his daughter a warm smile, pride shining from his eyes. It was an odd thing to see a father showing interest in a daughter, at least in my experience. Eliza was neither male nor an heir. She was widowed and determined to take the unconventional path for a woman of her station. And yet… Her father was proud. He was her mentor and teacher, dedicated to overseeing her education and her future in the medical profession. I was grateful Eliza had a purpose and a father who supported her in all things. It was simply a foreign concept to me. I hadn't even a letter from my father since our argument following my broken courtship. Frowning at the thought, I realized my father, the Marquess Middleton, likely had no idea where I was and he didn't seem to care.

"That's wonderful, Eliza," I said a moment later.

"Thank you," she began. "It was a lengthy birthing as it sometimes is for first-time mothers. I was very glad to attend to Lady Ramsey." Eliza cast a prolonged glance at her father.

He hastened to retreat behind his newspaper but did manage to ask, "No complications then?"

"No, Father," came Eliza's quiet reply followed by a sip of tea and a weary sigh. "Where were you last night? The servants were unable to locate you. That is the only reason I was sent for."

The moment stretched awkwardly while Dr. Finley's cheeks pinkened a bit. *Interesting*. He cleared his throat again. "I was unavailable, I'm afraid. But the Ramsey household knows how capable and skilled you are. You've assisted me on several births. It is no surprise you were sought-after for your services and not any other doctors in town. They could have just as easily summoned Dr. Miles, but they chose you. Take pride in your abilities, my dear."

As women were wont to do, Eliza ignored all praise, instead focusing on the mystery of her father's absence. "You were unavailable?" Her confusion was obvious, and I felt quite suddenly that perhaps I should not be in the middle of this family discussion. I made to stand and excuse myself, but Eliza quickly jumped to reassure me. "No, Jane. Stay." After I settled myself, she directed her attention to her father again. "No matter. All was well. It all worked out in the end." But her features retained their suspicion.

"Actually, I need to be heading off. Eliza, why don't you rest up this morning and join me in the clinic this afternoon? You've put in a full night's work already." Before anyone could respond, Dr. Finley gathered his paper and hat and fled the dining room.

Eliza stared after her father for a moment before turning to me. "That was odd, was it not?"

I nodded in agreement. "He seemed eager to escape."

"And where was he last night? It's not as if he was socializing. I manage all of our invitations and engagements. Do you think he made himself scarce so my presence would be required at Lady Ramsey's bedside?" Eliza mused.

"Perhaps," I offered weakly as I took another bite of bacon and chewed thoughtfully. "Although I don't see how he could possibly know when his patient was going into labor in order to avoid attending to her. Doesn't that violate the Hippocratic oath? Oh! Perhaps he was visiting a paramour?"

Eliza choked on her scone.

"Oh dear. I'm sorry, Eliza," I apologized after her coughing had subsided.

"Jane! That's my father! You know very well he adored my mother. He wouldn't have... a... a... *lover*." She was clearly scandalized. And really, I knew better than to push the issue regarding Eliza's views on love and marriage.

"He could have very well been in transit from one location to another when the messengers came round. I'm sure he was in a carriage on his way home from the club," I rushed to reassure her. Now was not the time to pressure Eliza. She was exhausted from delivering a human being, for goodness sake. I was merely tired from tossing and turning in my bedchamber. Eliza brought a life into this world. "What an accomplishment for you! Congratulations on a successful delivery and new patient of your own."

"Thank you, Jane." Eliza smiled shyly in the face of praise, but I could sense her pride. She stifled a large yawn behind her bare hands. I imagine her gloves had been misplaced at some point during the night.

Before I could suggest my friend get some much-needed rest, a footman entered the dining room and brought over a letter addressed to me. I regarded the elegant script rather suspiciously, remembering the calling card and handkerchief tucked securely under the mattress in my guest room above stairs. However, upon turning the parchment, I noted the seal and whatever anticipation had quietly been growing was suddenly quashed. It's not as if Lord Dashing would need to send a letter. Our plans were set for the upcoming week, and if he wanted to relay a message, he'd likely appear on my balcony with no warning. Mysterious dashing lords. No, the seal under my reluctant fingers belonged to the Earl Fairbanks. It seemed John was eager to seek me out again. I quickly scanned his blasted graceful penmanship.

Dearest Jane,
Apologies for writing so soon after our last meeting, but I wanted you to know that I've been thinking of you. I desperately hope you've been thinking of me and my offer. We could be happy together, Jane. You know this as well as I. We suit. And I care for you deeply. I hope to call within the week, if that pleases you. I do wish you'd write to me. Please know I only want to care for you, Jane. I hope you'll let me. I look forward to seeing you soon. Think of me.
Yours always,

John

"AND WHAT DOES Sir Soggy Britches want?" Eliza looked decidedly more alert.

I cut my eyes to her and met her mischievous expression with an indulgent one of my own. "Lord Fairbanks," I emphasized, "wishes to see me."

"Well of course he does. If he doesn't draw attention to himself every so often, you're likely to forget he exists altogether." Eliza seemed renewed by the appearance of John's letter and began eating in earnest.

"Eliza, that's cruel. I was planning on marrying the man. I can't simply write him off."

"He doesn't deserve you, Jane. He isn't worthy of you. You need passion and intensity. You warrant more than complacency," Eliza finished with bright eyes.

I didn't know what to say to Eliza or to John. Truthfully, I didn't wish to think of John at all right now. I planned to ignore the letter. He knew I detested correspondence anyway. I much preferred speaking face to face. I found it difficult enough to read intent and reactions while speaking in person. Reading between the literal lines of correspondence made me positively flummoxed. Besides, my penmanship was abysmal.

Putting John and his offer of marriage out of my mind for the time being, I took my final swallow of lukewarm tea and straightened in my chair.

Before I could offer a change of topic, Eliza's gaze sharpened. "Speaking of intensity, what happened with Lord Dashing after I left Foxworth's? Did you find out his name? Are you courting? Will he come to call on you?"

"Why would you assume such a thing? It was one dance at a masquerade." I found I had to look away as I uttered my reply.

"Jane, really. He was obviously enchanted by you. I saw him, and more importantly, I saw you. You never looked at Sir Soggy Britches like that," Eliza finished her statement with a flourish of her fork and a large bite of coddled eggs.

I knew what she meant. There was a name for the feeling I experienced when I was with Lord Dashing. Honestly, I didn't even need to be with him. I could simply bring up his countenance in my mind. The sharp masculine features, raven hair, and blue eyes that burned me from the inside out. I was attracted to Q. Evidence supported this. My pulse beat faster and my body felt warm. But it wasn't simply his face or his form that drew me in. My body longed for his. Yet I also desired his thoughts and his opinions. Q spoke to me like no other man ever had, like he wanted to know me. Seduction, indeed.

Eliza was accurate in her assessment, I conceded that I had indeed never known attraction with John. I assumed we could have a companionable marriage, a future with friendship and contentment. But now knowing true attraction existed and what it did to my expectations and longings, could I go back?

I brought Eliza back into focus from my woolgathering to hear her say, "Why is that so hard to believe? That Lord Dashing could be your future?" Her question was gentle and pleading. My friend, my Eliza, my greatest supporter. Of course she thought this magnificent male specimen had any interest in me.

"I don't know," I answered honestly.

"Well, at least tell me his name. We can't call him Lord Dashing forever."

I winced outwardly.

"Jane! You still don't know his name?"

"Q! His name is Q. Well, I heard his guard call him Q. Or was that his valet? I'm unsure. Anyway, he told me his friends call him Q, and there was only the address listed on the calling card." Eliza was unfazed by my steady stream of dialogue. She understood my ways and simply waited with raised brows until the verbal deluge abated.

"I think you should start from the beginning."

So I did. I told her about being off-balance from my exchange with Q in the garden. Without going into the details of our discussion, I related the confusing and overwhelming nature of our conversation which led me to retreat and ultimately flee the masquerade altogether upon Eliza's departure. I told her of the dangers I faced, the cutthroats in the alley, and my masked savior in the form of Lord Dashing. Next came the aftermath and our subsequent time in the tavern.

Eliza was very still and silent as I concluded my tale with Q's offer of employment and the less than respectable location.

"You—" Eliza's voice broke before she began again. "You could have *died*, Jane! You were reckless and irresponsible. Wandering away like that." Head shaking, she looked away from me as if unable to maintain eye contact in the face of my carelessness.

"Eliza—" I tried.

"No. The fact that you are sitting here at this table is a miracle. You could have lost your life. That was real danger brought on by sheer thoughtlessness."

She was right. I had no excuse. I required rescuing. If Q hadn't shown up when he did, unspeakable things would have been done to me.

"You're right. I'm sorry for frightening you. And I'm sorry for my reckless behavior. I'll… I'll…" Contrite and near tears, I promised, "I'll do better. I'll take more care. I'm so sorry, Eliza." I hiccupped as fear and remorse overwhelmed me.

"Shhh, shhh, I know. Don't cry. I'm sorry, too." She moved around the table and took the unoccupied seat to my left. Pulling me into a tight hug, Eliza rushed to assure me. "I'm so very glad you're okay. Unbelievably grateful to… Q, did you say?" At my nod, she continued, "Grateful to Q for protecting you with his life."

"I vow to be more diligent, more careful." I sniffled inelegantly, still embracing my friend. I was three and twenty. Too old to require a caretaker. I was a grown woman and needed to behave as such.

"I know. I'm sorry for being harsh. You scared me. I—" Eliza cut herself off abruptly. Seeming to make up her mind, she cleared her throat. "I don't want to lose anyone else." I squeezed her tighter in response.

Quiet for some time, the room was heavy with my silent recriminations and no doubt Eliza's reflections on the past.

Apropos of nothing, my friend said, "Lord Dashing must have followed you when you didn't return to the gardens. That's the only way he could have found you… in your time of need. How can you say he isn't interested in your affections, Jane? He followed you and made sure you were safe."

What Eliza said made sense, I supposed. I wasn't sure why he followed me exactly. But I did owe Q more than a debt of gratitude. More than my safety or a possible offer of employment. I owed him my life.

"Perhaps," I said in quiet acceptance.

Eliza rolled her eyes. "I do love you. Even if you are in denial about Lord Dashing. I'm just going to keep calling him Lord Dashing. Q sounds like some conspiracy pamphlet circulated by the fanatics in the East End."

I made a tolerant face but snorted at her ridiculousness. "I love you, too. No qualifier on my end, though." And I was suddenly overwhelmed with fierce affection for this woman. She had been my champion for so long, making sure I always saw the best of myself. All of my friends, really. Our circle was protective and accepting. They were my chosen family and I loved them all.

"Fine. No qualifier either," Eliza acquiesced with a smile in my direction. She squeezed my hand once more and then moved around the table to return to her seat. "Now pass the bacon. I'm starving."

On Monday morning, just before eleven, I stood outside Piker House on the cobblestones of St. James's and took in the building façade. A discreet portico hid what all of London knew to be a notorious, rowdy, and uncivilized establishment. I supposed I had never given this or any other gaming hell a serious thought. Aristocratic males frequented these clubs for entertainment and socializing but they also used such businesses to conduct meetings with like-minded individuals. Gentlemen with similar political leanings could be found congregating in certain establishments, but from what little I knew about Piker House, one visited when in search of vice. Gambling, whoring, drinking, and general carousing made places like this dangerous for anyone, but doubly so for a woman like me.

And yet it looked so innocuous in the dim gray light of a fall morning. The air was slightly chilled and rain was threatening. I found myself exceedingly grateful for the use of Dr. Finley's carriage. He and Eliza were ensconced in their duties at the clinic connected to their home. She assured me no one would notice neither mine nor the conveyance's absence for a short drive this morning.

I instructed the driver to return home after alighting from the carriage some moments earlier. I was still contemplating this strange turn of events and my presence in this location when a man joined me in my observations.

I wasn't alarmed. I recognized Daniel from our prior meeting. "Shall we head inside or continue staring at the front door?"

We were nearly the same height. Me with my abundance of size and he with a stockier build. His brown eyes danced as I turned to face him. "I suppose we should go in lest someone spot me on the street unaccompanied."

"My lady." He extended his arm and I took it. But we did not proceed to the front entrance. He led me down the block and through the side garden into a separate doorway. I didn't question our alternate route. Somehow, I didn't imagine I'd be conducting my business at the hazard tables.

"You're welcome to enter the offices through this side door and proceed up the servants' staircase to the third floor. There is a large library for you to conduct your work." He ushered me forward and up the staircase as he spoke.

I was distracted by my new surroundings, striving to take in the sights and sounds. It was remarkably quiet. We had obviously entered in the kitchens. It was warm, with a fire in the hearth, and the smell of something bread-like and comforting emanated throughout. The stairs were narrow and we passed no other individuals on our journey to the offices above stairs. The walls were all dark wood. Paneling lined the hall with thick rugs under our feet. The décor was a bit gaudy for my taste but no matter, gilt frames and baubles would not hinder me in my efforts.

Daniel finally paused by an open doorway and gestured for me to enter. Cautiously, I turned the corner and was met by ridiculous and unfounded disappointment. Perhaps my expression betrayed me, for when Daniel approached, he gave me a knowing smile and said, "Q is unable to join us this morning. He sent me along to fetch you and make the introductions. Lady Jane, this is Mr. Stevens. He's the solicitor." I bobbed a quick curtsey and mustered a small smile that did little to hide my disappointment at the news that Q was nowhere to be found.

Daniel continued his introductions. "And this is Mrs. Betty Hooper. She's the housekeeper for the offices and private living quarters. She'll be about to see to your needs and act as chaperone when required. Stevens here will get you started with your duties."

"Thank you, Mr.—" I paused in the hope he would introduce himself, and perhaps mention the actual name of our employer along with his own title.

"O'Connor," he supplied.

That was it. Nothing else. *Sigh.*

"Well, thank you, Mr. O'Connor, for your assistance this morning." An awkward silence followed my statement. I could only imagine what was happening with my facial expression. Nothing good, I imagined.

Mr. O'Connor shuffled back a few steps. "Of course. Think nothing of it, my lady." And with one final quizzical glance in my direction, he was off.

Those of us remaining in the library seemed frozen until Mrs. Hooper gathered her wits and some of mine as well and bustled over to offer a curtsey. "My lady, I'll be about should you require anything at all. How about a pot of tea for you and Mr. Stevens while you get yourself settled, hmm?"

"Thank you, Mrs. Hooper. That would be lovely," I offered with a genuine smile. It was obvious this woman had no idea what to make of me. With her steel gray hair and shrewd, assessing eyes, it was clear she was expecting my presence in the offices this morning. But it was equally clear she had no idea why I was here.

I was beginning to wonder that myself.

With a quick bob, she was through the doorway and in pursuit of tea for myself and the only remaining occupant of the room. And what a grand room it was. Large, wide windows allowed the gray morning to infiltrate the darkness that made the hallway and staircase seem oppressive. The library was very pleasing. Bookshelves lined the walls on either side of the windows and in front of those sat a large desk. Neat stacks of ledgers were stacked atop it. Parchment and quills, a pot of ink, and several candlesticks lined the sideboard on the wall to my left. There was an intriguing telescope tucked behind the desk and next to the bank of windows. Two high-backed chairs faced the desk and it was clear Mr. Stevens had been occupying one of them as he had awaited my arrival. His fingers tapped impatiently on the chair back as I finally concluded my visual appraisal of the room.

"My lady, won't you join me?" Mr. Stevens indicated I should sit at the desk across from him.

I removed my pelisse and placed it over the back of the chair and situated my reticule on the desk. Finally, I settled myself into the rather comfortable chair facing Mr. Stevens.

He sat as well. "Now, if we might get started. I have your employment contract here. Feel free to review it and prepare any questions you might have for me." He slid several sheets of very official-looking parchment across the table to me, but continued before I had a chance to speak. "These are the ledgers." Another pause to shift a stack of wide record books before me. "I'll let you get to work."

In my utter confusion, Mr. Stevens made it nearly to the hallway before I regained my faculties and blurted, "Wait!"

He reluctantly turned with a pained expression. "Yes, my lady?"

Baffled by the turn of events I said, "I'm sorry, Mr. Stevens. But what is it I'm supposed to be doing?"

With a resigned sigh, the solicitor returned to his seat. His expression distinctly read as frustrated and exhausted. As I looked closer, I noticed his disheveled blond hair and weary gray eyes behind his spectacles. He crossed his legs and leaned forward to place his elbows on the desk between us. "Jane, may I call you Jane?" Without waiting for an answer, he continued, "I am a solicitor. I am not equipped to decode secret ledgers. I'm used to managing estates and holdings, handling trades and sales and property acquisitions. But nothing has prepared me for my client suddenly purchasing this establishment and expecting me to work miracles." He releases a frustrated breath. When I didn't make a move to interject, he went on, "Now, I was told you would be arriving this morning to assist in my efforts to decode the records to determine what is owed to the institution by various debtors. As indicated in your contract, three days per week," he pointed to the parchment in front of me, "you will arrive in these offices to establish a cipher or system or whatever it is you do with numbers in order to provide a list of client accounts for the newly acquired Piker House."

Ah, so Mr. Stevens had been unable to decipher the numerical listings and it would be my job to untangle the notations. Likely, they had been unable to collect on the debts owed to the gaming establishment. In short, Q wanted his money and he wanted to know who owed it to him.

I tried playing dumb in an effort to gain more information. "Mr. Stevens, shouldn't we consult the previous owner in order to determine the accounts and straighten everything out?"

His expression went wide-eyed for a moment before he wrangled it into nonchalance. "I'm afraid that won't be possible. The previous owner of Piker House… is no longer… in London."

"Perhaps we could write to him," I suggested.

Mr. Stevens narrowed his eyes and asserted with some finality, "We won't be doing that, I'm afraid. Nevertheless, the ledgers are here. I'm confident you will be able to determine the client accounts and provide the answers that are so desperately needed."

So I wouldn't be getting any information out of him.

Mr. Stevens made to leave again and had almost made it to the hallway a second time when I called his name. He abruptly turned. It was then I detected true defeat in his features. I should really let him be. It wasn't his fault Q wasn't here to greet me and explain my duties. He didn't know I'd fretted over my first day of employment. How could he possibly suspect I'd worn my best sky-blue morning dress with matching slippers in hopes of… in hopes of something. My ruined expectations were not Mr. Stevens's problem. Q's solicitor had obviously been conscripted to this unpleasant task of managing my time until I settled in. I imagined Mr. Stevens had his own very long list of demanding assignments. He was likely quite out of his depth here at Piker House.

"Never fear, Mr. Stevens. I'll begin immediately and do my best to untangle these accounts."

Mrs. Hooper chose that moment to bustle in with the tea tray. She skirted the harried solicitor and began laying the tea setting on the far end of the desk.

I smiled in thanks before turning back to a relieved Mr. Stevens. "Well, after tea, of course."

THE LADIES WERE in rambunctious spirits the following afternoon. Cassandra was regaling those assembled with a humorous and outrageous account of her latest proposal. Footmen were delivering all manner of refreshments. We'd already consumed the initial wave of tea and biscuits. I spied lemonade and sandwiches on the recently supplied tray. The liveried servants were doing their best to quickly escape the room. Several were pink-cheeked from Cassandra's tale and decidedly uncomfortable in the lady's lively presence. I smiled to myself and met Kathleen's uncomfortable yet amused expression from across the room.

"...and that's when the geese attacked. Poor Charles did his best to appear unperturbed, but what gentleman could possibly continue a proposal when being chased by geese across Hyde Park? I feel ever so dreadful that I inadvertently antagonized them with direct eye contact, but honestly, how was I to look away?" We were all laughing at this point, but Cassandra continued on in dramatic fashion. "Have you ever seen the welts left by goose bites? I didn't even realize they *could* bite. I thought their danger lay in floggings. Who could blame poor dear Charles for crying like that? Eliza, have you ever cared for goose attack patients?"

Eliza valiantly regained her composure to say quite seriously, "No, Cassandra. I'm afraid my talents in the medical field have left me woefully unprepared for victims of geese."

"Aye, Cassandra. We have vicious biting geese in Scotland," came Ashleigh's dry rejoinder as she continued to direct her attention to her embroidery hoop. I'd abandoned all pretense of stitching quite some time ago.

"I did not know that," Cassandra remarked theatrically while reaching for a ham sandwich. "That settles it, I'll never visit the Winstead homeland. Well, unless I should ever need to marry in a hurry. I'm sure word will have spread, and the gangs of violent geese will surely be lying in wait for me in order to seek their revenge."

"Oh, Cassandra. You are a treasure," Fiona pronounced fondly from her seat by the fire, mirth shining brightly in her brown eyes.

"Well, I'm afraid my news isn't as exciting as all that." Mary smiled warmly and motioned toward Cassandra in an all-encompassing gesture. "But David is returning to London for part of the season." We all turned our attention to our lovely friend and made considerable effort to appear pleased by her news.

"Well, that's wonderful," came the duchess's response. Fiona had always been the best at mustering up enthusiasm where Mary's wayward fiancé was concerned. Perhaps it was her ability to support us unconditionally that kept her tone earnest.

"His sister seemed to think he'd stay on through the holidays," Mary continued with a bright if not slightly strained smile. We were all quiet a moment in digesting this tidbit and the likely assumption that Mary had not learned of her betrothed's upcoming return to London from the man himself but from his sister instead.

I had just taken an awkward gulp of tea to cover the fact that my mouth seemed unable to form a smile for Mary's announcement, when Eliza's raised voice caught me unaware. "Jane has some interesting news to share."

All gazes swung in my direction while I focused my attention on Eliza and her diversionary tactics. I knew she was shifting the spotlight from Mary in an effort to avoid awkwardness, as well as playing mischief-maker at my expense. Alas, I couldn't really fault my friend. She knew I didn't keep secrets from our group. It was only a matter of time before I confessed the events of late to our circle. If placing the attention on myself detracted from the odd tension that had settled over the drawing room in light of David's impending return, well, that was fine with me. I'd pay Eliza back later.

"Is it about Lord Dashing?" Kathleen surprised me with her quietly uttered question.

Eliza hurried to respond. "Yes, it is. They danced, and he saved her life, and she's going to work for him." The only sound following my friend's declaration was the sound of Ashleigh chewing a particularly crisp biscuit.

Raised eyebrows and gaping expressions awaited further explanation, so with a resigned sigh, I launched into a speech to recount the events of the Foxworth masquerade. This was met with *ohhhs* and *ahhhs* and a haughty exclamation from Cassandra. "I knew it! I knew he was enchanted with our dear Janie." I didn't contradict her, but instead continued on with my recollection of fleeing the ball and the danger followed by rescue that evening. I couldn't help but glance at Fiona to notice her complete stillness upon hearing I had been attacked by footpads after irresponsible behavior on my part. My brief pause didn't elicit recriminations as I imagined, so I picked up my tale with the encounter at the tavern and resulting offer of employment. That led to the conclusion of my story in describing my first day of service at Piker House on the morning prior.

"So, Lord Dashing, or Q rather, wasn't there? You haven't seen him since the evening he rescued you and escorted you home?" Kathleen again surprised me with her curiosity. Typically an observer at our weekly events, Kat never seemed entirely comfortable in our rowdy company. Perhaps her questions and willingness to engage showed she was finally letting her guard down after months in the duchess's employ.

"Correct," I replied. "I concluded my first day of employment with no Q sighting. His carriage did escort me back to Eliza's home at the end of the workday, though."

"And have you figured out who owes money to the gaming hell?" Mary's line of questioning was not one I was expecting either.

"Well, I haven't figured out the cipher just yet, but I'm not allowed to discuss Piker House patrons if and when I do decode the ledgers," I stated matter-of-factly. After Mr. Stevens had stayed for tea and a bit of conversation, I had reviewed the contents of the contract. It seemed I would be working three days per week, have discreet transportation from Piker House in the form of Q's nondescript black carriage, and I was bound contractually to never disclose the results of my decrypting efforts. I could see the need for secrecy in this respect, and I wouldn't have a problem honoring my employment agreement. I was surprised that Mary's thoughts had turned that direction initially. She shared an unreadable look with Fiona at Q's demands for confidentiality.

"This knowledge, once discovered, could put you in danger, Jane." Fiona searched my face for something. Her intensity was something I couldn't interpret. Before I could offer reassurance of my safety, she went on, "Well, more danger, that is."

This time I understood the censure in her tone. I acknowledged it with eyes cast down toward my lap and repeated the promise I had made to Eliza following the attack. "I know. I will not be so reckless again. I realize I was in very real danger and if Q hadn't arrived when he did, the outcome would likely be very different. I vow, I will take more care."

Fiona stared for a long time and finally nodded, her expression troubled. Kathleen surprised us all once again by saying with some strength behind her words, "I'm glad you're okay, Lady Jane. I'm grateful Lord Dashing followed you and made sure you were safe."

"Thank you, Kat. I'm grateful as well." I acknowledged her heartfelt statement but found I couldn't quite meet her eyes.

"But that is what happened, is it not?" asserted Cassandra. "Lord Dashing *did* follow you. He sought you out once again, Jane. And that has to mean something."

"If he really wanted to see me, I was in his place of business yesterday for several hours. Perhaps his interest only extends to my propensity for numbers and my ability to provide him answers."

As the ladies erupted into discussion, talking over one another and arguing their points, I couldn't seem to focus on their opinions. I could only consider the disappointment I had felt yesterday at Piker House when Q wasn't there. Admitting to myself that I had been looking forward to seeing him and talking to him was perhaps the first time I hadn't successfully moderated my expectations. With a selfish mother, an absent apathetic father, and two sisters who had quite easily left me behind, I did not allow my expectations to run wild and free as a rule. Anticipating disappointment just made my logical and pragmatic mind easier to manage. And for the first time in a very long time, I had allowed my hopes and the secret desires of my heart to get the better of me.

I wanted to see Q, and the sinking feeling in my chest told me I was expecting too much. I didn't know if anticipating disappointment where he was concerned would help prepare my traitorously optimistic heart at all.

The following morning found me distracted and irritable. It was a lovely fall day—mild and bright—which only seemed to aggravate me further.

I hadn't yet made progress in decoding the gaming hell's client list. I'd tried many known numerical ciphers in an effort to reveal Piker House's most notorious patrons. It was apparently wishful thinking to hope I'd quickly expose the secrets of the ledgers. But I hadn't given up. Not at all. I was merely getting started.

I used my time in the offices to balance the records from the previous owner. They'd been left coded and in a bit of a disarray. There was also the matter of the new registers being used by Q and his staff, namely Mr. Stevens, in an effort to track the debts owed by clients since the transfer of ownership. Apparently if you were an aristocrat, you were able to gamble as you wished and leave at the end of the night on the good standing of your reputation no matter how much money you had lost at the hazard tables.

The frazzled solicitor Mr. Stevens had come to appreciate my propensity for all things numerical. We got on quite nicely. He still seemed a bit secretive and undeniably confused about my presence at Piker House. And in all honesty, I was as well. Yet Q was the boss, and he did as he wished. It seemed, to me at least, he indiscriminately bought gaming hells with no rhyme or reason. Apparently, he also hired unmarried ladies. I got the feeling Mr. Stevens found it much easier to simply do his job and not question the motives of his employer.

With a sigh, my gaze strayed to the large bank of windows behind the desk in the library. Our shared office space was unequivocally distracting. If I wasn't determinedly avoiding the bookshelves by sheer force of will, the large and well-appointed gardens were beckoning me with their colors and delights. A small pond and bubbling fountains were closest to the structure we occupied, lined with flower beds that were surely a riot of blooms in the spring and summer months. The formidable hedgerow contained the large space with a wide-open area near the rear of the property and gravel pathway along the perimeter. Truly a hidden sanctuary in the midst of the bustle of St. James's.

"It's a nice day out. You could take your luncheon in the gardens." Mr. Stevens drew my focus with his quiet suggestion. I noticed his attention was firmly on the parchment in front of him.

I felt a bit guilty I had been caught woolgathering and so early in my employment no less. However, I wasn't quite ready to admit even to myself that my distraction was in some way related to my frustration at Q's continued absence. He had hired me. I assumed he'd be interested in the work I was doing. And a very small part of me feared that I yearned for his presence as more than an employer. I simply wanted to see his striking face and spend time with him. Talk to him about his work here and about my ideas. I did not want to consider the aching disappointment I felt at being denied his company.

"Well, perhaps I shall," I replied, gathering myself in an effort to focus wholeheartedly on the tasks at hand. "As you said, it is quite lovely out today, and it would be nice to explore more of the grounds."

Mr. Stevens abandoned his paperwork at my response. "I don't think that's a very good idea, Jane."

"Whyever not? You just said I should take my luncheon out of doors, not in this room. The gardens are exploratory, are they not?"

"The gardens would be appropriate for you to explore, yes," he clarified. "I just wouldn't want to encourage you to further your exploration to other areas of the estate. Q wouldn't like that."

I raised my eyebrows at Mr. Stevens's assertion. I hadn't been explicitly instructed to remain on this floor. Obviously I knew business was conducted on the lower floors. We did not however share working hours with the gaming hell. The doors didn't open to customers before eight in the evening. I was to be transported back to Eliza's at four of the afternoon on every Monday, Wednesday, and Friday. Home in time for tea. And to miss all the excitement of the gaming hell.

I'd noticed the movement of servants on this floor as well. Mrs. Hooper often bustled about. There were living quarters in a separate wing on this level in addition to the library we currently occupied and several closed doors that lined the hallway. I had occasionally passed additional maids in serviceable garb going to and fro on the stairs or in the passageway. But for the most part, our office remained quiet throughout the day. As if the beast that was Piker House was slow to wake, a sleeping dragon below us.

Obviously, a gaming establishment such as this was no place for a lady. But that didn't mean I wasn't curious in the light of day. I had no wish to further tempt gossip or tarnish my already smudged reputation, and yet… What would it be like to explore the empty rooms?

"Q wouldn't like what?" I inquired of Mr. Stevens in an effort to confirm the restrictions placed upon my person.

"He wouldn't like you testing the boundaries of this office. What happens below stairs…" He trailed off. "It would be better if you didn't know."

"Well, I'll just have to ask him myself, won't I?" I didn't know why I was pushing this. I *knew* a gaming hell was no place for me, even during daylight hours before patrons arrived.

"I suppose you could write him a letter." He eyed me over the rim of his spectacles as he thumbed through the contracts on his desk. "But you aren't likely to see him here that often. Q is mainly about in the evenings to manage Piker House. He has a few trusted men to assist him, but we're working on finding someone to fill a more permanent role. Someone to oversee the gaming nightly, so Q can go back to his real life."

I was overwhelmed by disappointment, so much so I overlooked Mr. Stevens's statement about Q's real life and all that might entail. It seemed I was unlikely to see Lord Dashing during my employment hours. My displeasure wasn't swift. It was a growing thing. I could feel it warming my cheeks and hollowing my stomach. My nose burned and I breathed deeply in an effort to moderate my physical response to my very one-sided expectations.

When would I learn to be more sensible? Apparently where Lord Dashing was concerned… not anytime soon.

~

I DID NOT HAVE luncheon in the gardens. Sometime later, I found myself wandering below stairs to the kitchens in search of nourishment. Mr. Stevens left shortly after our awkward conversation to attend to his own offices and other duties for a brief time. He assured me he would return later in the afternoon. I got the sense his presence at Piker House was in order to see me settled. With Q busy seeing to other tasks, there was no one to manage my employment directly. Perhaps Mr. Stevens felt sorry for me in my perceived neglect. No matter. Despite my earlier distraction, I was quite adept at time management. I knew my objectives and responsibilities and would conduct myself accordingly. I would be above reproach and prove myself invaluable.

Upon descending the servants' staircase and entering the kitchens, a startled Betty greeted me hesitantly. "My lady, did you need something?"

"Good day, Mrs. Hooper," I replied brightly. "I thought I might bother you for some refreshment for my noonday meal."

"Of course, Lady Jane. It's no bother at all." At her kind response, I noticed another individual by the stove. He was large and burly with dark hair and an apron about his waist.

Mrs. Hooper noticed the direction of my gaze and moved to provide introductions. "Lady Jane, this is our cook, Smith."

Smith gave me an assessing look, not so much an uncomfortable leer but definitely a once-over. He examined my attire critically from my sensible walking boots to the tight bun in which I'd wrestled my wayward auburn locks. He seemed confounded by my presence; nevertheless, I remembered myself and my manners. I stood a bit straighter before the middle-aged chef and finally found my voice. "Hello, Mr. Smith. A pleasure to meet you."

He regarded me a moment longer before turning wide eyes to Mrs. Hooper. She quickly clarified, "Lady Jane works above stairs, in the offices with Mr. Stevens."

Smith finally turned his attention back to me with a quiet nod and muttered, "Just Smith, my lady. And you're most welcome."

I couldn't be sure what their brief exchange had been about, but it struck me as quite odd, and I also got the distinct impression I was not at all what Smith had been expecting when a woman walked into his kitchens.

Mrs. Hooper distracted me from my reflections. "Would you care for a tray brought up, my lady? I can assemble a repast of cheese, fruit, some bread, a bit of chicken perhaps?"

"Oh, no. I do not wish to be a bother, as I said. What were you having?" I indicated her place setting at the work table. It appeared to be a bowl with steaming liquid, a hard roll, and a dish of tea from a nearby pot.

Her confusion returned as she looked to the table and the meal she was clearly enjoying alone before I interrupted with my entrance moments earlier. "It's soup, my lady. Vegetable soup."

I cut her off quickly before she tried to usher me back up the stairs with more promises of trays. I truly didn't wish to create more work for her. I could see the origins of the contents of her soup bowl simmering away in a cauldron on the stove. It was not my desire that she abandon her warm meal in order to serve my every whim.

"Might I have a bowl for myself and join you?"

"I… I…" Betty was slow to recover but eventually answered in the affirmative. "Of course, my lady. Let me fetch it for you." She kindly returned with my own steaming soup bowl and hesitated only a moment before placing it on the work table across from her own position. I retrieved my bread from the adjacent basket while she returned once again with a teacup.

I sat and quickly reached for the teapot and poured for myself. "Would you care for any more?" I indicated Betty's nearly empty dish. She could only nod.

I knew what was happening. Mrs. Hooper was astonished by my actions. I should not have poured my own tea, and I categorically should not have offered to assist her with her own beverage. It made little sense to me when it was just the two of us dining to stand on ceremony. I didn't believe in the ridiculous societal rules that demanded I act incapable. She was bothered by my actions and yet I couldn't feel sorry about it. There was no harm in pouring my own tea in the privacy of this kitchen. I was alone upstairs, could I not simply be practical and take my meal here where it would be easier to serve?

However, it was obvious practicality was not prized in our society. Mrs. Hooper's reaction, though well hidden, confirmed my outlandish behavior.

"I apologize if I made you uncomfortable. I'm used to a small household and do my utmost to never burden the staff unnecessarily. If you prefer I leave you to your meal alone, I shall retreat above stairs." I made to stand but her wrinkled and work-roughened hand upon my arm stopped me.

"No, my lady. Of course you are welcome. Forgive me, I'm unused to gently-bred ladies in residence." Betty shared a very brief look with Smith before meeting my eyes once more. This time, her unease bled away and genuine warmth entered her features for the first time. It seemed my act of contrition had softened whatever opinion she had been harboring. Apologies had the ability to illicit a myriad of responses, I'd found. Perhaps my earnest tone and honest claim struck the appropriate chord to smooth our future interactions. And whatever knowledge she shared with the cook appeared to relax her stance and diffuse the tension in the room even further. I caught a fleeting smile on Smith's lips before he turned for the larder, leaving us alone. I wondered what that was about. Knowing when to leave well enough alone, I had no desire to push my luck. The mystery would stand.

Giving her a nod of understanding, I spooned up a bite from my own bowl and blew across the hot liquid before commenting, "Not many daytime employees at Piker House, I would imagine. I've seen very few individuals beyond Mr. Stevens and a few of the staff above stairs."

Wiping her mouth with a linen cloth, she inclined her head in agreement. "That's quite true, my lady. This building comes alive at night. Piker House is quite forgotten during the day."

I knew what Mr. Stevens had indicated regarding Lord Dashing's schedule, but it couldn't hurt to receive confirmation. A little innocent snooping during luncheon couldn't hurt. Despite my curiosity, I tensed for disappointment before striving for subtlety and likely missing the mark with my next inquiry. "And Q… He's here in the evenings to see to the gamblers and the like?"

Mrs. Hooper searched my face. Whatever she saw there had her softening before responding quietly and with a measured amount of sympathy. "Yes, my lady. It's rare to see the master here during the daylight hours."

Ah, well. Missed the mark, indeed. Subtlety was never my strong suit. Too direct for that. Not to mention my ability to wear facial expressions like a windowpane. Reflective, transparent, and with a tendency to crack.

We continued our meal in not-quite-comfortable silence but something like it. Smith bustled in and out with supplies from the pantry, likely preparing for the evening's service. Piker House didn't provide full provisions to customers, but nobility often made demands the majority of establishments did their best to accommodate.

Mrs. Hooper whisked away our dishes and bid me a good afternoon. I decided to visit the gardens after all. A quick trip out-of-doors to take in the glorious sunshine would certainly do no harm. I wouldn't stay long enough to impact my productivity nor my fair complexion.

Quietly exiting the side door into the gardens, I emerged into tranquility. The bubbling fountain and serene pond drew my immediate attention. My boots crunched on the gravel pathway and the mild London air provided a much-needed distraction. I settled myself on a stone bench overlooking the water and simply closed my eyes and turned my face toward the sun.

What must have been just moments later, I heard the telltale sound of boots making their way along the path and looked up in startled surprise to see Lord Dashing approaching. My shock must have shown on my face, but he made no comment, merely lifted an amused brow.

"My lady." Q gave a brief bow in greeting. "Might I join you?"

"Of course," I managed through my shock. After telling my hopes to settle themselves, here I was, facing the very object of my anticipation. "What are you doing here?" The words came out breathless, much to my dismay.

Lord Dashing—I'd given up on thinking of him as simply Q—leaned forward conspiratorially. "I work here."

Unfortunately, I wasn't in the mood for his amused eyebrows nor his open and charming expression. Why couldn't I simply be happy to see him? This was what I'd wanted. What I had hoped for, against all reason and common sense. And now I was buggering it up because his appearance conflicted with my expectations. I was told he wouldn't be here and yet here he was.

Attempting to reign in this unjustified frustration, I took a deep breath and asked, "But I thought you were only here in the evenings to oversee the gaming hell?"

If he was surprised by my knowledge of his schedule and habits, he didn't show it. Q remained unaffected. "Typically, I suppose, I'm here in the evenings. I thought I might check in and see how you were fairing. I apologize for not being here on your first day to get you settled. I had some unavoidable business to attend to."

I nodded in understanding. "Oh, that's quite all right. Mr. Stevens has been very amiable and welcoming."

"Is that so?"

"Indeed," I replied, falling into our familiar pattern. Lord Dashing met my smile with a small one of his own.

With my irrational frustration at his surprise appearance nearly abated, I finally took in his appearance. In a dark gray wool suit custom fitted to his immaculate form, Lord Dashing looked very fine in the afternoon sun. The white of his cravat contrasted with his slightly bronzed skin, as if he'd been outdoors recently and enjoyed the fading warmth of autumn. But his eyes, they fairly glowed, seemingly lit from within.

I was starting to feel very warm indeed.

Thankfully Q seemed oblivious to my scrutiny, and remarked, "Betty told me where to find you. Are you enjoying the gardens?"

"Oh, yes." I nodded eagerly. "It's lovely. Mr. Stevens thought it would be a good idea to take my luncheon out here, but once I found Mrs. Hooper in the kitchens, I just decided to join her instead. Perhaps another day I could enjoy dining alfresco." A victim of nerves, I finished with an odd Italian pronunciation. *Why did I do that?* Less talking, Jane. No accents.

Q grew very still as I spoke and, I must admit, looked quite stunned by the end of my speech. Perhaps the gardens were off-limits. Or maybe my use of the Italian language was as offensive as I feared.

But before I could question his reaction, he said, "You… You took your meal in the kitchens with Mrs. Hooper?"

I looked down at my hands in order to avoid his confused expression. I was always doing this. Not behaving quite the way a gently-bred lady should, saying the wrong thing, speaking my mind, priding the practical and logical over the socially acceptable. I finally answered without looking up. "Yes. She was kind enough to accept me at her table and indulged my interruption. I didn't wish to further inconvenience her by requesting a picnic on the lawn."

"You didn't wish to inconvenience Mrs. Hooper, the housekeeper?" he said slowly, seeking to clarify.

"I suppose—" I cut myself off before meeting his gaze, unsure what I would read on his handsome face. "That's accurate. Yes. I didn't wish to inconvenience her."

Naturally, he remained unreadable. Q had perfected the mask of indecipherable calm. I barely knew him and had already determined that fact. And yet as we stared at one another, my face open and trying to convey honesty and his in Q-like assessment, his expression transformed. It was subtle to be sure, but his features relaxed and I detected an odd sort of approval. It was a rare thing to find members of the *ton* who respected and valued their servants. At best, they were ignored. I supposed for a man like Q who held such progressive ideas about elitism and our society, it was only natural that he didn't conform. Of course he would approve of my appreciation and gratitude for the hard work of his staff.

For once I didn't feel alone in my awkwardness. I felt alive.

Perhaps sensing the need for a change in subject, Q cleared his throat and asked, "How are the ledgers? Have you made any progress there?" He seemed merely conversational, not anxious for a status report.

I liked the way I felt while talking to him, but made a concerted effort to transition to work-related topics. "I'm still working through possible ciphers. I'm confident I'll be able to crack the code and translate the client list for you. For now, I'm balancing your current accounts since taking over Piker House and making headway there."

"That's good." He shifted in his seat, turning toward me as he spoke again. "Are you enjoying the work? That is, are you happy with your duties?"

I found it hard to stare directly at Lord Dashing for a protracted period of time. His eyes were so intense in their regard. I feared if I didn't take frequent breaks, I'd stare openly and make this conversation exceedingly uncomfortable. "I'm quite content with my responsibilities here," I answered honestly.

"That's good," Q said on a sigh.

"Besides, it's not as if my former clients are likely to return for consultation. Those that were remaining sent letters to end our arrangement. So I'm very thankful for this position and your kindness." Again, honest. I was very grateful for our serendipitous meeting.

"I'm not that kind," came his surprising reply. Before I could refute his claim, he continued, "Would that bother you? If your society matrons continue to rebuff you and turn away your services for good?"

"I would be disappointed, I suppose. I appreciate certain measures of loyalty. But I enjoy my work here, brief though it has been. It feels exciting and secretive. As if I am a spy working to decode hidden messages."

"You desire the life of a spy then?" I could tell he was teasing, but it didn't seem the mean sort of mocking I was so often accustomed to.

"Oh, of course. I am definitely spy material. I'm sure the War Office will come calling any day now," I managed to tease back, indulging in a mirthful laugh. Were we having a flirtation? I wondered if I was doing it right.

I was suddenly struck with a bout of nerves. I didn't know how to carry on a flirtation with a man. Being with John didn't require flirting on my part. We simply conversed. I never made a concentrated effort to amuse John and be amused in return. Coy and coquettish were more in line with Cassandra and her interactions in a ballroom. She laughed loudly and often, usually flapping her eyelashes in a pleasing manner. Lords were simply drawn to her. Now that I considered it, it was likely just her outgoing personality. I was… not like that.

This bantering, the back-and-forth with Q in the garden, was multifaceted. I warred between self-consciousness and butterflies erupting behind my sternum.

His eyebrows remained amused and my pulse leaped once more. "Well, I hope the crown doesn't steal you away just yet." Warmth pooled low in my belly at Q's admiring look. Those butterflies were approaching maximum velocity.

In a show of sheer survival instinct, I straightened on the bench. "I should probably get back to work."

Q's gaze was questioning. Perhaps signs of self-preservation weren't evident in my expression, but I felt certain he could read some inner turmoil there. Q stood slowly and held out an arm. "I'll escort you back to the library, if that's all right?"

I nodded and felt grateful I hadn't ruined our time together with my abrupt decision to depart. These feelings were so new and utterly overwhelming.

We made our way along the gravel path, through the kitchens, and up the service staircase in quiet contemplation before emerging in the long hallway of the third floor. His heat and nearness were addicting. The simple act of walking by his side was fraught with tension—the good kind. The best kind.

"Perhaps you could enjoy a picnic in the gardens another day. I could let Betty know in advance and she could pack a few items for you. So you wouldn't feel like an imposition," Q said as he slowed our progress outside the library doorway.

I appreciated his consideration for my concerns and for Mrs. Hooper's time and energy. "If it's not too much trouble, that sounds lovely. Thank you." Genuine pleasure sufficed my demeanor, chasing away my previous doubts.

"And perhaps I could join you." At these quietly uttered words, my head snapped up abruptly to meet Lord Dashing's patented intense stare. "If that's agreeable, that is," he murmured, seemingly unsure of his welcome.

I smiled then. Full and wide. I often had difficulty interpreting the reactions of others, their hidden smiles and secretive expressions. Conversing with nobility was often an exercise in subterfuge and subtlety. Both elements I struggled with and didn't see the need for. I preferred honesty and directness. Therefore, I wanted Q to read the authenticity in my smile when I replied, "I'd like that very much."

Lord Dashing escorted me the remaining distance to the library before lifting my hand from his arm. I assumed he'd simply deposit me at my desk and be on his way, but he lingered. Twining our fingers together, Q raised my hand to his lips. Slowly and quite deliberately, he rotated my hand and placed a kiss on the inside of my wrist just beyond the fabric of my kid gloves. The heat from his mouth was deliciously obscene and I felt my breath stutter on an inhale. I should have been shocked by his behavior and scandalized by his forwardness. And yet… All I could muster was a sense of regret that I'd cut our afternoon short in a moment of weakness.

Eyes locked, Q pulled away from my skin. Lowering my hand to my side, he retreated a pace before turning slowly and exiting the room. I stood frozen in place, staring after his departed form. With my opposite hand covering my inner wrist, I could feel the heat from his scandalous touch and sought to trap it within.

What was happening?

I spent the afternoon mostly absorbed by the ledgers lining my desk, but couldn't help but allow my attention to stray to the gardens a time or two, remembering the sun on my face, the man at my side, and the butterflies wreaking havoc on my carefully laid plans.

Ten

"What's that face you're making?" Mr. Stevens's sudden question startled me out of the data I was reviewing.

"I suppose it's my thinking face." I blinked away the endless columns of numbers to take in the waning light entering through the window. It appeared to be much later in the afternoon than I realized. I rolled my shoulders back to alleviate some of the stiffness from sitting so long.

It was Friday afternoon, two days after my surprise run-in with Q, and I'd come to work today wondering if Lord Dashing would arrive and we'd have that picnic. I hated to admit, even to myself, but I'd been looking forward to the prospect of more time alone with my mysterious employer. I found myself thinking of him at the oddest times. I never felt that way with John. I was much more likely to encounter an article or publication that roused my interest and left me longing to discuss it with my circle of friends, the embroidery ladies. But recently I'd wondered what Q would think about a pamphlet I'd reviewed on the suffragettes and their cause. Would we agree? Disagree? What conclusions would he reach regarding the information? Would he care at all or simply find my interests boring? Somehow, I got the impression Lord Dashing enjoyed our discourse. He listened attentively when I spoke and often engaged me in questions that furthered our discussions.

Was I starting to think of Q as a friend? I thought about seeking his opinion on subjects similar to how I sought Fiona's. But the simplicity of friendship didn't seem to necessarily fit what I was thinking and feeling for Q. It was a complex, layered sort of desire. I wanted his ideas and his company, yes. But I also wanted something else. Something I couldn't put a name to just yet.

I also wanted to learn his bloody name, but found myself diverted on that front. Everyone I'd encountered at Piker House simply called him Q as I had been instructed. The mystery was maddening, and yet when I was in Q's presence, I didn't seem to care about learning his surname or his title, whatever it may be.

"Now *that* is not your thinking face. What's happening over there?" Mr. Stevens once again startled me out of my own thoughts.

I could feel a blush high on my cheeks. Unwilling to admit the direction of my inner musings, I said, "I was just surprised it was so very late in the day. So absorbed was I in the latest figures, I didn't realize the time nor did I remember my luncheon."

A peek out the windows behind me showed another lovely autumn day as the sun slowly made its way closer to the horizon. Another day without Q in residence. There was no word from him and I'd come to the conclusion our unexpected encounter earlier in the week was just that, highly unexpected and unlikely to be repeated any time soon. I worked to keep the disappointment off my face lest Mr. Stevens's keen eye detect my inner turmoil. After all, there was plenty of time for a picnic. Q undoubtedly didn't mean we would immediately dine together. Yet I still felt disappointed, and then silly for entertaining such disappointment.

Moving on.

"Should we ring for tea and have a break then?" came Mr. Stevens's suggestion.

I smiled warmly in response, content to stay a bit later today. "That sounds lovely, yes."

Several minutes later, we were settled on opposite sides of the large desk in the library. Mr. Stevens added milk and sugar to his cup and sighed after a long sip. "That's perfect. I needed that. I'm exhausted."

"The life of a solicitor, I imagine." I blew along the surface of my cup before finally taking a small drink.

"It does keep me quite busy managing estates and multiple clients."

I didn't know that much about Mr. Stevens. Our interactions had been mostly work-related. I did know he was unmarried and kept his own offices in a space nearby on St. James's.

"So it's not just Q and his affairs that have you overworked?" I inquired lightly, knowing the solicitor must contain a multitude of secrets. Confidentiality, and so on.

"Not at all. I have a myriad of clients and duties that require my attention, but Q does seem to necessitate more involvement than most."

Oh really. "The sudden acquisition of a notorious gaming hell will likely do that." I briefly glanced to Mr. Stevens before looking away, once again striving for subtlety but mostly more detail.

"Honestly, if it had just been the purchase and procurement of Piker House, that wouldn't have been such a strain on my time and energy. But it was everything else that went along—" He abruptly cut himself off from saying more. With a guilty squint from behind his spectacles, Mr. Stevens simplified, "Yes, Q does keep me busy."

I supposed I could push for more information, but decided I wasn't likely to be successful extracting secrets from a solicitor. Besides, I enjoyed sharing my time in the office with Mr. Stevens. He was kind. I didn't want to make things strained and awkward.

"Well, it can't be easy rushing back and forth between here and your rented office space. If you're running yourself ragged on my account, I would feel terrible. I'm settling in nicely. I have Betty and occasionally Q or Mr. O'Connor."

"It's no trouble. I actually enjoy working here with you and sharing the space. I maintain my main office in order to have a suitable meeting location for clients, but I like being here when my schedule allows it." I didn't get the sense from Mr. Stevens's words that he was seeking my company for any romantic purposes. He seemed a trifle lonely, if I had to guess. Perhaps this was an opportunity to acquire a new friend, someone who shared his vocational interests.

"I'm happy to have you here as well. But please do cease rushing about if you become too exhausted. I don't want to negatively impact your work or worse, your social engagements," I rushed to encourage him as I placed my remaining tea back on the desk.

"Oh, I—" A huff of laughter interrupted his words. "I assure you, there are not ever so many social engagements demanding my attention."

"I can hardly believe that, Mr. Stevens. In all honesty, I do my best to avoid them. You have a genuine wallflower in your midst. Although I will say, I rather enjoy dancing." I recalled Q at the masquerade and the closeness of our bodies. The proximity and heat, the overwhelming desire to follow wherever he led. Realizing I had fallen silent for too long, I quickly added, "With the right partner."

Mr. Stevens's focus abruptly sank to the desk in front of him as if his gaze were weighed down. His cheeks flushed, and he blew out a frustrated breath before meeting my eyes resolutely. "I'm afraid I haven't found the right partner, and if I had," he asserted with a sad smile, "it's unlikely I'd be able to dance with him."

I worked determinedly to keep the shock from my face, knowing instinctively that Mr. Stevens was trusting me with something precious. The knowledge of his proclivities surprised me, but I was firm in my regard that he should only have my support. Therefore, I endeavored to meet his smile with one of my own before confiding, "I thought I had found a partner, but no amount of dancing in ballrooms could make him the right one." Courting John meant we danced together the requisite number of times, took a turn about the room, and then spoke quietly while drinking watered-down lemonade. It just took my absence from a single event for John to cast me from his thoughts completely in favor of doing God knows what with an unchaperoned young lady.

Wishing to impart wisdom but knowing our situations were in no way similar, I gentled my voice and carefully said, "Perhaps your right partner, your perfect person, isn't waiting for a dance. Perhaps he's just waiting for you to enter a room."

"Maybe you're right, Jane." Mr. Stevens gave me a quiet smile and a brief nod.

"Oh, I am. I'm nearly almost always right." I saw his nod of acknowledgement and raised him a wide smile of my own.

"Then we shall get along just fine, for I am never wrong," he teased with eyes bright and amused.

We laughed together as the sun stretched across the sky.

My chosen family was not bound by blood. Honoring friendships was something very important to me. Mr. Stevens was a new friend, but I valued his honesty, treasured his trust, and would guard his confidence.

~

I DIDN'T REALIZE the time for a picnic with Q was nearing. Perhaps if I had, I wouldn't have gotten caught snooping about on the lower floors of Piker House.

During my second week of employment, I was finally feeling settled. Betty and I were conversing regularly and dining together often. Mr. Stevens was an efficient and productive partner in our shared office space. We had decided to take tea together in the afternoons when he was available, and it suited our growing friendship quite nicely. I'd still only seen Lord Dashing on the one occasion in the gardens. And I took the plain black carriage back home to Eliza's residence every afternoon. I had a routine and followed a schedule which felt important, purposeful. I liked it.

Even as I was establishing new roles and relationships, I felt the absence of my female companions. Eliza and I were a bit off as of late. Dr. Finley had grown more and more absent; therefore, Eliza was filling in for him more frequently. Her career was flourishing as she strove to insinuate herself in the male-dominated medical community. I was happy for my friend, but I missed her greatly. I hadn't returned to our Tuesday ladies' salon since the week prior when Cassandra regaled us with her latest proposal and I'd confided my masquerade encounter with Lord Dashing. This week's meeting had been cancelled as Fiona was feeling a bit under the weather. All in all, I'd been focused on my new employment and running through ways to crack the cipher and decode the ledger.

Wednesday morning at Piker House, I found myself alone in the library. Mild, sunny weather had returned after several days of typical London misting rain and fog. I was happy to see the sun again.

While glancing at the clock over the mantle and fantasizing about Smith's roast beef I would likely be served for my midday meal, a bright flash of red caught my attention near the open doorway. It wasn't unusual to hear and see maids moving about on this floor. I knew there were other rooms and living quarters nearby. But I didn't know any maid who wore red. I couldn't fathom what the sharp burst of color might be other than a crimson-colored skirt moving quickly down the hallway.

Interesting.

Rising from the desk, I didn't pause to consider my actions, I simply moved out into the passage, intent on… what, I didn't know. As I emerged from the library, I caught sight of a woman. A very tall woman wearing a bright scarlet gown, vanishing around a corner.

Maneuvering quickly down the hall, I heard the clack of slippers descending the main staircase. I hadn't ventured into this area of the establishment. Despite my curiosity, there had been no reason to. I honestly didn't require Mr. Stevens's warning about exploring the grounds to know a gaming hell was dangerous in many ways, my reputation being chief among them.

Nevertheless, I continued down the stairs after my target. The pull was instinctual. I didn't know why I was so adamant to discover this woman, but something niggled in my subconscious and pushed me to hasten my descent.

I wound around the corner, hand gliding along the newel post as the mysterious woman vanished down the next flight. Her auburn hair was fashionably curled and up about her crown, jeweled pins throughout. If I hadn't already deduced from her colorful garb that she was no in-house servant, then the perfectly styled coiffure would have given her away. Perhaps it was the flash of profile I caught on the final turn before reaching the second-floor landing and the gaming hell proper, but I could have sworn this woman looked familiar.

It couldn't be.

I was already scanning left and right to determine the direction the lady had taken, and that is perhaps why I failed to take in the surroundings of the gaming hell or the wall of chest I smacked into with a bone-jarring thud.

Strong hands grasped my upper arms and held me away from his body. I knew without looking up it was Q. His subtle cedar and parchment scent filled my head and distracted me from my mad pursuit. What was I doing? I was chasing some woman who showed a passing resemblance to a ghost from my past… from the side… and with no evidence whatsoever. If she heard me in pursuit, she probably thought me insane. Then again, why didn't I call out and why didn't she stop?

With a deep breath, I finally lifted my head to see a concerned frown on Lord Dashing's lovely face.

"Are you all right?" he inquired steadily.

I pulled out of his arms and brushed my hands along my dress as if dusting off our collision were physically possible. "Quite well, thank you. I apologize for intruding on… your person. I-I was distracted and not watching where I was going."

Q looked down the hallway to his right and then back toward me. "What were you doing down here? I didn't think I needed to warn you away from the lower floors. It seemed obvious that your presence here would be hazardous for many reasons."

He stepped closer and regained the space I had put between us when I'd removed myself from his embrace. I longed to look beyond him to take in Piker House's main floor, but I couldn't see beyond the irritated gentleman in front of me. It was easy to forget how large he was. As an above-average height woman in London, I frequently found myself eye to eye with most men, well, eye to forehead, if I was honest. Having Q in my personal space reminded me of our dance at the masquerade and how well we fit together. How close his face was to mine. His lips.

That slightly full upper lip was now pressed in a tight line. Oh yes, waiting for my response. "I-I…" I was unsure how to proceed. Should I admit I was chasing someone down the stairs? I didn't think the scarlet woman was an employee, but I didn't wish to get anyone in trouble if that turned out to be the case. "I wished to have a look around. I didn't think it would be a problem so early in the evening. I do know to avoid the gaming hell during business hours. I'm not completely inept."

In a very ungentlemanly maneuver, Q rolled his eyes. "I never said you were inept. But you are apparently very curious and have a tendency to wander away from your desk. First the gardens and now the main floor of a notorious gaming establishment. I wonder…"

Unable to look away, I realized I was very warm. Must have been the race down the staircase. And the collision. Surprise can make you feel a bit overheated. I believe I'd read that somewhere.

"I wonder," Q repeated, voice low and dangerous, "if I need to tie you to your desk to keep you out of trouble."

I found myself for once at a loss for words at the image his threat immediately conjured. I managed a strangled, "Oh my…" I hadn't looked away from his face so I saw the change come over him. The challenge of his words reflected the challenge in his gaze. Those blue eyes were no longer icy. Heat lurked in their depths, liquid pools displaying mischief and something else. If I didn't know better, I'd say he liked the idea of restraining me, leaving me at his mercy.

Well.

This entire day was completely unexpected. From the mysterious women in red to this odd and frankly heated exchange with Q, my mind was having trouble processing. And my body. My body was feeling off-kilter as well. From the intensity of his nearness and his heat, the scent of him and the wicked turn my thoughts had taken. Attraction was bubbling to the surface again. Was he feeling it, too?

In a move of subtle self-preservation, I looked down, only to realize that my hands were no longer merely hanging from my wrists but for some strange reason were pressed to Lord Dashing's chest. When had *that* happened?

Cheeks and neck and basically all body parts flushing in embarrassment, I stepped quickly away and clasped my hands in front of me. "Yes, well," I mumbled, unsure of where to lead the conversation. I found there was no segue between being tied to a desk and, well, anything really.

Valiantly and with much effort, I drew myself up. "I think you're just trying to distract me from exploring these lower floors."

Q allowed the shift in discussion and merely raised a skeptical eyebrow before replying, "You must admit, Piker House isn't the best place for a lady such as yourself."

That made me compare the kind of lady I appeared to be with the scarlet lady I had followed onto this floor. Were we so different?

Before I could voice my objection, Q rushed to add, "Even during the daylight hours."

My huff of indignation was barely audible, but he heard it. Q noticed everything. He let out an amused breath before offering, "But perhaps with the right chaperone, you could explore the fixtures on this floor."

My focus detached itself from my clasping, nervous hands and snapped up to his face to gauge the sincerity of his proposition. I narrowed my gaze before agreeing outright. "Are you making more promises you don't intend to keep?"

Q's confusion drew a small V-shaped furrow between his brows. "What promise did I break?"

At his genuine question, I realized how silly I must sound. A nagging woman demanding to know where her man had been. He wasn't mine, and yet I had allowed this… this hope to fly away with itself. The idea of spending time with Lord Dashing, whether for picnics or future tours of the lower levels, would all lead to disappointment on my part. I'd never truly longed to spend time with a man in such a way. I was getting muddled just considering it.

Feeling silly and embarrassed, I finally admitted, "I wasn't sure if you truly meant to join me for luncheon. I don't often see you in the offices and I'd begun to wonder where you were and if you were coming back." The weight of my mortification had my eyes glued to the elaborate carpets beneath my feet. Luckily the intricate designs were quite interesting.

Q placed a finger just under my chin and lifted until my gaze connected with his. "Jane, it's better if you don't know where I am, nor the business I conduct."

It was the gentle understanding in his tone and perhaps the curious wonder in his expression that someone could possibly be eager for his company that allowed me to continue with a bit of confidence. "I can't be expected to wait around all afternoon for you to join me. I'll get light-headed. I might swoon."

Q let out a disbelieving snort. "You're too practical to swoon."

Secretly pleased with Q's assessment, I replied, "You could leave a note if you're to be delayed or unavailable. It would be the considerate thing to do."

As if he knew I'd missed him, he bit his lip to stop his smile from spreading. "You are *angry* with me."

"I am not angry. I'm just… just *vexed* by your vague plans. I have expectations. I enjoy a schedule. It keeps everything tidy."

Smile finally wrangled, Lord Dashing attempted a solemn nod. He fell short, but not by a lot. "Absolutely. You're right. I shall endeavor to improve my behavior. We wouldn't want anything to get too messy." Sparkling blue eyes urged me to join in his mirth. Before I had the chance to respond, he continued, "In fact, I think you should leave notes for me as well."

"What? Why? You know where I am and what I'm doing," I protested.

His expression turned wry as he looked theatrically from side to side. That eyebrow rose in an attempt to make his point that for the second time now he'd found me in an unexpected location on the estate.

"Yes, all right. But most of the time, I'm in the library above stairs *working*," I conceded with a noble amount of exasperation. But really? Correspondence is grossly overrated. What good is a letter? I can't read a letter's facial expressions or tone of voice. I can't deduce based on a letter's judgmental eyebrow. I prefer face-to-face interactions. I needed that intimacy in order to better perceive intent. It's hard enough to interpret the subtle meaning and nuance in a conversation with members of the *ton*. Letters and correspondence added another layer of frustration and ambiguity.

Q cleared his throat and turned my attention away from my inner tirade on nonverbal communication and back to him. "Well, perhaps I'd like an update on your progress, and I might also be interested in knowing if you were thinking of me as well."

Quite sure I'd heard him incorrectly, my stare intensified and my mouth likely hung open, catching flies. But, wait. What did that mean? He wanted to know if I was thinking of him? As if such a thing were desirable. And we wanted that? Suddenly the entirety of his suggestion permeated my fog.

As well.

Had two words in the English language ever held such potential, such possibility?

Did that mean he was thinking of me in return?

Fairly certain my brain was malfunctioning, I offered no response at first. We had drifted closer once more. Q was merely a breath away. Luckily, my hands hadn't risen of their own accord again. We weren't touching but it was a near thing. One synchronized inhale would cause a brushing of our bodies, and then where would we be?

"That seems… I should say…" I inwardly cursed my inability to form a coherent response.

Q let out a long breath. Were the tips of his ears a bit pink? "You are one of the smartest individuals I have ever met, and yet you—" A huff of humorless laughter interrupted his statement. It was a moment before he continued, "You seem to miss my obvious intentions."

And with that, he raised his hands to my face, cradled my jaw, and kissed me.

Eleven

Warm gloved hands held my face and my own rose to cover his, to feel him embracing me. To confirm this was actually happening.

Lord Dashing was kissing me.

And I was kissing him back.

His lips were firm but yielding, soft in a way I hadn't imagined. Admittedly, I had speculated over his mouth quite a bit. As he moved over me, tasting me, I felt surprised by how gentle he was. Despite my surprise at his kiss and how intense he seemed in everyday interactions, this kiss was tender. Perhaps he thought me a hapless virgin who'd never been kissed. Well, he'd be half-right. This wasn't my first kiss, but it was the first one that ever made me think of more. Of reaching, grasping hands, breathless exchanges, and the sounds I'd make if he descended and ran his lips along my neck.

This was mild-mannered seduction. I felt barely restrained and he seemed utterly contained.

So I opened my mouth and darted my tongue along his lower lip.

He froze.

Our hands were still interlaced as he cradled my jaw but at the movement of my tongue, he grasped my fingers and moved our joined hands down my neck and shoulders, skimming my sides, and anchoring them behind my back to pull me flush against him. My arms were bent in such a way that our hands locked us in an embrace that I was powerless to escape.

Perhaps I wouldn't mind being tied to my desk.

I was overwhelmed by the feel of his body, the hard planes and muscle, the heat. Unsure if the pounding I felt within was his heart or my own, I relished his embrace. Q held me tightly as he deepened the kiss, taking over the brief seduction I'd initiated with my tongue on his lower lip. He invaded and dominated, but I felt secure in his grasp. My body responded much the same way it always did in his presence. I was drawn to him and that swooping sensation in my stomach had returned. I had the sudden urge to shuck my passive participation in our secret kisscapade, longing to touch him. Who knew when I'd have the chance again?

I unlaced our fingers and brought my arms up to clutch him to me. One hand slipped to the back of his neck feeling the soft short hairs there, and the other hand slid around his back to keep him close. His hands stayed on my lower back, an anchor in the storm. And I was lost. Lost to his attentions and this overwhelming attraction that made me reckless and unmoored. I didn't know it could feel this way. This sense of urgency, devastating in its intensity.

Q broke off suddenly, his mouth leaving mine. He didn't release his hold, however. We stayed together, bodies locked, breathing the same air, arms pulling each other close. He rested his forehead against mine and closed his eyes before finally saying, "I didn't mean for that to happen."

I stiffened at his admission. Was he saying he didn't mean to kiss me? Feeling the disappointment settle like a weight in my stomach, I moved to extricate myself.

Correctly interpreting my attempt to flee, Q hurriedly added, "That's not how I intended it. I just meant… I didn't anticipate the moment getting so out of hand. Losing control that way. You seemed so stunned and oblivious that I could want even a letter from you. That I could want your thoughts and attentions. I wanted you to know. I wanted you to finally see."

"I see you," I whispered.

Our breathing quieted, but we remained, foreheads pressed together. As if Q needed a moment to gather himself as much as I did. Thankfully there were no sounds or interruptions. Piker House was still a sleeping beast before the dawn of a new evening of vice and frivolity. I was grateful we hadn't been discovered.

"I take it you were sufficiently distracted from exploring the lower floors," came his amused voice very close to my ear.

"You—!" I broke off as warm laughter radiated his pleasure. He anticipated my exasperated attempt to whack his shoulder and snagged my hands in his.

Placing a soft kiss on first my nose and then the fabric of my gloved palm, he murmured, "Good." He moved my right hand to link through his arm and said, "Come, let's have our picnic."

~

SITTING in the afternoon sun on a blanket in the gardens of Piker House gaming hell, I found myself eating and conversing with Lord Dashing.

"Did you do this as a child?" I inquired cautiously. I still didn't know all that much about this man, a man I'd kissed quite soundly not half an hour ago.

"Yes, I ate quite a bit as a child," Q replied dryly.

"Ha, I meant picnics out-of-doors, in the country maybe? With your family?" I pressed innocently, popping a bit of cheese in my mouth. Mrs. Hooper had packed a lovely basket filled with bread and fruit, cheese, and wine. Sadly, the food was nearly gone as we'd been enjoying our luncheon in the gardens for some time.

"I suppose I did my fair share of picnicking as an adolescent. We were often in Southampton in the summers. When the weather was fine, as it often was, we'd do everything outdoors, eating included." Lord Dashing reclined languidly, propped on one elbow as he squinted at me over the rim of his cup. The sun was rather bright this afternoon.

"And who is we, might I ask?"

He paused only briefly but turned his head to gaze out over the small pond adjacent to our position. "My brother and sister. We ran wild those summers."

"I have siblings also. Two sisters. We weren't terribly close, but I have fond memories from childhood," I offered to help ease the discomfort I read in his body language.

At my familial admission, his attention returned to my face, searching. "Two sisters?"

Scandal is never far from the lords and ladies of the *ton*. It was possible Q didn't know the particulars of the gossip surrounding my sisters. "June is the eldest and Gemini is the youngest. The three Morrison sisters. I haven't seen either of them in quite some time," I finished with a frown.

Q looked at me for a long moment, assessing. I didn't know what he was contemplating at my confession. An indolent lord, coat removed, lounging in his shirtsleeves and waistcoat, but his serious expression ruined the whole air of relaxation. Being the sole focus of his intense stare was more than a little disconcerting. My nervous butterflies were returning.

In an attempt to lighten the atmosphere, I inquired, "Are you the middle child as well?"

"No, the youngest. I have an older sister, Rochelle. She prefers life in the country and the company of animals to people, I'm afraid. She has a menagerie of creatures and raises horses at her estate outside the city."

"And your brother?"

Q took a deep breath and once again turned his attention to the pond beyond. "I had an older brother. He passed away several years ago. Desmond and I weren't so very much alike, but he protected and supported me. I always looked up to him." He finally looked back in my direction and with a very small, sad expression, he said, "A better man you'd never meet."

Grateful for his trust and the knowledge of his family, I returned his look with an understanding one of my own. The urge to comfort and console was overpowering, but I remained seated on the blanket across from him. I could sense that while my touch might be welcome, Q didn't want pity. Grief is a hollow thing you carry with you. And every so often it fills to the brim. Q's grief appeared to carry the weight of his anger, sadness, and a hundred other things I could never understand. My own grief toward my lost mother was consumed by my feelings of betrayal and abandonment at times, and often filled that hollow ache to bursting. And then other times I didn't allow it to skim the surface. Death and loss are unchanging, but our grief fluctuates like the tide.

Before I had the chance to offer any condolences on his loss, Mr. O'Connor entered the courtyard. Boots crunching on gravel, he made his way to our picnic.

Daniel offered a tip of his hat. "Good day, Lady Jane."

"Hello, Mr. O'Connor."

I could see Daniel surveying the scene. A private garden luncheon, reclining employer, and his employee. My cheeks heated with awareness and sudden shame. I should be working. This wasn't a social call.

While I didn't necessarily sense judgement in Mr. O'Connor's very open perusal, I did however detect some censure in his gaze. "Q, the boys have a problem. Could use yer assistance, if ye have the time." He concluded with an odd look in Q's direction.

But I was surprised to find my employer's eyes still on me. Without looking away, he replied, "Yes, of course." Lord Dashing rose smoothly from his position on the ground, donning his coat and hat. Mr. O'Connor waited a few paces away while Q took my hand for a quick kiss on my knuckles. "I'll see you soon."

"Are there any of those orange cakes left? Those are me favorite," interrupted Daniel, eyes suddenly alight with mischief.

Q scowled in response and joined his friend on the path. "Let's go."

I watched them exit the courtyard with a smile on my face. An odd relationship those two had. Q was obviously Daniel's employer, but they had an easiness about them, as if they'd known each other a long time and shared each other's secrets.

A few moments passed before Mrs. Hooper bustled out and together we packed up the remains of the picnic.

I eventually made my way back to the third-floor library to return to my duties for the remainder of the afternoon. Imagine my surprise when there on my desk was a note bearing my name on the front. I opened the folded parchment to see a short missive in small, precise script.

Jane,
Apologies our luncheon was cut short. As recompense, you can expect a guided tour of the second floor in the upcoming week. I'll endeavor to improve my thoughtless behavior and provide correspondence at regular intervals to assuage your curiosity regarding my whereabouts. While I can't promise specifics, I'll do my best to keep you informed. I fervently hope to never cause disappointment again. Please avoid the lower floors until the time we can visit together. It isn't safe for you there, Jane. I wasn't lying about that. Business will keep me out of London for the remainder of the week. I look forward to our next run-in.
Q

Twelve

The following nine days were exceedingly long, for a myriad of reasons, I'd wager. The looming promise to explore the main floor of Piker House was like a dangling carrot to my curious nature. Like my visit to John's pub some weeks past, any activity or experience outside my typical sphere felt exotic and mysterious despite being mundane and frankly ordinary to most Londoners. I was excited to discover the secrets unknown to a lady of my station, and if I was being honest with myself, which seemed the prudent thing to do, I was eager to spend more time with Q.

Our kiss was reckless and irresponsible, but I was undeniably attracted to the man. I still didn't know his full name, but I knew what he tasted like. I knew his heart beat wild with my body pressed to his, and I knew beyond a shadow of a doubt, that things would never be the same.

With Q away from London on business, working in the office the following Friday was a bit lackluster. Mr. Stevens was there for a portion of the day and kept me company, but it wasn't quite the same. Just knowing there would be no chance meeting with Q improved my productivity but reduced my pleasant mood. Nevertheless, I persevered and made quite a bit of progress on balancing Piker House's current ledgers. The cipher still eluded me, but I had every confidence I would make headway on cracking the code. I'd started taking the smaller record book home with me in the evenings to Eliza's residence should inspiration strike, but alas, nothing so far.

Eliza herself was becoming a sought-after physician. We became like ships passing in the night. Little to no time for tea or conversation, and definitely not the amount of time required to discuss the recent happenings at Piker House. I felt a bit guilty that I hadn't divulged my kiss with Lord Dashing to any of my friends. Our Tuesday embroidery meeting was once again called off due to Fiona's illness. She sent a note round assuring everyone that she was in no danger but was still not feeling up to hosting. And with Eliza away so often, when she was home, she needed her rest. Therefore, my interlude with Q had remained a lovely little secret, something for me alone. I'd take the memory out, hold it delicately in my palm, and remember it fondly... Usually with a flush about my cheeks.

Several letters found their way to my person that week. One note delivered by Botstein from Eliza warning, or rather informing, me of an upcoming ball at Lady Vega's. She had apparently sent ahead our intent to attend the countess's ball the following week. Lady Vega's parties were quite popular as she rarely hosted sedated affairs. I wasn't terribly excited about joining Eliza; however, my friend assured me that nearly everyone from our circle had accepted invitations as well. At least we would all be there together. Cassandra would be surrounded by suitors, but odds were high that something disastrous yet amusing would happen. Ashleigh would be entertaining in her assessment of the gentlemen present.

Mary was the consummate guest and perfect role model for any gently-bred lady. I could learn a thing or two about conversing with my peers from Mary, but generally she provided the perfect distraction and enabled my general laziness when dealing with lords and ladies in attendance. They all sought Mary's sparkling company, and therefore Eliza and I could assume our roles of observers and wallflowers. Fiona would be there, in all likelihood without her husband. His Grace Gregory Bowen, the Duke of Compton, was often out of London. He managed several country estates that held a large number of tenant farms. The Duke seemed more comfortable in a dirt field with farming equipment or conducting soil enrichment procedures than dancing in a ballroom. Fiona didn't seem to mind. She had responsibilities in town during the season that required her attention, but often conducted herself and the children to the country in the spring and summer months. So, while I wasn't particularly thrilled to attend any such ball, at least I would be in good company.

Another letter found me reluctantly one morning while breakfasting alone. Dr. Finley was unaccounted for and Eliza was already in the clinic for several early appointments. One of the footmen delivered a letter bearing a familiar seal that made my kippers sit rather unwell. Lord Fairbanks was again urging me to write to him and to consider my position regarding our engagement. I don't recall ever actually being formally engaged to John. It was as if he took the news of our broken courtship and used it to assume an entirely new role in my life without consent. I made the easier yet potentially irresponsible decision to ignore his bloody letters. Hopefully that wouldn't come back to haunt me in the future.

On the following Monday, I readied myself for Piker House. Meg, Eliza's lady's maid, seemed oddly helpful and offered to assist me with my hair. I allowed this despite my distrust of her cross attitude and my general unease with being attended. I dressed in a lovely pale violet patterned day dress with matching heeled slippers. I was quite embarrassed to admit to taking more care with my appearance. It wasn't so much wanting to impress Q as much as I wanted to feel utterly confident in his presence. I longed to be on equal footing. Feeling wholly off-balance for the majority of our encounters had created this anxious anticipation surrounding Lord Dashing. At least, I assumed that's what the feeling was. It wasn't necessarily a bad thing, but I desired appearing more at ease and self-possessed. I've always prided myself on being a practical sort of person, but clearly attraction makes those inclinations irrelevant. My heart was destined to beat faster in his presence and my wits to suddenly abandon me.

But upon entering the library on that misty gray morning, another letter awaited me.

Jane,
I'm afraid other business matters require my attention at present and I will be unable to visit Piker House before Friday of this week. I'm sorry for my continued absence, but feel even more sorry for myself for being denied your lovely company. I read the daily papers and find myself longing to hear your thoughts on nearly everything within. Perhaps we can compare notes upon my return. Until then...
Q

EQUAL PARTS DISAPPOINTMENT and hope flooded my consciousness upon reading Q's letter. Well, perhaps not equivalent. Disappointment was winning the battle. And yet it was rather lovely to hear that he was thinking of me and anticipating my company. What person of my acquaintance had ever longed for my thoughts and opinions, my oddities in all regards? The list was frightfully small.

It was going to be a long week, but I was determined to use the time to work with no distractions. I could remain a competent employee and not allow whatever was happening between myself and Q to affect my work.

What *was* happening between us? Was I to be a dalliance? Despite my independence and minimal involvement from my father, I preferred to avoid being the subject of gossip. Being the secret mistress of Q, was that what I wanted? Was that what *he* wanted? I knew we needed to discuss these matters, but it all felt so new and tenuous. I wasn't ready to question motives and second-guess every sentiment. All I knew for sure was that when Q looked at me, I liked the way it felt.

WHEN I ENTERED the library of Piker House on Friday morning, Mr. Stevens inclined his head and gave me a knowing smirk. "Good morning, Jane. How are you today?"

"I'm well, Mr. Stevens. And yourself?"

"I'm having a delightful morning. There's a letter for you on the desk." He paused in his writing and brought his full attention to my face, so he likely saw disappointment wash over me like a garden hose.

"Oh," came my unenthusiastic response as I removed my pelisse and walked over to the desk to examine the aforementioned letter. I braced for disappointment. This was undoubtedly Q writing to let me know he'd been called away again or detained in some way.

"What ever is the matter? I thought—" Mr. Stevens sat up straight. Obviously Mr. Stevens didn't know the contents of the letter or that it likely held frustrating news for me. I didn't actually know why he seemed interested or eager in the first place.

"Nothing. Nothing is the matter," I assured him distractedly as I reached for the parchment, unfolding it and reading the contents. It was short but brought on a triumphant smile in response. I'm sure Mr. Stevens was even more confused at my shifting moods. I let my eyes scan the letter once more and felt that delicious sense of anticipation flood my system. Butterflies took flight in my stomach once again.

Be ready this afternoon. We're exploring. See you soon.
Q

~

LORD DASHING HAD REMOVED his jacket at some point upon entering the main floor of Piker House, leaving him in his shirtsleeves, steel gray waistcoat, and snowy white cravat. His dark hair seemed longer. It had only been a short while since I'd last seen him, but my eyes drank in all the changes. He seemed tense. We'd lost a bit of the easiness we'd had with one another during our picnic in the courtyard, speaking about our families and learning one another. Perhaps he was as unsure as I was about how to proceed since the kiss. I know my mind had considered every possible motivation and outcome in numerous combinations.

Or worse, perhaps he hadn't considered it at all.

I'd been missing him and building up our next meeting in my imaginings. Expectations are like that. Provide them a bit of freedom and they'll lead a revolt.

The main gaming room was one wide, open space with tables arranged systematically. Extravagant carpets covered the floors and equally excessive wall coverings lined the large room. Sconces were affixed equidistant along the wall, and I could imagine the illumination from elaborate chandeliers throughout. I took in everything in wide-eyed wonder. As interesting as the surroundings were, I wished I could see them at the height of service. With the energy of the space, the noise, the excitement, I could only imagine the experience that was Piker House at night.

The staff would be in to light the many candles present before service began this evening. As it was, Q and I were alone. No servants scurried about preparing the gaming room for patronage. But it was still early in the afternoon. Q had come to gather me with little fanfare just after two o'clock.

"These are for whist." Q pointed perfunctorily to the tables surrounded by chairs for the favored card game among the peerage. "And those are the hazard tables." He indicated the long tables containing dice. Preferred and played more frequently by the working class, hazard still found its way into a gaming hell that served the aristocracy. Apparently not every rich noble found themselves skilled enough for card games. Games of chance would always have a place, I imagined.

"Do you play?" I inquired, searching his passive expression. I was desperate to crack this awkward shell surrounding us.

With a barely noticeable wince, he replied, "I'm not much of a gambler, I'm afraid."

"Is that so?" I lobbed the opening at him, praying it would ease some of the tension he was carrying.

Q's eyes met mine and the tiniest of smiles tugged the corners of his lips. "Indeed."

I smiled warmly in response. "So, if you don't care for gambling, what made you acquire such an establishment?"

At my statement, his gaze dropped and he resumed a meandering path around the tables. "Well, I suppose it was a sound investment." I followed in Q's wake as he continued walking. "Also, the previous owner… Well, safety wasn't a priority here. The changes I've made to how Piker House is run have greatly improved the profit margins."

"So it was a business decision then?" I made an effort to simplify.

Bringing himself to a stop, he said quietly, "It's complicated. But now that I'm in it, it's very much a business decision."

I was still unsure what all of that meant, but I allowed his non-answers to steer the conversation, despite my frustration. "I suppose a gaming hell is a lucrative acquisition for a bachelor. A sound investment, as you said."

He nodded along with my statement until I had a sudden thought which I immediately blurted out. "You *are* a bachelor? I assume there is no Mrs. Q?"

He seemed to choke a bit. "Of course I'm not married, Jane. Are you serious?"

"Well, admittedly, I don't know that much about you," I said matter-of-factly. Inwardly I was quite relieved.

Running his hand through his hair, he finally settled both hands on his lean hips and turned to face me fully. "I kissed you. I would not have done so if I was married." His voice was an exaggerated whisper by the end.

His comment surprised me, but I tried not to let it show on my face. Q was already riled by my questioning of his marital status. I didn't want to make it any more awkward. But in general, wealthy affluent men didn't see a problem with having a wife and kissing whomever they wished. It was rather expected in society and quite commonplace. Perhaps Q didn't feel like it should be discussed so openly. Before I could ruminate on that any further and torture myself with the possibilities, he continued, "Obviously it was wrong of me to take advantage. You are a proper young lady. It shouldn't have happened. And yet I can't make myself regret it."

I didn't want him to regret it, and I didn't want him to say it was wrong. For goodness sake, I was three and twenty. Another two seasons and I'd be firmly on the shelf. It wasn't even my first kiss. No advantage was taken, and honestly it had been my goal to provoke a response. I took things further. And neither did I regret what happened as a result.

He undoubtedly anticipated my forthcoming argument, but he persisted before I could open my mouth. "Nevertheless, I would not have kissed you while promised to another. That might be accepted in society. But you can add that to the list of rules I refuse to follow regarding the *ton*. Should I ever take a wife, she'll be mine and I shall be hers alone."

I supposed this coincided with what I knew of Q and his rather progressive views surrounding the aristocracy. His passionate and emboldened words from the masquerade floated back to me. There was little love lost between Q and the standards and expectations surrounding the nobility. Perhaps the idea that he supported fidelity and commitment in a marriage was not so far-fetched.

Interesting.

"So you're not resolved to marry?" I asked with no subtlety whatsoever, as one does. If one is me.

Pink-cheeked and more than a little flustered at my brazenness, he replied a bit sheepishly, "I haven't been, no."

Ah, there it was. I doubted he was celibate. Based on our kissing encounter near the very stairwell we were facing once again, Q was well practiced in the romantic arts, shall we say. He was obviously a confirmed bachelor and preferred the company of a mistress or three. And I'd just made him allude to that fact aloud to a young, unwed lady with whom he'd engaged in a recent… flirtation. The poor man. He probably thought I planned to demand a proposal any moment now.

"Just because I haven't been interested in marriage previously, doesn't mean I couldn't be interested now or… in the future," he finished with an exasperated exhale.

Q was noticeably uncomfortable with this line of questioning; therefore, I did my utmost to suppress my amusement at his expense. I pressed my lips into a firm line and rocked back on my heels a bit. Reminding myself to avoid eye contact lest a laugh escape, I failed miserably and ventured a brief glance to find Q watching me, eyes narrowed in suspicion and arms crossed defensively.

"Well. What about you?"

"What about me?" I sought to clarify.

"You were practically betrothed. You must believe in marriage." From Q's glorious lips, it sounded like an accusation.

I proceeded very carefully, getting the sense he was trying to turn the tables on me. "Yes. Lord Fairbanks and I were courting last season and had discussed the possibility of marriage, before." I decided honesty was required. "And well, now as well. John is sort of still planning on marrying me."

"Excuse me?" came the dangerous-sounding question from the gentleman facing me. He began advancing until we were quite close, slippers and boots nearly touching.

"Well, you see..." Perhaps honesty was overrated. "He hopes to put the past behind us, which frankly is such an odd statement. Where else would one put the past? Obviously behind... one." I snorted an odd laugh.

"Jane," came Q's rough reply, patience nearly gone with my attempt at humor and distraction.

Ah well, honesty it is then. "John wants to reconcile, and continue with our original plans to marry," I finally got out.

"Are *you* still planning to marry him?" Q's eyes were searching.

"No, I am not," I answered, hoping the sincerity in my tone would convey the honesty of my words.

"Are you—" Q uncrossed his arms and let them hang at his sides. I wasn't convinced his posturing was no longer defensive, but he appeared more at ease. He continued, "Are you just working for me until your next engagement comes along?"

I broke eye contact and looked at the room beyond without really seeing it. Hating the thought that a woman's only option was to marry in order to secure a future, I answered rather resentfully, "I don't know, Q. I'm trying to make my own way, financially and independently if possible. I don't want to be beholden to some lord twice my age or someone incapable of honoring marriage vows. I don't want to play into the illusion and take my place in that gilded cage. If I married John or anyone like him, that's where I'd be."

I couldn't see the impact made by my pronouncement. If he felt one way or another at having his own words used in support of my argument, he didn't show it. Impassive, unreadable Q. It was that expressionless face that allowed his words to land surprise assaults. "Would you entertain other suitors?"

Well, you could have knocked me over with a feather duster.

"What do you mean? Other suitors? I told you I'm not reconsidering John's offer of marriage."

"Might I call upon you?"

"Call upon me?" I parroted.

"Yes."

"I thought you weren't interested in marriage." It wasn't a question.

I felt off-balance again. No amount of confident dressing or preparation could prepare me for this man.

Exasperated was the best way to describe Lord Dashing at this point. "I said I hadn't been. Past tense. Might I call upon you?"

"Courtship and chaperones, promenades and waltzes, calling cards in the afternoon. You would really follow society mandates in this regard?" I questioned. I could not understand this. It was a bit of a shock to the system, and let's not forget one's pride, when you think you have someone all figured out and they attempted to prove you wrong.

"In this regard? I think I would." Q's face had taken on a determined glint as if preparing for battle or dancing in really uncomfortable shoes. "Might I call upon you?" he tried once more.

There went my pride. "Yes, you may call on me."

Without allowing myself to panic too much at this turn of events, I decided to compartmentalize for the time being and hope that Eliza would be home this evening to consult. I needed a sounding board. I needed a friend. I needed someone to keep me from squealing into my pillow like a ninny.

We were still staring at one another. Q looked frankly smug at this point, and I had no idea what my face was doing.

About that time, a woman's laughter drifted up the stairs to our left and my head turned automatically in that direction. We attempted to speak at the same time, "What's downstairs?"

"We should go, it's getting late."

Q cleared his throat, tension tightening his wide shoulders.

More laughter from the direction of the staircase.

"Is the tour over then? What's down there?" I asked again.

"Just the staff below stairs. We should get out of their way so they can prepare for this evening." I could tell Q's answer was technically honest, but I still felt like there was more going on here. Reluctantly, I let it go.

"Very well."

"Come, let's gather your belongings from the office and I'll escort you to the drive. Vincent will take you home." He then plucked his forgotten coat off a nearby chair, gently gathered my hand in his and escorted me up the main stairs.

Mr. Stevens must have had an appointment because he was no longer working in the library when we arrived. I retrieved my pelisse and reticule and we made our way, hands clasped, to the waiting carriage.

I filed away the events of the day for later examination and analysis. If I stopped and allowed myself to consider how nice Lord Dashing's hand felt in mine, I feared I might lose my nerve.

"This is a little like the first night we met. You whisking me away to your carriage. Luckily, my dress is still intact." I laughed, feeling my cheeks flush with remembered embarrassment. Phantom embarrassment, if you will.

"Yes, lucky that." Q glanced at me sideways with amusement. "And again, business is pulling me away. I should have liked to escort you home that first night as well."

He placed a soft kiss on my gloved hand and then helped me into the carriage. "I'll see you soon."

I nodded a goodbye and settled back as the carriage bustled down the drive and out onto St. James's.

A short while later, I was entering the Finley residence as a beleaguered Botstein took my things. "Lady Morgan is taking tea in the second-floor family room if you care to join her."

I thanked Botstein and took off toward the stairs. I could hear the butler's sigh from behind me. I'd forgotten myself and been less than ladylike in my haste to finally see Eliza after so long apart despite sharing the same household.

Making quick work of the stairs, I walked briskly down the hallway until I reached the cheerful yellow family room on the second floor. Typically unused for receiving callers, Eliza and Dr. Finley often enjoyed tea together here to discuss patients and medical practice. They didn't usually stand on ceremony and used the room in a very relaxed capacity.

I entered the room and was happy to find Eliza alone by the fire with a dish of tea in her hands and a book in her lap. "Jane!"

"I am so happy to see you. It feels like it's been ages."

"I know! I've been so busy. I don't know what is going on with Father, but he breezed into clinic this afternoon with nary an explanation as to his whereabouts and fairly shoved me out the door to go rest." Eliza embraced me briefly as I sat beside her on the settee. "I didn't argue as I *am* quite tired, and I knew I could catch you after you finished for the day at Piker House. So, what's been going on with Lord Dashing and the ledgers? Have you seen the gaming hell yet? Did you see that new letter from John that arrived today? Anyway, tell me everything."

So I did.

I told her about working to discover the cipher, the strange sighting of the scarlet woman and subsequent chase, the resulting run-in and kiss with Lord Dashing, the letters and the gaming hell tour, and then oddest of all, the indication that Q would be my potential suitor.

"I think you're right in assuming that he has only entertained mistresses in the past," were Eliza's first words after my deluge of information recounting the past several weeks. "Would you consider being Lord Dashing's mistress, do you think?"

I wanted to say I was scandalized by her question, but I wasn't. It was something I had considered and something I thought Q had likely considered as well. Besides, my friends and I often discussed all manner of scandalous behavior. Cassandra was a fount of inappropriate knowledge.

"I don't know," I finally answered.

Leopards didn't change their spots. But what if they could? Might Q's earnest insistence on courtship and following the traditional path in this instance be trusted? I didn't know. Was it what I even wanted?

"You're not exactly on the shelf, Jane. There's still a chance you could land a husband if you wanted. Not Sir Soggy Britches, of course. He's dreadful. But there might be another someone out there for you." Eliza placed her book and teacup on the table in front of us before taking a deep breath and continuing, "Or you could assert your independence, follow whatever path you wish, and be the mistress of a mysterious lord. As long as you felt safe, this could be an opportunity to decide your own future and live for yourself, for your own enjoyment."

I reflected on her statement with a small twinge: *live for yourself.* I had a mother who had done just that. She lived for her own pleasure and with little regard to the impact her actions had on her husband and her children. I lacked a husband and children to dishonor with scandalous behavior. But still, the idea of acting solely in my own interests felt exceedingly selfish and I wanted no part of that. It seemed a slippery slope, one my mother had descended to her grave.

"I think…" I found myself unable to meet Eliza's eyes. The subject of marriage with my friend often made me feel guilty, but despite her unwavering support, I still kept my eyes on my lap. "I think I do want to marry. Some day. I like the idea of marriage, a tangible show of commitment, dedication, and loyalty. And the mere thought of being someone's mistress—for favors or jewelry or protection—I don't think it would be enough for me. A trade-off I couldn't make. I want affection and mutual respect and a sharing of ideas. I suppose I want love or at least the potential for it."

I looked at Eliza then, noting the paleness of her face and the faraway look in her eyes. Her focus had strayed to the fire. "It's okay to want that, Jane. I wanted it, too."

"Do you think," I began very gently because this was something we had never discussed, "you'll ever marry again?"

I assumed her response would come quick and sharp, but she surprised me by shaking her head very slowly before finally saying with only a slight wobble to her voice, "No, I… I don't imagine I will."

Deciding I should turn the conversation away from Eliza, for her own sake, I looked at my friend and asked, "Do you think Q is serious about courting me? Or is that just what he's calling his plan to tempt me into mistressdom?"

Smiling at my attempt to lighten the conversation, Eliza said, "I don't know. But let's see what happens, shall we? He practically begged to call upon you. Let's give him a chance to prove himself, and if he attempts a quick seduction, well, you can tell him that's not want you desire. And if Lord Dashing wants to keep your beautiful, gigantic brain in his employ, he'll respect your wishes."

She brought up a very good point. Q was my employer. I didn't want to lose his respect in that capacity, nor my position. My work at Piker House allowed me the measure of freedom I had gained. I didn't plan on living forever with Eliza, although perhaps we could continue our friendship into spinsterhood and a shared estate. I didn't know what the future held, but I did know I didn't want to jeopardize the only one I'd ever have.

I thought of my friend and her sound advice. I would give Lord Dashing a chance. I could trust him enough to allow that. "You're right, of course. Thank you, Eliza."

Realizing how much I valued Eliza's counsel, I squeezed her hands in a show of affection. In all but the legally binding way, she was my sister. My found family. She took more care of my heart than June and Gemini ever had. I knew I could count on my friends to support and honor me, and the idea of marriage coincided with the life I was already leading. Building my family and choosing who to let in. Perhaps finding a husband was in my future after all.

Eliza returned my embrace and turned her head to give me a mischievous grin. "Have you thought of this, Jane?" She paused dramatically before continuing, "Perhaps courting Lord Dashing will lead to a betrothal and then you could even marry the man. If nothing else, we might actually learn his full name."

Thirteen

Saturday morning callers were often few and far between in my experience. Back when John and I were courting, he would occasionally call upon me, but he generally understood my dislike of standing simply on ceremony. The tedious expectations of marriage-minded mamas who often welcomed lines of suitors for their debutantes were of little consequence to me. I didn't have a mother to force a connection between myself and any eligible gentleman within marriageable radius. I had a long-standing suitor with the assumption of marriage. And I had a regular meeting time on Tuesdays with my circle of ladies in which to gossip, visit, and consume large quantities of tea and cakes. Therefore, I had little use for the concept of setting aside time in one's day to welcome guests for uncomfortable and idle chitchat. Meaningless frivolity. I'd prefer to read a book.

So that's what I was doing the following morning.

Dr. Finley was in clinic and had a light day from what he'd indicated over breakfast several hours prior. Eliza had joined me in the formal receiving room on the main floor. Like any well-bred lady, she was embroidering… something… onto a linen square? Perhaps a napkin?

"It's a handkerchief, Jane," Eliza smoothly said after my befuddled examination of her current work in progress.

"Right. And it looks lovely," I replied brightly.

She rolled her eyes. "Would you prefer I play the pianoforte while we await our plethora of callers?" she inquired demurely, the picture of refinement and decorum.

I slid her a look. Eliza was well-known for her love of upbeat music that was often inappropriate in nearly any setting. She fancied regaling all the embroidering ladies, myself sadly included, with obscene lyrics and shanties inappropriate for society gatherings, even intimate ones among our group of friends. Cassandra often joined in during the choruses.

Eliza's statement was doubly amusing in that a "plethora of callers" was highly unlikely.

"That won't be necessary, thank you very much," I assured my friend. Laughter was her only response and I resumed reading once more.

Several beats passed before Eliza wondered aloud, "Do you think he'll come?"

"What?"

"Lord Dashing. Do you think he'll call upon you today?" she clarified.

"Do I think Q will call upon me less than twenty-four hours after declaring his intention to call upon me?" I asked skeptically. Honestly, my flippant response was my attempt at tempering my expectations. No use in hoping if I was destined to be disappointed. It was much easier to snap out a denial to Eliza than examine too closely the likelihood that Q would or would not show.

No day or time had been set. No arrangements had been made. My expectations were quite literally all my own at this point.

Well, except for my hopeful friend arranged on the settee to my left.

"What? Yes. He could have very well meant today and plans to call on you presently." Eliza's exasperation was obvious. I was determined to be an unwilling participant in whatever made people irrationally optimistic, my friend included. This was all very exciting to her. Q had shown an interest in me and declared his intent… Whatever ambiguous intent that might be. He was not John, therefore Eliza was quite happy with the turn of events and invested in the outcome.

I wasn't quite so sure. "We shall see, I suppose."

I retrieved my book from my lap and removed the ribbon bookmark from between my current pages. I scanned the words without comprehending. Reviewing them a third time didn't help either.

Sighing in reluctance, I turned to Eliza. "What if he doesn't come?"

My friend glanced up from her embroidery with sympathetic and knowing eyes. "Then he doesn't come. Maybe not today and perhaps not tomorrow either. But let's give it time, shall we? Hmm?"

I nodded, fidgeting with the edges of the pages in my hand.

"It's okay to want this, Jane," she began. "It's okay to want him: in friendship, as an employer, as a part of your life. Perhaps it will be nothing." She turned her attention and resumed her needlework before concluding, "Or perhaps it will be everything."

What a frightening concept. *Everything*.

That was an enormous responsibility to place on someone. Becoming someone's everything.

I was tired of feeling frightened. Frightened of my position in society, the gossip, the temptation, the helplessness. And I was honestly tired of fighting with myself. Of being frightened by my attraction to Q, something I'd never felt before. Scared of what it could mean. And completely terrified of letting myself hope. Could I be brave? Could I wait and see as Eliza had counseled? Or would it be too late by then? Would my hopes and expectations have taken flight to new heights beyond my control or ability to manage?

I wanted to be brave. I wanted to trust in Q and his motives. But all prior evidence and my own wealth of experience pointed to the simple fact: people often let you down.

While I was still lost in thought evaluating Eliza's words, commotion from the front of the house caught my attention. I heard voices, several of them. Eliza's head raised as well. Footsteps approached from the hallway and a beleaguered Botstein entered the receiving room and announced, "Lord Fairbanks."

John waltzed in determinedly, holding a small bouquet of flowers. Eliza's sigh was wildly audible and caused the earl to pause in his progress across the room.

Eliza and I both stood to greet John, but it was then we noticed another man entering on his heels. John followed our gazes and spared a brief glance over his shoulder. He didn't seem surprised at the other man's presence but was decidedly put out by it. Q, on the other hand, seemed more than a little amused to be intruding on John's announced arrival. Botstein lingered near the doorway obviously conflicted by the newcomer, but seemed to err on the side of letting the aristocrats do whatever they wished, and fled without announcing Q or asking him to wait his turn in the front parlor.

Both gentlemen made their way to us with polite bows. I believe I managed a passable curtsey, but who could say because *what was happening and how did I make it stop?*

"Welcome, gentleman, would you care for some refreshments?" came Eliza's greeting with much more enthusiasm now that Lord Dashing had arrived and seemed to be causing John a great deal of annoyance.

"Greetings, Lady Morgan, that would be lovely." I caught Eliza's imperceptible flinch at John's formal address. She nodded with a tight smile. "Jane, how are you?" John moved to cradle my gloved hand for a kiss above my knuckles.

"I am well, thank you, Lord Fairbanks." It was John's turn to flinch away from the use of his title. He was far too familiar and seemed to forget that I had, in fact, ended our courtship.

My stare swung to Q. I could feel the heat rushing to my cheeks and my smile turning shy. "Good morning, my lord."

"I'm relieved to hear you are well, my lady." Q looked dapper in a navy-blue suit with a silver embroidered waistcoat. Dark hair gleaming and blue eyes shining with mischief. He turned to address Eliza. "And good morning to you as well, my lady."

She smiled and bobbed a quick curtsey before moving toward the doorway. "I'll go see about some refreshments. Gentlemen, have a seat. I'm sure Jane can keep you entertained in my absence. I'll be back shortly."

There was a brief awkward struggle as John and Q made for the same settee and some male posturing engaged before a conclusion was reached. I was too busy making ridiculous eyebrows at Eliza and attempting to convey both my panic at their arrival and my incredulity at her abandonment. Eliza faced me on her way into the hallway behind the backs of our callers mouthing what was very well "OH. MY. GOD." And then she was gone.

She'd left me alone with them. In this receiving room of awkwardness. Perhaps she needed assistance with the refreshments.

"Jane, come join me," John called from his spot near the fire, preventing me from retreat. I noticed he was still clutching the small bouquet of colorful flowers in his hands. His light hair was styled longer on top and smoothed away from his face. His green eyes looked so hopeful.

Oh, hell.

I slowly made my way to the seating area near the fire. The pianoforte and a small cluster of chairs were placed on the opposite end of the room. Q and John had taken opposing sides on small sofas facing one another with a low table between them. My book lay abandoned on the tabletop. Both gentlemen had left an open spot beside them on their respective sofas. The decision of where to sit felt like a test.

They needed to learn that I wouldn't engage in whatever game was taking place.

I resumed my seat in the single high-backed chair adjacent to them both.

John appeared crestfallen by my decision. Q's lips twitched at my obvious evasion. Awkward silence descended as both men looked at me expectantly. My gaze fell to the table. This was beyond my capabilities. Small talk was one thing. I could stumble through a generic discussion around the weather or the latest fashion, but being trapped with both men felt like a new level of torture.

Abruptly, my stare snagged upon the bouquet of flowers in Q's hands. It was lovely and thoughtful. He was clearly attempting this courtship, to do the things society commanded with arbitrary rituals. With the presence of both Q and John and the discomfort surrounding their simultaneous arrival, I hadn't really allowed myself a moment to examine Lord Dashing's appearance during calling hours.

He was here.

Finally meeting Q's stare, I offered, "Thank you for the beautiful flowers. I love them."

"You're welcome," both men replied in unison.

And the awkwardness returned, if it had left at all.

I'd forgotten John had a small bouquet in his grasp as well. Both men were frowning at each other once again. I immediately turned my attention to my former betrothed. "Yes, Lord Fairbanks. Thank you for your thoughtfulness as well."

He seemed to be taking in the size of his bouquet relative to the large and colorful flowers held by his rival across the way. "Think nothing of it." He placed the flowers on the table atop my book and swiveled his body to face mine.

Before I could protest or reach for my discarded hardback, Lord Dashing lived up to his namesake and smoothly retrieved it from beneath the blooms and greenery. I smiled gratefully and was rewarded with a wry twist of his lips as Q settled the book in his lap.

Attempting to garner my attention, John began, "Jane, I had hoped we would have the opportunity to discuss some personal matters." He flicked an annoyed glance in Q's direction but he either didn't notice or didn't care because Q was still examining my book. However, Q's amused expression told me he'd heard John's little gibe.

"Yes, well. I'm not sure what that would be, my lord. I believe I've said all I needed to on the matter. I remain unchanged."

"But if we had but a moment to talk, I think we could reach an acceptable conclusion," John tried again in an urgent, lowered tone.

This was not a matter I wished to discuss with Q in the room. Why was John forcing this? Attempting to stake a claim in front of this stranger? He likely didn't know Q or why he was even here during calling hours.

However, before I could attempt an exasperated reply, Q cut in while smoothing his fingers along the spine of my forgotten novel. "Are you enjoying your story, my lady?"

John huffed in frustration as we both turned our attention to the large man whose interruption brought me nothing but relief. I could talk about books endlessly. I'd rather not openly discuss the failure of my past relationship with the Earl Fairbanks.

Brightening visibly, I straightened in my seat and opened my mouth to reply in the affirmative but was cut off before I could utter a sound in response.

John could no longer contain his annoyance. "And why are you here, sir? I don't believe I've seen you at the club or in the park or at any society engagements. I don't believe I recognize you at all."

Q's attention finally diverted from my concerned expression to Lord Fairbanks's impudent face. The transition was not a pleasant one. Q's stare intensified and his expression neatly blanked. Eau de Unaffected Gentleman wafted from his person, and John visibly wilted. It was like witnessing a wildlife interaction in nature. There was a clear alpha presence in this drawing room. I was suddenly feeling rather warm.

Eventually after a protracted silence, Q spoke, "That's interesting because I recognize you, Lord Fairbanks." The words were measured, Q's tone even and unhurried. As if his pronouncement was an arrow meeting its mark, John's face morphed with dawning awareness. He paled and moved quickly to stand, breaking decorum.

John offered no response but abruptly grabbed my hands and drew me up and out of my armchair to quickly guide me across the room to the pianoforte. It was far enough away so as not to be overheard, but only just. "What is he doing here, Jane? What is going on?"

"So you know each other?" came my curious reply. What did Q's presence here mean to John and how could they know one another? John said he did not recognize Q from polite society. What was the alternative?

"No," John immediately assured me before amending, "not really."

I raised a skeptical eyebrow and glanced behind me to see Q looking on with that same passive, unreadable expression. Tugging my hands out of his grasp, I finally turned back to John.

"That is, we haven't been properly introduced," John said in a rush.

"That doesn't really answer my question."

His voice was low and hurried, a frantic whisper as he completely ignored my query. "The better question is what in the world is he doing here calling upon you? Or… Is he here to see Eliza?" he asked hopefully.

My eyes narrowed. "Not Eliza."

John's eyes widened and he grasped my hands again, moving even closer and saying in an urgent whisper, "You mustn't listen to him, Jane. Whatever he says about me, whatever he tells you. Don't believe him. You know me. We've known each other for years. We're getting married for Christ's sake."

That was the absolute wrong thing to say and simultaneously the perfect way to end our current discussion. Yanking my hands from his fevered grip and stepping back, I raised my voice for likely the first time ever in John's presence. "We are not getting married!" Striving for calm in the midst of calamity, I continued at a more reasonable volume. "We may have been acquainted for years, John, but I do not know you. Not like I thought. The John *I* knew would have valued and respected my position as his intended and avoided obvious dalliances. Avoided humiliating me, making me a pathetic paragraph in *The Ton Tattler*."

Despite knowing male aristocrats are rarely monogamous creatures, I had hoped John could at the very least spare me from public ridicule during our courtship. And perhaps it was shortsighted of me, some vindictive part of my nature that made me this way, but once my favor was lost… I didn't really believe in second chances for someone so careless with my future. Because that's the truth of it. My future would have been irrevocably tied to John's had we continued on our projected path. He cast me aside before we were even wed. What were the chances our union would have been an amicable one after countless affairs and humiliations?

His expression fell. Unable to meet my eyes, he uttered, "I am sorry. It was but a momentary indiscretion. A regrettable mistake. It won't happen again."

"I have forgiven you for your momentary indiscretion." At his hopeful expression, I hurriedly continued, "But I won't give you the opportunity to humiliate me again. I valued your companionship for a long time, but—"

John interrupted. "I'll go, alright? You need time to see my intent. To build trust again. I won't hurt you."

"John, no. That's not—"

"We'll talk again. I'll see you soon," he cut in once again. As if knowing if I concluded my statement that my favor would be lost forever, he rushed toward the exit with a murderous glance at Q.

I stood staring after Lord Fairbanks, reflecting on the odd turn of events. This morning had started so very awkwardly, it was almost comical. What were the chances? Two suitors arriving at the same moment when I rarely had any callers to speak of. From awkward to strange and a bit mysterious. Something was going on between Q and Lord Fairbanks. Some sort of game was being played here, and I was exceedingly tired of being the unwilling spectator.

I wanted answers.

But I had a feeling my mysterious gentleman would remain elusive. I audibly sighed my disappointment.

I rejoined Q near the fireside, taking the recently vacated space across from him. Our positions felt very much like we were in opposition now. After such an exchange between the two gentlemen, he had to know I had questions.

I wouldn't be denied my answers.

"Well, that was interesting," I began. Nice and easy. Best to let him warm up to the idea of being forthcoming.

Q seemed both wary and amused, if that were possible. Something about the tilt of his lips led me to believe he enjoyed my subtle opener. "Indeed."

"Are you planning on telling me what that was all about? With you and the earl?" I twirled my finger to encompass… all of that. So much for subtlety.

"I think you should ask him when he calls again."

"Why don't you save me the effort and let me in on the secret?"

He considered me for a long moment before cryptically saying, "Interesting phrasing. Lord Fairbanks does have a secret, but it's not mine to share. You should ask him."

"You're enjoying this," I accused. "You like having the upper hand."

He shifted in his seat and leaned forward over the central table, forearms balanced on his spread thighs. My traitorous eyes tracked the movement. "I like having information. Knowledge is power in this town," he confirmed. "But I'm not enjoying your frustration, your confusion, or your hurt. I came here with good intentions, Jane. I told you I wanted to call upon you, obtained your permission, and here I am at the first opportunity." His expression was open and honest. "I didn't anticipate running into Fairbanks. He's spoiled enough of our morning. Can we please forget about him and move forward?"

Moved by his sincerity, I nodded in agreement, but inquired honestly, "What do you mean by that? Liking information and it providing power in London? That sounds borderline nefarious. Villainous, even."

"Is it bad to want control?" Q's stare was no less direct and honest, but he seemed hesitant now, as if worried he'd frighten me away.

I narrowed my eyes in consideration. "Manipulative, perhaps."

"I can hear the distaste in your tone."

"Well, manipulation itself can be good or bad depending on the intent behind it."

"Good or bad. Is everything either one or the other?" Exasperation bled into his tone… and his eyebrows. Those were definitely exasperated eyebrows.

I paused to formulate my response and, forgetting myself, shifted forward on my forearms, mirroring his pose. "No. I realize there is light and dark within us all," I offered in earnest. "But aren't we the sum of our parts? Standing mostly in shadow reflects a life of predominately bad choices. If not bad, then immoral or unjust. Shouldn't we as a society strive to remain in the light?"

Q looked toward the fire and appeared thoughtful, considering. "What if…" He ran a hand across his mouth. "What if society's expectations aren't always right and good and true?"

"What do you mean?"

At my question, Q's eyes focused on me once again. "For instance, most lords rarely marry for love and are often discovered in the arms of mistresses or frequenting brothels with little regard for their wives. It's known and accepted within society. Does that make it good and just because it's approved by the masses?"

My hackles raised. He was making this about John and me. Painting me as this naïve debutante, voicing my objections and unrealistic expectations. My voice was cool when I responded, "Where are you going with this?"

"Just a hypothetical," came his reply in a bored tone, but his gaze was unyielding. He was waiting for a response.

Or an explosion.

"You know my position. I've made it quite plain that I have different expectations for my intended. I won't be made a fool of." I took a deep breath to steady my racing pulse. Honestly, where in the hell was Eliza with those refreshments? "But what I want does not matter."

Q's brow furrowed.

I huffed a laugh lacking any amusement whatsoever. "I am a woman in London, Q. I have little reputation, no means, no family fortune. I have nothing to offer a partnership, no matter how sincerely I may seek one. I have few choices. Be seen as merely a… a… womb in exchange for an heir, a mistress in exchange for security, or a spinster wallflower in exchange for a lifetime alone with my principles."

If Q was surprised by my candor, he didn't show it. He said very softly, "Don't you believe people marry for love, Jane? Your friends, the Duke and Duchess of Compton? It's well known they're a love match. Women have more to offer than their bodies, more currency than that. What about their ideas and thoughts, their minds and affections?"

"Tell me, my lord. What gentleman would want me for any of that?"

Q finally seemed affected by my position. My surrender to societal standards. Stating the obvious and reminding him of the London in which we resided. Running a hand through his hair and schooling his incredulous features, he said simply, "I disagree."

Another disbelieving laugh erupted, and I felt it necessary to abandon this conversational topic and return to what I really wanted to know. To what Q had successfully distracted me from. "How do you know John?"

His expression turned dark and somewhat foreboding. "He's not who you think he is."

"Oh really?" I said incredulously. *This* man was going to correct my assumptions on Lord Fairbanks? A man I had already assessed and found wanting. Lord Dashing, the mysterious and unknowable, was going to give me this cryptic response about misjudging someone. "And who are *you*?"

I am rarely the kind of person who has the perfect response at the appropriate time. Actually, I rarely stumble upon the most fitting retort at all, much less at a time for maximum effect. But, oh. This one hit its mark. Q seemed to acknowledge the perfect irony of the situation because I received a reluctantly admiring nod and a bitten-off smile.

Literally. He smiled and bit down on his lower lip to prevent his amusement from growing.

I most definitely did not stare.

"Well then." Icy blue eyes sparkling, he asked, "What would you like to know?"

I gifted him a wide smile to indicate my unasked question. *Of course*. Of course, I wanted his name.

And he knew it. Q's smile flattened. "Not that. What else do you want to know?"

"Tell me about Piker House and your army of men. Where do they come from? What do they do?" I pivoted easily, drawing on my absolute wealth of questions. My curiosity was limitless where Lord Dashing was concerned. I could be momentarily appeased from the name issue if he conceded on other counts.

He rolled his blue eyes and leaned back on the sofa as if settling in for the inquisition. "It's not an army. I have a handful of men who maintain the security of Piker House, as you well know. They're in-residence day and night to make sure the staff as well as the patrons are safe. Most of them I've known for some time and they're trusted employees. A few of them have additional tasks and accompany me in my business and travels."

"Do you travel often?"

At my follow-up question, Q's face closed off a bit. He was less casual in his response. "Not like I used to."

"What does that mean?" I, too, leaned back against the settee, all but squared off against this mysterious gentleman. If he was willing to answer my questions, I was going to get comfortable and find out as much as I could.

Mouth tight with strain and reluctance, Q finally gritted out, "It doesn't paint me in the most flattering light. I… don't want to tell you."

I had not expected that. "Why ever not? I'm not trying to judge you. I'm merely trying to become better acquainted. You are such a mystery to me, my lord. Can't you see that?"

"And I want you to know me. Truly. I am just aware of your propensity to categorize actions as either bad or good. I worry my past plants me firmly in the shadows."

I didn't say anything, just allowed my gaze to convey my earnestness and sincerity and hoped he'd continue speaking.

After a protracted staring contest that I didn't mind one bit, Q released a long breath and offered, "I told you I had an older brother who passed away. Well, Desmond was the heir. Very responsible. He took his duties to the family seriously and was the perfect man to assume my father's title someday. I… was not that. I felt lucky to have been the second son with less obligation and no one dependent upon my reputation. So, I often acted in my own best interests. After university, I travelled much of the time. Gallivanted would be a better word."

I considered Q's admission. Despite avoiding my original question of his name, he'd given me some clues to consider. His brother had been the heir, which indicated a title in his family. Desmond was not a name I recognized, but I seldom troubled myself with *ton* gossip unless I couldn't avoid it. "So you thought I'd disapprove of your gallivanting? That I would have expected you to act the part of heir apparent?"

"I was reckless and selfish."

"You were also young. It doesn't sound like anyone expected you to be like Desmond. It's okay to not be. Like your brother, that is," I finished softly. And truly I didn't judge him for his wild and youthful ways. He had obviously grown up and assumed his responsibilities. Q was a business owner and had many individuals in his employ. I didn't know his obligations now that he was the heir. It may be too soon to ask. The subject was obviously difficult to discuss.

With a sardonic smile and shake of his head, he looked down and away. Perhaps the softness in my tone held too much compassion, too much of something he wasn't willing to accept. "Well, there's no chance of that. I'm heir now only because I am next in line. My parents and I… We don't speak. They were too devastated after Desmond…" I could only imagine how difficult it would be to lose a child. Before I could offer any response, Q continued with a small amount of determination. "You asked before, why Piker House? Why purchase the gaming hell? The truth is, my brother died leaving Piker House several years ago. He was out enjoying an evening with friends, and Piker House wasn't safe back then. The owner… He didn't care if his patrons were safe leaving his establishment. He encouraged the thieves who took advantage of high-society lords leaving the premises with their pockets heavier and their wits lighter. I don't know why Des left alone that night. I only had secondhand accounts. His worthless friends probably abandoned him to the blackguards who cut him down for his purse. They left him in the street, and where was I? In the Mediterranean, enjoying my days in the sun and swimming in the ocean."

He stopped for a moment, eyes on the dwindling fire and seemingly unable to look my direction. I wanted to cry for Q, for this man who blamed himself and cursed fate. But I knew showing that kind of emotion would be unwelcome. He'd held on to his guilt for so long and had likely never had the chance to mourn his brother.

When he began again, he met my stare with a sort of grim determination. "So, I came back to London and vowed to honor my brother. I acquired the gaming hell in order to ruin it, hold the owner and the proprietors accountable, leave their lives in shambles. Shame the clients and patrons, call in their debts and ruin them all. But once Piker House became mine, things became… complicated. Too many livelihoods depended on the day-to-day running of the establishment, and I couldn't even determine the clients' accounts, as you well know. My plans adapted and changed. But the streets around Piker House will be safe. My men and I will see to that. It will never be how it was before."

"You're avenging your brother's death. Honoring his life and making your corner of London safer for everyone else as well. I don't believe you're as far in the shadows as you think."

Admiration must have leaked into my tone because a humorless laugh escaped Q's lips. "I am not a martyr, Jane. Nor am I some hero or vigilante. But you are correct in that I do seek vengeance. I find it hard to forgive anyone involved. And, I fear, my mother and father will never forgive *me* for taking over the business that destroyed their family."

I took but a moment to absorb this. Fearing Q would be overwhelmed by his own self-loathing, I pushed forward, eager to turn the conversation. "What about your sister? You mentioned her before. Are you still in touch?"

He allowed a small smile. "Yes. Rochelle and I write to one another often, and I visit her country estate several times a year. It's difficult to be close to her. It's just her way, but I know she cares for me. And I would do anything for her."

Thank god he still had someone. I'd witnessed his friendship with Daniel first-hand, but knowing his parents had essentially cut ties with him despite his future inheritance made me immeasurably sad. I knew what it was like to have no connection to your past. And I would never want that for Q, for anyone.

"Thank you for telling me," I said meaningfully. I really did value his honesty. This wasn't small talk about horses and the English weather. This was real. What was happening between us was equally genuine.

Q made a humorous sound that I could tell wanted to be a laugh once it outgrew its leading strings. "I fear I did this all wrong. We were supposed to sit stiffly and discuss lady so-and-so's scandalous gown and lord whatever-his-name-is embarrassing himself in his cups last evening."

I did laugh at that, a full-grown one. "Well, that is typically how one spends a Saturday morning call. Although there are usually tea and cakes to make the tiresome gossip go down much easier." Looking over toward the doorway once more, I muttered, "I think Eliza got lost in the kitchens."

When I turned back to Q, he seemed hesitant and unsure, which was so very unlike him. Usually unflappable and stoic, this new version gave me pause. "What is it?"

"I don't know how to do this, Jane."

"Do what?"

"Court you properly. I've… never done this. I want to do it right."

My heart took off at a gallop. He wanted to court me and he feared he was failing. It was unbelievably adorable. In an effort to both lighten the conversation and reassure him, I said, "Well, seeing as I have vastly more experience in this area, I will be happy to tutor you in the ways of courtship. Never fear."

"All right," he drawled. "What should I do first, professor?"

"You should come sit by me," I replied with no small amount of brazenness. My heart was pounding in my chest, craving and dreading Q's nearness in equal measure.

His lips quirked and his reply was to stand smoothly before coming around the table and settling himself beside me. "And now what?"

"And now I will tell you about my friend Cassandra and how she led a suitor to be attacked by geese in Hyde Park. You may want to take notes to ensure you don't repeat his courtship errors."

We proceeded to talk for the next hour. Me with stories from my friendships and Q with tales from childhood. We talked about his travels and all the places I longed to see. Upon discovering Q's love of books as well, the discussion evolved into comparing and contrasting our favorite works. We laughed and argued and at one point I playfully shoved his shoulder in exasperation. It was then I realized, Lord Dashing was real. I held him less in my mind as this mysterious stranger who was too beautiful for words. A handsome automaton. He had flaws and a history and regrets. I even began to notice physical imperfections that made him all the more arresting and lovely in my mind. The scar on his dark brow (childhood roughhousing), his broken nose (from boxing with this men, of all things), and even his longer hair that was slightly out of fashion but fell so lovely when he raked his fingers through it in frustration.

So many little things to remind me that Q was here and present, not the unattainable Lord Dashingham of the Hallway Encounter. This was Q, a man with intentions. He wanted me, and I honestly couldn't fathom it.

Unsure of how long I'd lapsed into silence following our last discussion topic (touring the continent versus visiting Scotland), I followed the line of my internal musings and blurted with little regard to embarrassment, "Why me? Why now? I don't understand. I imagine you have any number of mistresses to choose from."

He choked. "Any number? Jane, it's not like that."

I waited but he didn't offer any further explanation, however his ears did appear slightly pink and he eyed me from the side before admitting, "Yes, I've had mistresses in the past. But that's not what I want any more."

He turned to me more fully with an arm behind my back and his forehead pressed to mine, finally admitting, "I want you."

And there it was: wanting. I didn't understand why Q wanted me specifically, but because of him I could understand the concept. Despite our time together today filled with openness and candor, there was still so much I didn't know about him. And yet some part of me had already decided.

I didn't care. I wanted him, too.

Breathing the same air with brows touching, I closed my eyes and whispered, "Tell me your name."

I could feel the movement along my temple as he slowly shook his head. "Not yet."

"Why?" I pleaded.

"Because I'm not ready for this to be over."

I pulled back to meet his tortured gaze. "I don't understand. Why would anything change?"

"It just would, Jane. Give me a little more time. Please."

I was sure uncertainty painted my features, but I nodded because the simple truth was this: I wasn't ready for this to be over either. I didn't know what the future held. Wrangling my wild hopes into submission would be a problem for another day.

"Can I kiss you again, my lady?"

Instead of answering I asserted, "I won't be your mistress."

His reply was serious as he took my hand in his. "I don't want you for a mistress, Jane. I want to court you, properly."

"All right," I said finally, honestly answering the previous question regarding kissing.

But he seemed determined now. "We'll go for a ride… in Hyde Park… tomorrow. That's something courting couples do. What do you say, professor?"

I smiled in answer and murmured as I closed the space between us. "My student is doing so well. Tomorrow, it is."

He met my advance, pushing flush against my upper half. And then he smiled against my lips before fitting his mouth against mine.

Fourteen

I have memories of watching my mother as a young girl. In the mirror, I'd witness her doing this magical feminine preening that doesn't appeal to me now, as a grown woman. But as a child of seven or eight years of age, I was completely entranced as my mother, this beautiful and elusive woman who adjusted her jewelry or tried on cloaks, fiddled with the curls along her hairline. It was like being admitted entrance into a secret world in which women were not always perfectly attired at all times. Seeing this version of my mother, witnessing the transition from woman to marchioness was captivating to my young mind.

As I grew older and later after her death, I came to realize that those were times my beautiful mother had been readying herself to meet one of her paramours. As I sat unnoticed and ignored in her chambers while maids bustled about with discarded fabric and curling implements, my oblivious father wasn't preparing for a night out at all.

Perhaps that is why now, as a woman who should enjoy being attended to and made society-ready in appearance, I often found myself resentful of the excess. The jewelry, the lip color, the extravagant hairstyles, and lavish gowns. It was just one more deception. The circumstance and ceremony signaling the fraud and selfishness within.

It's strange that that was all I could think of now as I watched Eliza fuss over my appearance in the standing mirror in her dressing room. Eliza's lady's maid,

Meg, assisted with my riotous auburn waves and neatly managed them into a braided chignon at the base of my neck. I had a hat ready to pin in place, but Eliza was busy fluffing my dress. The palest of pinks, my morning dress was nearly white, with lace at the neck and sleeves. It was snug along the bodice and mostly modest near the neckline. Nearly.

"Stop fidgeting," Eliza scolded.

I worked to still my nervous fingers and return my hands to my sides. Despite my lack of response, my friend seemed to know exactly what was troubling me. "You're completely covered. Not immodest in the least. Calm down."

"You don't think it's too much?" My eyes narrowed on my ample bosom in the gilt-edged mirror.

Eliza followed my gaze. "Nonsense. You look beautiful. Lord Dashing will swallow his tongue when he sees you."

"I don't want him to swallow his tongue. And I don't want tongues wagging at my appearance. We'll be parading through the park. Everyone will see us. No tongues whatsoever," I insisted.

"Fine, take my shawl. Will that make you feel better?"

"Yes, thank you," I said with genuine relief.

"Why are you so worried about this? You've promenaded in the park before with Lord Fairbanks." Eliza's voice was muffled as she dug through her wardrobe to find said shawl.

I wasn't nervous, per se; more cautious. I still felt the sharp edge of past gossip quite keenly and being seen with another gentleman so openly was inviting curious glances. I wished… I wished we could enjoy another picnic in the Piker House gardens instead. Talking and laughing and getting to know one another in a quiet and comfortable setting. But I could also understand why Q felt compelled to plan an outing in the park. It was a sure sign of courtship and he appeared to be making every effort in that regard. I just wished there was a way to do so without members of the *ton* taking such an obvious interest.

"I'm not worried. I'm just unsure and trying to manage my expectations," I assured my friend.

Reemerging from the wardrobe, shawl in hand, Eliza huffed. "Not this again. Lord Dashing asked to call upon you. He *did* call upon you. Then he asked to court you. And today he will commence courting you. What expectations are there to manage, Janie? The man wants you."

"Yes, but what does that even mean? Hell, *he* doesn't even know what that means. He's never courted anyone. He's used to mistresses and liaisons and assignations." I didn't want to think about that too closely. Did he have arrangements with widows or actresses? Surely not married society matrons.

"So. That's his past and he obviously wants you to be his future. Lord Dashing has never seen fit to court someone before. He realizes you're special and wonderful. And he's done with all the trollops and opera singers. Trollopera singers!" Eliza finished with a grin in the direction of my mirrored reflection.

"You're ridiculous," I countered.

"And you deserve someone who wants you for you, Jane. Not Sir Soggy Britches."

~

ONCE ELIZA FINISHED FUSSING and my coiffure received one final adjustment, I watched with mounting horror as Q arrived by curricle in Dr. Finley's circular front drive.

I exited onto the main portico as Q passed his reins to a waiting groom and made his way up the front steps to join me. He bowed low over my gloved hand and straightened to meet my troubled gaze. "You look lov—What's wrong?"

I could feel my mind spinning, my vision darted all around. How could I make him understand? Why couldn't I just get over it and ride in his conveyance? I should try. He would think me a lunatic.

Q stepped closer and lowered his voice, "Jane, what's happened? Are you well?" The concern in his voice snapped my attention back to his face. He was so close I could catch his cedar and parchment scent, even out-of-doors with the slight breeze on this gorgeous fall day.

Q filled my vision, blocking out the street, the drive, and the cursed curricle beyond. He was all broad shoulders smoothed over in gray wool and snowy white cravat. I finally gave my eyes permission to seek his visage, the strength in his clenched jaw, the concern written all over his glorious face. His eyebrows made two anxious slashes over eyes lit by blue fire. Definitely apprehensive eyebrows.

Regaining myself and clearing my throat, I attempted a smile. "Nothing is wrong. I apologize. You surprised me. I was expecting horses… for a ride," I stammered. "Not the curricle."

He looked behind himself to where I'd indicated and found a normal-looking open carriage balanced on two wheels behind a matched pair. Finally turning back to face me, he said, "I thought you might prefer this mode of transportation what with the lovely weather." He eyed me a bit suspiciously, but when I offered no further explanation for my increasingly odd behavior, Q hesitated. "But we could always walk. If you'd prefer?"

I smiled gratefully in return. He wasn't pushing me and I didn't have to compromise my fears to retain his affections. I vowed to tell him about my mother and the accident in due time. Q would understand. He wouldn't judge me, I was sure of it. But for now, I would take this gift of acceptance. I placed my arm in his and told him honestly, "I would be most grateful."

Q scrutinized my smiling face but finally nodded in return.

We made our way the short distance from Dr. Finley's residence to Hyde Park, arm in arm, discussing the London weather and our favorite places to frequent in the park. He joked that we should avoid the geese by the pond, and we finally settled on promenading the pathway along Rotten Row at the south end. All manner of individuals were out and about. Couples and families, servants, and covered tents along the path. It was such a fine day. I wasn't at all surprised by the turnout. I should not have been so shocked at Q's arrival by open carriage. But the mere sight of the curricle triggered all my irrational fears.

I knew… I *knew* the situations were not similar in nature. There was little chance that Q would be wild and reckless with my safety. I was not my mother. I would never be my mother. Selfish. Careless. Out for a good time with a forbidden yet-not-so-secret lover.

It was madness to expect Q to know of my eccentricities, my adolescent traumas surrounding my mother and her untimely death. He likely thought me unhinged and bound for Bedlam based upon my paranoia and anxious reaction.

"So, how are the accounts coming?" Q inquired cautiously, as if I were a rabid animal. His words had been careful on our walk over as well. I vowed to act normally to put him at ease. It wasn't his fault I reacted badly.

"Oh, well. I'm still working to decode the cipher that will reveal past clients and their debts before your takeover of Piker House. I feel close, but I've been unable to translate the text thus far. Honestly, I'm a bit frustrated by my progress. I have, however, balanced all the accounts since you've acquired the gaming hell and can indicate the current gentlemen in your debt. Mr. Stevens has the updated list." I recited my progress in a straightforward manner so Q would know I was taking my work seriously. Despite my lack of progress in deciphering the coded client list, I had made great strides in managing and untangling the money coming in and out of Piker House since Q's acquisition of the property. "I've also been working to figure out the one ledger that seems unusual among the others."

"Jane, I wasn't expecting a full report of your duties. I wanted to inquire as to how you were enjoying the work. Is it challenging? Are you getting along with Mr. Stevens and the staff? I know it's not the same…" He trailed off momentarily as we passed a group of young women who seemed very curious about Lord Dashing judging from their interested stares and tittering behind wildly fluttering fans. Once we'd ventured further down the path and out of earshot, Q continued, "I realize it's not the same as working for yourself, as you were before. But are you happy in your current position?"

I looked over to meet his earnest expression and suddenly felt terrible. I was utterly unfit for polite society. How could I have overlooked showing my gratitude? He wondered if I was satisfied with my work. This position that practically fell in my lap and would never, under normal conditions and societal constraints, be offered to a woman of my station. Despite his mysterious nature, I owed Q my continued independence. Because of him and my work at Piker House, I had a future. I wasn't beholden to some outdated construct that stated marriage would be my one and only option. Despite this new attempt at courtship, I didn't feel threatened by Q's position at the gaming hell. My work felt oddly removed from his ownership. This sense of separation and protection was likely all imagined on my part, but until he gave me a reason to worry about my current occupation, I was determined not to punish him for wanting to both court and employ me.

I halted abruptly and turned to face Q, pulling him off the path and into the grass. "I am. Happy, that is. And so very grateful for your kindness. I—"

"I'm not kind," he asserted. His stare was penetrating. There was demand and intensity in his voice. Q was either insulted by my assessment or trying very hard to convince me of his wickedness. He paused after his interruption as another group of ladies paraded past, eyeing us all the while. Our position off the path made us far more conspicuous than if we were simply following the flow of foot traffic.

"Come, let's continue," I said, making my way once again on the gravel walkway. I decided to let the ridiculous assertion of his unkindness go. I could argue until blue in the face, but I'd never change his perception of himself. Self-awareness is just that. Singular, focused, and entirely inward. You can be on the outside peering in, but your point of view will never match those within.

I remained quiet as we resumed our stroll. It seemed we were still attracting attention. I noticed whispered conversations and meaningful glances in our direction. My gaze bounced around the landscape as I took in the curious gentlemen and nosy matrons tracking our every move.

Noticing my distraction, Q muttered, "What's the matter?"

"Doesn't it bother you?"

"What's that?"

"All the attention. Lady Stanton whispering to her daughters and fairly pointing in our direction. The pause in conversation as we walk by. Everyone watching us and likely placing wagers on our chances of matrimony."

Q seemed to consider that for a moment before passing me a sidelong glance. "I believe White's has us at four to one odds for a spring wedding."

My bulging eyes and horrified expression met his teasing one before he released an indulgent chuckle.

I increased my speed and stomped determinedly away.

Q's long legs kept pace easily. "Apologies, my lady. You looked so serious. I couldn't resist." His smile was still firmly in place. As was my indignant scowl. "Why do you care what they think?" He seemed honestly curious.

"How can you not?" I challenged frostily. But I continued before he could reply. "Simply by being seen together, everyone in London will assume we're bound for the altar. Walks in the park lead to courting, and courting leads to betrothal, and betrothal leads to marriage in their eyes. All because I walked beside you in Hyde Park on a Sunday afternoon."

"I suppose I don't see it that way. And frankly, their assessment doesn't matter."

"Then you are willfully ignorant."

With a perplexed frown, Q replied simply, "We've already discussed my views of the *ton* and expectations therein. They can think whatever pleases them. They don't know my mind. If they want to label me your intended, that's fine."

I sputtered dramatically. I was actually aware of how dramatic I was being, but I could no more control my reaction than the gossip surrounding me. Q's response was measured and calm, completely rational. And that seemed to intensify my indignant sputtering.

"Jane, I have no use for labels. I am of my own mind. A grown man. Why do *you* care what they think?"

Exasperation bleeding through, I whispered furiously, "Because I am a woman and their opinions obviously affected my former employment, and where I can take my tea and with whom I can be seen. And that all matters. There will be assumptions. If you aren't prepared for that, then we shouldn't be seen together."

Q examined me once again in that measured way. "It seems *you* are the one concerned about being seen with *me*."

I opened my mouth, but no words emerged to defend my position. He was right. I was the one causing a fuss, reacting badly yet again.

A lip twitch indicated his amusement at my befuddled appearance. "So, tell me, Jane. If gossips are to be believed, you must be expecting and longing for a proposal at the end of this stroll."

"What? No!"

"Then let us court, as I've said. Just as you agreed," Q was quick to remind me.

In my defensive state, self-conscious wonderings spilled forth from my mouth. "But why would you ever want to court me? I'm odd and bookish, tall and a poor conversationalist. I will never be at the top of anyone's guest list. I'm practically another species." It was true. I might as well have been a Neanderthal for all the similarities between myself and my peers.

"Is that truly how you see yourself?" Q inquired calmly.

I ignored his question and forged ahead in my misgivings. "You've never wanted to court anyone before."

He raised a questioning eyebrow. "I'm allowed to change my mind, am I not?"

"How convenient for you."

My snipe brought him up short. I was letting my resentment for my peers ruin everything. "I apologize, my lord. That was a reflection of my own insecurities and not in any way appropriate." My honesty and genuine contrition seemed to set his feet in motion once more. As we resumed our way down the path, I attempted to explain. "I am just cognizant of my place, and I don't want to be the subject of scandal once again. What happens when you tire of me and my oddities and are seen with a new mistress? A trollopera singer, no doubt."

"A what?"

"I don't want to be made a fool of again. I just want to be… me. My mother was selfish. She… She died when I was a girl." At this, Q's hand reached up to cover my own resting in the crook of his arm. "It's fine. She died in a curricle accident. That's why I panicked at your arrival today. Why I refused to ride in one. She was with her paramour. She was reckless and constant fodder for the gossips in this town and started our family down the destructive path in the scandal sheets. Father was a cuckold, and she made a fool of him. He was despondent without her, never mind her obvious betrayal. It's all anyone could talk about growing up. Made bitter fools of us all. I never want to be that again."

Q had directed us off the main throughway at some point during my rambling deluge of personal history. We were now seated on a stone bench under a tree. The afternoon sun filtered through the scattered autumnal leaves that remained on the tree overhead. We were still visible to curious onlookers. Yet the fall foliage gave the illusion of privacy; there was no one nearby to hear our conversation.

He was looking at me with that quiet intensity of his as if trying to read my mind. I didn't want that. I didn't want him to know the fear and anxiety that lived within. How deeply I'd been affected by John's betrayal and subsequent scandal. Our relationship had seemed complacent on the surface, companionable and modest. Certainly no great love affair with simmering attraction and unbridled passion. Even without those messy emotions and impeding sentiments, John *still* made a fool out of me. Whatever was happening with Q… It was not complacent nor was it modest. I couldn't fathom the havoc he could inflict on my emotions and expectations. Not to mention the damage to my reputation. Our relationship, if one could call it that, was new and unestablished. But I could connect the dots to scandal and ruination quite easily.

"Jane, I don't want to hurt you. It's not my intention to cause you strife or to instigate gossip. I have no nefarious plans. Nor would I want to shame or humiliate you. There is no one else I want. No other women. No trollopera singer, whatever that is. You're the one I want." Q seemed sincere in his attentions. I needed to stop assuming the worst. My protestations and unfounded accusations said quite a bit more about me than they did about Q.

I was devising my own ruin. Like a self-fulfilling prophecy, I was bringing trouble to my own doorstep, and Q was, thus far, the innocent bystander.

It was some time later that I became entirely distracted by Q's tongue.

We had salvaged the afternoon by continuing our conversation and purchasing lemon ices from a nearby seller. Typically a treat for warmer months, the fine weather provided an opportunity for the merchants to fit in one more day before the weather turned and London shifted to a misty gray thundercloud.

I had vowed to really give Q a chance. To trust in his earnest declaration and commit myself to the idea of courting him, and to the idea of him not hurting me.

It was difficult for me to trust anyone with myself, especially someone new in my life. More specifically, someone like Q. Mysterious and beautiful. He was vastly out of my realm. I didn't see the appeal of being with me, but I'd put up enough blockades and voiced my concerns. It was time to let him prove me right or prove me wrong. Wringing my hands and challenging his sincerity was only going to drive him away sooner.

But back to the lemon ices and his tongue.

Q seemed unaware of my fascination as I openly stared at his mouth at work. His lips, typically so firm and unyielding, seemed to meld to the domed ice as he lowered his head to feast on the cool treat.

My own lemon ice melted in my hand.

"Did you know men typically have longer tongues than women?"

Q did look up at my blurted comment. I rushed to continue, feeling the warmth in my cheeks. "The average adult male's tongue is 3.3 inches long and a female's is 3.1 inches… long," I finished slowly as he took one last lick from his ice and raised his head, considering my freakish fact recitation.

His eyes twinkled and he gave his lips a final lick as if chasing the tartness left behind. "Is that so?"

"Yes, and did you also know that tongues have a unique signature? The impression of the tongue is as distinctive as a fingerprint. So, my tongue print is specific to me, and your tongue print is specific to you." I literally could not stop speaking. I needed to bite my tongue. Ha.

Q's eyes focused on my mouth as he finally responded, voice low and faintly rasped, "I had no idea."

Sucking in a shuddering breath, oxygen helped return function to my brain and therefore halted the continued use of my mouth.

"Any more ideas regarding our tongues?" Q inquired innocently.

I could think of a few.

Shaking my head slowly, Q chuckled and turned to dispose of our ice containers. "I should probably return you to Dr. Finley's. Are you ready?"

Face still flaming, I managed a nod and placed my arm in the crook of his elbow and we strolled out of the park.

The return walk along the cobblestones was… challenging. I felt like I was strung tight as a bow. That gnawing desire had returned to the pit of my stomach, and every time I thought of Q's smile or his laugh or his tongue, my belly gave a little swoop. It probably didn't help that we were in such close proximity. I could feel his heat, his strength, and his presence at my side. He was reassuring and safe.

I liked the way I felt when I was alone, but I also liked the way I felt with Q nearby. It was this push and pull. I couldn't settle. My mind was cataloging all the ways I wanted him, and with a mind so unused to wanting… Well, I felt rather frantic to make up for lost time.

Perhaps if I hadn't been so lost to my attraction I would have noticed the man who stepped out of the alleyway into our path. Q recovered before I did and moved me to stand at his back.

The man was large and wearing an ill-fitting suit, as if it struggled to accommodate both the width and breadth of his shoulders and his barrel chest. He appeared bald beneath his bowler hat and seemed very interested in my presence behind Q.

"What are you doing up here with the toffs, *my lady*?" The man, for I could not accurately refer to him as a gentleman, emphasized my honorific with exaggerated sarcasm. I had never seen this person before. I could not for the life of me understand why he would address me at all.

"Don't look at her. What do you want? You can't approach me in the middle of Mayfair. What are you thinking?" Q's tone was lethal.

While no one was close enough to hear the conversation taking place, ladies and gentlemen were strolling across the street and carriages rolled by. It felt as if time had stopped with the appearance of this threatening stranger, but indeed, we were in the middle of Mayfair in the afternoon. There would be witnesses.

"You'll take a meeting with Seamus, and soon. What the boss wants, the boss gets," came the stranger's reply.

"The answer is no. So pass that along to your unfortunate employer." Q's tension was palpable. I could feel his muscles vibrating with uncontrolled fury, but his tone was even and unaffected. He was not cowed by this giant, dangerous man.

"You'll regret this, Q. Don't say I didn't warn you." And with a final sneer in my direction, the man in the bowler hat retreated down the alley from which he'd come.

My mind was warring with the racing of my heart. As adrenaline buzzed through my system, I was consciously trying to piece together the situation. "Why did he act like he knew me?" I knew my voice was overly loud, but I couldn't see to modulate the volume.

Q turned to face me then, taking my clammy hands and watching my face closely. "Pay him no mind. He was trying to intimidate you and subsequently threatened me. He's someone I used to do business with and is bad at taking no for an answer. Come, let's get you out of the street." Q tucked my arm back into the bend of his own and resumed our walk down the cobblestones at an increased pace.

We didn't speak again until we'd reached the front steps of Finley House, my mind whirring all the while.

"Q, come in. Stay and explain this to me. I'm so confused and frankly a little frightened."

"Don't be frightened. He won't bother you again. I'll see to it."

At my pleading expression, he softened. "I'm sorry. I can't come in right now. I have things I need to attend to. I'm sorry to end our time together on such a sour note. Don't let this interruption ruin our day, Jane. Our first outing together."

I realized he wasn't going to explain himself. There were so many parts of him that were off-limits to me, his name being the least of them. What kind of partner could I be if I didn't know the man before me? Alternately, what kind of partner would Q be if he wasn't willing to share himself with me?

Who was Q and what kind of business could he be involved in if it included the sort of man that we'd met out on the street? In the name of self-preservation, I backed away and moved to brush my hands down the front of my dress as if wiping the whole encounter from my person with the nervous gesture. I found I could no longer meet Q's steady, assessing gaze. Feeling the distance between us growing and unable to do anything about it, I reached for the door handle.

"I'll see you tomorrow. At the office?" Q asked in an attempt to divert my attention from escape.

I inclined my head in his direction but refused to give him my eyes. "Yes, of course."

And with that, I opened and closed the door behind me, adding a physical barrier to the emotional one I had just hastily constructed.

~

On Monday morning, I found a letter waiting on my desk. I knew before I opened it that the contents would leave me raw and disappointed.

Jane,
I'm afraid business takes me away from Piker House this week. I will not be in-residence. I'll see you when I return.
Be safe,
Q

I didn't know where this left us, but I felt a sense of loss. As if it was over before it had even really begun. No matter how much I tried to convince myself that I hadn't known Q long enough to feel disappointed by his absence, the bite of sadness was keen nonetheless. I couldn't find logic and rationality. I could only feel.

Based on the pressure in my chest and the stinging behind my eyes, I'd let my hopes get away from me after all.

Fifteen

"Perhaps yer mystery gentleman is a spy," guessed Miss Winstead from behind her embroidered fan. Her eyes narrowed in contemplation. "And in a vow to protect ye from his professional proclivities, he has right distanced himself from ye."

"But he doesn't want to, and he's just as miserable as you are," Mary speculated on the back of Ashleigh's wild conjecture.

Fiona watched me with a concerned frown as the rest of the ladies put forth their two shillings regarding this whole situation with Lord Dashing.

We were in the corner of the ballroom at Umberland House attending Lord and Lady Vega's soiree. I was stationed near a potted fern with Eliza hovering close by. The other ladies in attendance formed a loose half circle as they discussed Q's sudden disappearance from my life.

It was now Friday, four days following the mysterious letter stating Q would be absent from the office. And five days from the odd encounter with the rough-looking man with the bowler hat. I was confused and hurt. And I didn't know what that chance meeting with a stranger had to do with Q's decision to abandon our courtship… If that was even what was happening.

It felt like that. I felt like everything was over.

I'd considered the situation from every angle, fretted over my continued employment, and compared this new sense of loss to all my prior experience with disappointment. I was still confused and at a loss. But I knew my friends meant well and were attempting to help me reason everything out.

The air was stifling in the ballroom. The quartet played a waltz for the revelers and the candles glowed across the space. I wasn't in the mood for dancing and the card about my wrist was blank. The ladies had joined me in support and thus far had refrained from partaking in the merriment of Umberland House. But the reprieve wouldn't last long with both Cassandra and Mary in our midst. Gentlemen fought for dances and attention where they were concerned. I was certain any number of gentlemen would be approaching shortly. It would likely just take one brave stag to venture forth and the others would follow.

"Jane," Fiona murmured, drawing my attention to the motherly worry stitched upon her face. "Perhaps he simply *is* away on business, and you'll hear from him again next week. Sometimes the simplest answer is the one our brain tries to reject. He could be telling you the truth and he's just... away for some time. There is likely no ulterior motive or spy plot." She cast Ashleigh a beseeching glance.

Before I could agree or refute or beg everyone to stop talking about Lord Dashing, Eliza chimed in, "Yes, well. We aren't likely to deduce the answer or reach any conclusion this evening. Let's talk about something else." I passed my perceptive friend a grateful smile.

Cassandra caught on quickly and eagerly diverted the conversation. "Did you hear? Lord Sullivan is supposed to be in attendance tonight."

"Oh, where?" came Mary's interested reply.

"I haven't seen him, but the ladies in the retiring room were gossiping while I adjusted my coiffure and mentioned his presence this evening."

Lord Sullivan. I couldn't place the earl in question. It was his ball I'd escaped from with the tear in my dress. The same event in which I'd met Q. But I couldn't remember an introduction, nor could I recount his likeness.

"They said he never showed up to his own ball at Benton House some weeks prior. And that every marriageable lady, and some matrons, are attempting to get him on their dance cards tonight." Cassandra finished recounting the gossip and flagged down a waiter for champagne. Only the best for Lady Vega's events. No watered-down lemonade here.

The liveried footman approached with a beverage tray and Cassandra fanned herself theatrically. "Thank you ever so much, my good sir. I was decidedly parched. You are just the man I needed." She gave a flirtatious little wink and selected her champagne flute. Cassandra was outrageous with servants generally, but she was always kind and offered her thanks no matter what—usually in dramatic fashion that elicited reddened cheeks but amusement nonetheless. But instead of amusement, this footman gave an indelicate snort and muttered just loud enough for our small group to hear, "I seriously doubt that."

Cassandra has just raised her glass to her lips and promptly sputtered out a shocked reply. The footman spun on his heel and continued on his way, seemingly unaffected by my exuberant friend.

"Did he—" Cassandra coughed again while Fiona passed over a linen square to wipe her chin. Once recovered she said, "Did he just roll his eyes at me?" She stared off in the direction of the footman, his broad back retreating through the crowd.

I found myself looking around at my friends in astonishment. Collectively, we'd never seen a man react that way to Cassandra. She was the belle of every ball, sought out for conversation and dancing. And she had more proposals than I had fingers. It was beyond strange to see a man, of any station, not fawning all over her. This was interesting. The five of us were speechless as we watched Cassandra narrow her eyes. Oh dear, she was likely plotting.

Nevertheless, the distraction provided an excellent change of conversation. I was beyond appreciative to no longer be the focus. I knew my friends meant well, but I didn't need them to speculate about Q and his motives, whatever those may be. I wanted freedom from my own thoughts surrounding him, and that was difficult with Fiona, Ashleigh, Mary, Cassandra, and Eliza all weighing in. Between our recent Tuesday embroidery circle, sharing meals with Eliza for the week, and generally replaying in my own mind what could have possibly gone wrong, I was overwhelmed.

Naturally, it was when I'd decided I didn't wish to think of Q any longer that he should suddenly appear.

Of course.

As I watched him move through the crowd completely unaffected and totally at ease, I realized I'd never seen him in this setting. His time at the masquerade had been utterly devoted to me. I couldn't remember seeing him interact in polite society. But engaging he was, in more ways than one. Lords stopped him for hearty handshakes and indulgent slaps on the back. Ladies with their fluttering fans and overactive eyelashes curtsied and demurred as he made his way through the assemblage with nods of greeting and little else.

I could vaguely hear my friends in the background, so mesmerized I was by Q's presence in the ballroom. It was like seeing a peacock strutting through the kitchens, completely and wholly out of place while also remaining untouchable and confident.

Unnoticed, I continued watching him mingle with these people he claimed to abhor, his peers. And there was no doubt about it. He was one of them. One of us.

And I was a fool.

He noticed me then, but if he was surprised to see me in Lord and Lady Vega's ballroom, he didn't show it. Unflappable Q. He made his way toward me and much to my dismay, eyes all over the ballroom followed in his wake.

My fluttering heart was only rivaled by my lofty expectations. And then I recalled Q's unwillingness to share his secrets with me. His disappearance this past week and the uncertainty his absence had wrought in me.

Confusion and surprise gave way to hurt. I became reacquainted with it. Wielded it.

Q approached with intent, undeterred by my undoubtedly hardened expression. He bowed low, and then his perpetually cool gaze met my own. "Will you dance with me?"

If it had been a demand, I would have balked. But his quiet question was uttered in a way that pronounced his uncertainty. Despite his self-assurance in all things, he didn't know if I'd agree to dance with him.

Well, at least he was perceptive.

I placed my hand in his without speaking and he led me to the dance floor for the next waltz. I heard Cassandra, or perhaps Eliza, whisper my name in earnest, and when I looked back to my friends, they were staring after me with concern. All of them. This gave me pause, but then the musicians began, and Q and I were in motion. I'd find out after this dance what those dire expressions and whispered warnings could mean.

I genuinely wanted answers from Q, and this seemed the best way to go about it. It was time Q was honest with me, and if I needed this excuse, this dance, to receive my answers… Then so be it.

Opening my mouth to begin, I was cut off by Q's low voice, "I'm sorry." His hand on my waist was warm through the layers of silk. "I'm sorry for being away this week. It was… wrong of me to shut you out. I'm not used to being held accountable to another person or explaining my motives."

He paused as we turned in time with the music and moved with the other dancers. Once my hand settled again on his shoulder, Q continued in a rush, "But I do want to explain, Jane. About the man in the street and why I left. He works for someone I no longer do business with. He's not a good man and I wanted to distance myself from him. When he saw you on the street, I was concerned. I was afraid he would hurt you simply for being associated with me. So, I left to handle the situation myself. I thought the sooner it was dealt with, the better for you and for me. For us."

"What did you do?" I asked in worry, hand tightening on his shoulder.

"I took a meeting with Seamus, my former business associate. He's unhappy with my position, but I'm done with that part of my life."

Our dance was ending, but he didn't relinquish me to my friends. We began moving together into the next quadrille. The pace and positions didn't allow for continued conversation, but I was formulating questions as we danced.

Upon completion of our second dance, I started toward the edge of the ballroom, but Q refused to surrender my hand. "We cannot dance together again this evening," I hissed as gentlemen and ladies moved into position on the dance floor.

Q escorted me a short distance away and huffed a disbelieving laugh. "Why does it matter whether we dance once or twice or twenty times?"

"You know exactly why." He could not be this obtuse. Tongues would be wagging as it was. I was conscious of the stares accompanying our continued interaction.

His hard expression showed me exactly what he thought about perception and the demands of polite society.

"Why are you even here if you detest these practices so much?" I bit out.

"I was tired of waiting. I wanted to see you."

"You could have seen me all week long at Piker House," I countered. Tugging subtly on his arm to put more distance between us and the dancers, we finally cleared the dance floor and slowly made our way through the revelers.

"I needed to maintain my distance for your safety. But my men were watching you, protecting you, and making sure Seamus stayed away." I frowned at this. I didn't recall any guards.

Seeing my confusion, Q muttered quietly, "They were discreet. Accompanying you at a distance to and from St. James's."

My mouth formed a surprised O. I had no idea. And I didn't know what to think of all this new data. I needed time to consider these developments. Was life with Q destined to be a dangerous one? Did I still want a life with Q? Did he?

Before I could reply, Q halted our progress and turned to face me. "Jane, I was tired of staying away." His blue eyes had lost their glacial quality. There was only a frustrated, desperate male before me. I could feel my cheeks heat at Q's earnest words. Yet despite his sincere pronouncement, I couldn't help but notice the attention we were attracting. Paused on the farthest edge of the dance floor, people were watching our exchange. Society could scent scandal brewing in the ballroom.

I never claimed bravery in the face of the gossipmongers of the *ton*. And I wasn't proud of the fear and uncertainty I knew Q could read all over my face. After a few hesitant glances around the space, I made to step back and away. I just needed some space from all the prying eyes to think. To consider Q's explanation and to figure out what it meant for our future… should there be one.

However, before I could retreat, a man approached from behind. I was startled by his proximity and likely inebriated state. "Sullivan, my good man! Good to see you finally out and about." His joviality and volume were inescapable, and to my extreme confusion, he moved directly to Q and clasped his shoulder in benevolent greeting.

My eyes narrowed, unsure. "Sullivan?" I murmured.

Q had yet to respond to the gentleman and didn't look away from my pinched features. He took a deep breath, looking resigned to his fate. The knowledgeable interloper seemed to finally notice my presence and turned with a good-natured, "Apologies, my lady. I haven't seen Lord Sullivan since his return to society and was eager to say hello." The man hastily turned back to Q, apology already forgotten. I took the opportunity to back away.

"Jane!" I looked up sharply at my name from Q's lips. Gaze darting from face to engrossed face, my vision tunneled even as my heart galloped wildly. The whispers were overwhelming. Here I was, once again at the heart of scandal. Q paused in his advance as if finally noticing the onlookers. His thunderous expression made his frustration plain as day. He stayed where he was, the oblivious lord blathering in his ear.

I turned then, blood rushing in my ears, and made my way to the closest hallway at a measured pace. I made my steps controlled and careful in an effort to appear unfazed. Head held high, chin up.

I was crumbling inside.

How could I have been so stupid? Q was Quinton Jameson, the Earl Sullivan, the future Duke of Benton. The very subject of gossip tonight. I had met him at his own ball in his family home with a torn dress. I felt sick with embarrassment.

This whole time it had been him. Rakish lord returned to society on the heels of his familial estrangement. This was my employer. And he never wanted me to find out. He said as much. *I'm not ready for this to be over.*

I'd let the charade continue for far too long. I could have demanded his name. But I'd held on to my ignorance like a shield, protecting me from a truth that was more than I could bear.

I had been naïve in my assumptions, in my easy acceptance of Q as a mystery lord, my vague employer, and man of business within the *ton*. I didn't know his title. But it was clear from my observations this evening: Q was part of the upper echelon of London society. He was someone. Everyone knew it.

I was a fool.

And he'd willingly made me one. Finding out this way, in a crowded ballroom, while the truth had been fairly staring me in the face was too much. The hurt far outweighed the humiliation of finding out Lord John had been seen with another woman. I didn't care to examine that too closely just then.

As I made my escape, I thought back to all the times I should have realized the truth. All our illuminating conversations. Only the son of a duke could afford to have such outlandish views of society. All the eyes pointed our way as we'd promenaded in the park. I should have realized.

I continued internally berating myself as I discovered an unlocked door and an empty study. I slipped inside and breathed a sigh of relief to finally be alone with my thoughts. The room was modest with bookshelves, a desk, and a window filled with moonlight. A sense of romantic déjà vu was threatening, but I beat it back with the blunt force of my righteous indignation.

Turning back toward the closed door, I pressed my forehead to the wood and breathed out a deep sigh. My fingertips bit into the smooth texture and I took one more breath to focus my careening thoughts.

I really believed Q wanted me, or at least wanted to try. But Quinton Jameson was heir to one of the oldest and most distinguished dukedoms in the kingdom. I was so very far out of my depth, once again finding myself embroiled in scandal thanks to a thoughtless earl in a ballroom. There was no way our exchange went unnoticed.

I needed to leave.

As if a prayer had been answered, footsteps greeted my ears and a harshly whispered, "Janie!" followed. I opened the door a crack and peeked out in time to see Eliza's blue frock race by.

"Eliza!" I whisper-hissed in return, hoping to gain her attention before she continued her search along the hallway.

Spinning on her slippered heel, she caught sight of me through the sliver of space between the door and its frame. "There you are! Come. Let's get you out of here."

There were many, many reasons to love Eliza and value her friendship. We didn't agree on everything, choice of music chief among them. And I didn't always live my life the way Eliza would hope, but this… this unwavering support in the face of public ruination and spectacle, my throat nearly closed. She was a gem. I may not have my blood relations in my life, but I wasn't the poorer for it. Sometimes it takes forming your own family to really understand the depths of love.

So it was with watery eyes and a turnip-sized knot in my throat that I removed myself from another stranger's study and escaped through the kitchens once more.

Sixteen

I didn't go back to Piker House on Monday.

I didn't return on Wednesday either.

Which is how I found myself in a bit of a standoff in the foyer with Botstein on Wednesday midmorning. Apparently Q, or Quinton as I'd taken to calling him in my head out of spite—not that I was thinking of him anyway—*Quinton* had sent his own carriage and driver, Vincent, to retrieve me when I failed to report to the Piker House offices.

I knew it was irresponsible. I had contractual obligations and was behaving most unprofessionally. But I needed time. I wasn't ready to see Quinton.

So, I told Botstein to pass along my regrets to Vincent.

In a manner of speaking.

"My lady." Botstein's sigh was overwhelmingly put-upon. "You want me to tell Lord Sullivan's driver that you are unwell?"

"Yes. I would be most grateful," I replied with a pitiful cough thrown in for emphasis.

Then, without waiting for me to vacate the foyer, Botstein turned with a dramatic eye roll and opened the front door to convey my message. I quickly dashed into the front receiving room to avoid being seen and may have peeked out the front window to ensure there were no occupants in the waiting carriage. From what I could tell, it appeared rather empty inside with only Mr. Stanley accompanying Vincent in the driver's box as they finally made their way off. Breathing a sigh of relief, I realized I needed to figure out a plan. Was I surrendering my employment and independence? Was I willing to be driven away by another highhanded lord? Was I going to live with Eliza forever?

I had no answers for myself. Knowing I would eventually have to speak to Q, er, Quinton, made my chest ache. See? I was practically ill. Botstein hadn't lied on my behalf after all.

Once the crisis on the front drive was averted, I wandered back up to my guest suite. Dr. Finley was mysteriously away again and thus Eliza had been busy in the clinic for the last several days. Upon our escape from Lord and Lady Vega's, I'd relayed to her Q's apology from the dance floor and his subsequent identity reveal by Sir Whatever-His-Name-Was, Lord of Poor Timing.

Eliza had then recounted what had occurred after my departure from the ballroom. Duchess Fiona, Lady Cassandra, and Lady Mary had known Q was Quinton on sight. Eliza, unfamiliar with Lord Sullivan herself, had confirmed for the remaining ladies that he was in fact the mysterious Lord Dashing I'd danced with at the masquerade some weeks prior. It was Mary who'd whispered a warning at my retreating back. My friends had attempted to gain my attention whilst dancing, but I'd been unaware of my surroundings. In truth, I hadn't been able to see past Lord Sullivan. And that was the problem. I'd been distracted by him since the first.

With my ladies keeping a close watch, and the intruding gentleman conducting his reveal at top volume, they'd deduced I'd been unaware of Quinton's true identity as I'd fled the ballroom. Eliza had volunteered to retrieve me and spirit me away to avoid the scandal I'd left in my wake.

Fiona, Kathleen, Mary, Ashleigh, and Cassandra had all called upon me to make sure I was well in the days following the Vega ball. Cassandra and Eliza alternately cursed Lord Sullivan, while Ashleigh and Mary had attempted to offer explanations for his deception. Kathleen had given a completely out of character yet impassioned speech about how sometimes the people we love feel compelled to hide who they are in order to keep us safe. I don't know. I didn't quite follow. She seemed rather worked up about it. And most disturbing of all, Fiona had remained rather quiet and thoughtful, offering no advice on how I should proceed. She gave me a tight hug and merely encouraged me to take some time to think.

And that was exactly what I was doing.

Was I angry that Q had withheld part of himself from me? Of course. A lie of omission is a falsehood nonetheless. Could I understand why he'd done it? Yes, I suppose I could.

As a daughter of scandal and gossip, I was predisposed to want to avoid the upper echelons of society. Those high-ranking peers who were always watched and scrutinized. I'd learned my lesson with Lord Fairbanks as well as my mother.

The crux of the matter was that Q had allowed me to find out his true identity in such a public and embarrassing spectacle. He might have the name and backing to support his progressive views of society, but I most certainly did not. I couldn't pull off the eccentric nouveau aristocrat routine. As a woman, I'd be ostracized and openly mocked. What if by some stretch of the imagination we married someday? Our lives would be under a microscope. One false move on my part, an awkward conversation, or a single societal misstep would paint us as the most ridiculous match of the season.

I knew I sounded preposterous. Realizing one shouldn't concern themselves with the small-minded was unfortunately difficult to put into action. Perhaps my trauma from adolescence had damaged my self-worth and confidence beyond repair. I didn't want to be this way.

As I lay on top of my duvet and stared upon the canopy overhead, I couldn't help but imagine what a life with Quinton would be like, if that was something he even sincerely wanted. And truthfully, I didn't hate all of it. Some parts didn't make me fearful. I thought about what it would be like living as man and wife, what it would feel like.

My breath gusted out of me and I draped my arm over my eyes. Thinking about Q's perfect lips and his solid form beneath my hand would do little to help in this situation. I needed time to consider my future and what that would mean.

~

"AND THAT, my dear friends, was when the horse bucked, and I tumbled right off into the arms of a startled groom. Here I thought equines and all manner of beasts enjoyed my attentions." Cassandra fluttered her lashes and the assembled young men chortled and rushed to assure her that everyone did, in fact, enjoy her attentions.

I suppressed a laugh as Cassandra winked at me over her fan. She was the perfect companion this evening. I was so grateful she'd agreed to meet me at Lady Eugenia's musicale on this misty gray Thursday evening. Eliza had been overwhelmed by patients and was unable to attend. She'd previously accepted the invitation on our behalf to a musical performance featuring the Countess of Langston's talented daughters. This annual recital was often a highlight of the season. Lady Eugenia's three daughters were quite gifted in song and a variety of instruments. Eliza always enjoyed the affair. I was disappointed that she couldn't attend, but she encouraged me to take Cassandra as a societal buffer and do reconnaissance on the damage done to my reputation during last week's ball at Lord and Lady Vega's.

Thus far, Cassandra had been a lovely distraction. Her admirers flocked and she included me in her circle of merriment. The whispers and eager eyes of the assembled ladies had been surprisingly absent for most of the evening. Perhaps my misstep with Lord Sullivan wasn't the disaster I had assumed.

I should have known better.

As the gas lanterns dimmed to signal the upcoming performance, Cassandra and I made our way toward chairs near the front. It was then I noticed Q in the room. With all the assembled bodies moving toward a common goal, he was noticeable in his stillness. It seemed he'd been waylaid by some young bucks eager to converse.

I couldn't get over the changes in him. Yes, his face remained as passive and as stoic as ever, yet in this setting, he appeared cold and untouchable. The ultimate lord presiding over acquaintances beneath his notice. There was no comradery or joviality typically seen between gentlemen who frequent the same club or share similar circles. Here, the Q who spoke animatedly with me in private was entirely absent. Or perhaps seeing him surrounded by other high-ranking society members reminded me he was one of their own.

I'd stopped in the middle of the row without meaning to. Cassandra smoothly tugged me down into the seat next to her. She quickly followed my line of sight and cast an irritated glance in Quinton's direction. "It's fine," I assured her while smoothing my dress into place beneath the chair.

But my mood was quickly plummeting. I remembered the ease with which Q and I had conversed. He seemed so stiff, not like himself at all. But did I know the real Q? Perhaps it had all been a game, an act. It had felt real though. But the seeds of doubt are small and take root in the barest of cracks. Seeing the stoic man, the future duke, before me, it seemed impossible to think he'd ever cared about me.

I was glad he hadn't noticed me yet. I couldn't imagine what emotions he'd be able to read on my face just now. All of them giving too much away, that was for sure. That's why I was staying away from Piker House and any potential run-ins with Q. I didn't relish the thought of his pity, or worse, his regret. He'd see my hurt and anger and realize that I cared more than I should. That I'd let my hopes soar too high yet again.

The musicians took the stage and for the next hour we listened to Lady Eugenia's three daughters delight the crowd with their talents. I did my best to focus on the music and not the sidelong glances of whispering ladies in the audience. My discomfort must have been noticeable because at one point, Cassandra reached over and squeezed my hand in a show of silent support and commiseration.

Following the performance, I said my goodbyes to Cassandra and made my way to Dr. Finley's carriage. I assured my friend I was well and retreated before she could offer further objections.

Feeling eager for time to myself, I was waiting for the conveyance to arrive in the procession of departing guests when a throat cleared and a rough-accented voice asked, "Lady Morrison, might I escort ye to yer carriage?"

"Mr. O'Connor, how do you do?"

"Oh, I've been better, I suppose," he replied sardonically, eyes alight.

I didn't understand why Daniel was here or why he was seeking my company, but polite conversation was ingrained. "I'm sorry to hear that," I said sincerely while pulling my cloak tighter. The evening air was damp and chilly.

"Not to worry. All will be well. I have a feeling." He winked and offered me his arm as we progressed slowly down the drive with the other awaiting guests.

"Did you know that Q and I grew up together?"

I shook my head and Daniel continued, "That is his name, by the way. He prefers Q. Well, he prefers those close to him to call him Q. His brother started it when we were young."

"Oh," was all the reply I could muster.

"I told the idiot he should have told ye who he was. Once I realized ye were important to him. Anyway. I've known him me whole life. Me mam was the housekeeper for the Duke and Duchess at their estate in Southampton. She and the Duchess are close. Mam used to be her lady's maid before she started running the household. So I was raised there, and every summer I ran wild with Q. Des and Chelle, too, but they were older and outgrew us after a time. We've been through a lot together, me and Q. I might work for him or appear as his valet or bodyguard at all these high-society functions," he said with an eye roll, "but he's still me best mate."

I nodded, absorbing the words that Daniel had offered so freely, obviously in the name of friendship and support of Q.

"Don't tell him I said that." Tugging awkwardly on his hat, he continued, "The point is, Lady Jane—"

"Just Jane," I interrupted, offering a small smile.

"The point is, Jane. Q isn't like the rest of 'em. And I think ye know that. I don't need to stand here in the rain and sing his praises. But if ye need a little encouragement to hear him out, I'd ask ye to consider it. He's right miserable, and I'm not saying he doesn't deserve it. He does, the fool. But I imagine in this moment yer feeling like ye don't know him or yer questioning what you do know. And as his oldest and most attractive friend, I thought I could help."

I smiled at that. "Is that really what you're doing, standing here in the rain with me?"

"It is. That, and he asked me to make sure you were safe since ye came unescorted out of the house. Guarding and giving advice. Two birds, one stone."

I found I couldn't quite meet Daniel's eyes. "I saw him inside. Why didn't he wish to ensure my protection himself?"

"Because, my lady, he knew all those vultures would delight in having a go at ye." The Finley carriage pulled up on the circular drive just then. Daniel stepped forward before the driver could make his way down and opened my door with a flourish. Beaming a smile in my direction, he handed me up into the carriage. "Besides, he had somewhere important to be."

And there, sitting inside the carriage, was Lord Quinton Jameson himself.

~

"WHY HAVEN'T you been to work?" It was too dark to see his icy blue glare, but I could feel it even across the short distance between us.

The carriage trundled down the drive. I pointedly looked out the window to track our progress before replying, "Really? That's what you're leading with?"

He bit off a curse before leaning forward, arms on knees. "Where have you been? I've been worried. It's harder to keep you safe if you're unpredictable and away from Piker House."

I refused to be cowed by this, by him, but I lowered my eyes to his clasped hands before replying, "I needed time."

I could feel the frustration rolling off him in waves. The tension was thick inside the carriage. But despite the rigidity in his posture, he took my hands in his tenderly as if they were made of spun sugar. "Do you still need time?"

My anger flashed hotly. "Oh, should I be over your deception by now? Is a week the standard allotment for righteous indignation? You lied to me!"

Q opened his mouth, but I pressed on. "And don't say *technically* you didn't lie. It was a deception nonetheless. You *knew* how I would feel. You knew I'd be mortified to find out that after all this time, all this secrecy, you were actually the Earl Sullivan, back to claim his title and be the talk of the *ton* this season."

"I don't want them talking about me. All the women forcing their daughters upon me. The insufferable lordlings slapping my back and acting like we're old friends from Eton. Do you think I like it?"

"I don't know, *Your Grace*." It was petty and small, but so was my capacity for his bullshit in this moment.

He dropped my hands. "Don't call me that unless that's what you think of me. If an heir and a title is all you see, then carry on."

Truthfully, he'd never fit that mold so much as during the musicale this evening. But it was true. I could read his discomfort when standing on ceremony. I'd never felt like I was in the presence of a future duke when we were alone, just the two of us. I couldn't meet his gaze.

The carriage had stopped bumping along the cobblestones at some point. We were likely back to the Finley residence.

"You knew, Q. That's the part I can't get over. You knew how I would feel, and that's why you withheld the truth, withheld yourself from me."

Giving his head one firm shake, he asserted, "I've only ever been myself with you."

"Then you made me a fool, just like John. Left me to the wolves with our names on the lips of everyone in the ballroom. You could have confessed your identity at any time, but instead, you let me find out in the worst way possible. I felt like an idiot. *Feel* like an idiot. I thought… I thought…" But I found I could not finish that statement. Couldn't admit to Q that I'd hoped he cared about me, wanted a future with me. "I should not be alone in a carriage with the future Duke of Benton."

He winced at my pronouncement. "I'm still just a man, Jane. I can't look at you any other way. When I'm with you, I see a woman, not the scandalous daughter of a marquess. I see you, all of you. And no one else."

"I don't know how to be with you. Your name and title, your reputation, all seem more than I can bear."

"As much as it pains me to remind you, you courted the Earl Fairbanks," Q countered flatly.

"Yes, and I knew his rank all along. Look how well that turned out."

"Do not blame me for his mistakes."

I huffed a laughed. "No, you damn well made your own."

We were getting nowhere and I could sense Q reaching the same conclusion. But instead of silent regret and acquiesce, he took my hands once again and strove for earnest determination. "Janie, I'm sorry. I never meant to hurt you. I would never willingly sacrifice you to those sharks. I should have told you who I was. I just… needed time." He paused, having borrowed my words from earlier. "I wanted you to see only the man who aided your escape from the ball in your ruined gown, the man who would have protected you with his life in that alley-way. I just wanted you to see me as a man, as myself. That is the only part that matters. I'm sorry you found out in such a public way. I never wanted you to see the spectacle and attention I receive in a ballroom. I had hoped by the time you found out, it wouldn't matter. That nothing would change your regard by simply knowing the title I bear."

I was confused by his words, couldn't understand the outcome he had been hoping to achieve. I'd focus on that later. "So you never intended to tell me your-self? You, what? Swore Mr. Stevens and Mrs. Hooper to secrecy to aide in my ignorance?"

"No, of course not. I knew you'd find out. As you well know, London runs on gossip and my return to society has been much discussed," he added with a disgusted sneer. "It was childish of me to hope. And it was ignorant of me to fail to anticipate this outcome. And worst of all, I was cowardly. I should have confessed myself."

I nodded in response. I appreciated that he'd finally apologized and admitted his wrongdoing. Looking down at our joined hands, I realized at some point mine had clasped his back tightly. I had a death grip on his elegant, gloved fingers. Pulling myself away, I admitted, "I don't know what to do."

If Quinton was frustrated by my indecision, he didn't show it. He looked calcu-lating. "Will you come back to work? I don't want to be the reason you abandon your goals. I can stay away from Piker House if that's what you require. I'll… give you space. If you need it."

That seemed reasonable enough an offer. "Very well. I'll come back to work Monday."

Quinton nodded, satisfied.

"And," I ventured, "you don't have to. Stay away, that is." I could feel the heat crawling up my cheeks and felt grateful for the darkness of the carriage.

He nodded solemnly, but I couldn't helping feeling like I'd fallen into a trap. Proximity to Q had always been a needy, distracting thing. I didn't know what the future held for us, but I was glad we'd spoken. This conversation felt important. Communication was necessary.

While I still had my reservations about courting an earl, I couldn't deny the fact that I wanted more time with Quinton. He made me feel seen. And I felt like I could be myself with him, my odd bluestocking self, with my strange facts and my ability with numbers. I didn't think he'd judge my poor singing voice or my inability to play the pianoforte or paint a lovely landscape; all those things prized in a delicate lady of society. Q seemed to see past all the pomp and circumstance and lived his life freely as his own.

Perhaps we could do that… together.

Seventeen

Saturday afternoon found me tucked up in front of the fire with a book. The weather had turned mild again but I could tell the coming night would be chilly. Eliza was once again busy with her father's patients. I was thumbing through the small, odd ledger from Piker House, the one with only columns of coded names and dates. No transactions or debts or reimbursements. It was small enough that I could easily pack it away in my reticule and I had taken it home on my last day in the office before discovering Quinton's identity.

I felt guilty for abandoning my tasks in my emotional state and decided to get a start on my work by reviewing the records for any potential clues. I also found work to be a healthy distraction. Having studied this particular notebook several times, I wasn't sure what I was looking for, but the fact that it was different from the others made me think there was something special about it. I was simply hoping some new discovery would lead me to the hidden content in all the ledgers. I'd exhausted all the common ciphers in my attempts to decode the note-books. To say I was growing frustrated was a vast understatement.

As I reached the final leaf, I noticed a corner of one of the pages folded back on itself. In my previous review, I'd been so focused on the data within. I'd completely overlooked the blank pages beyond the coded names and dates. Seeing the layers was now overtly suspicious, but the light from the fire clearly illuminated ink written behind the overlapping parchment. Brows drawing low in confusion, I peeled the paper away from itself and smoothed it back into position, aligning with the surrounding pages. The resulting text came into view. I straightened in my chair, unfolding my legs from beneath me, and sat forward in my chair.

It was a series of letters.

I flipped back to the beginning of the book, memorizing the sequence.

This was the key to unlocking the mysterious ledgers.

The owner of the accounts had used substitution cryptography, words or phrases standing in place of other words or phrases. But instead of requiring an entirely new translation document for each substituted phrase, only a section of the alphabet had been rearranged and substituted. It was just a matter of using the same alphabet from a different starting point and translating the coded text.

I quickly moved over to the desk on the other side of the study and uncovered parchment and ink to begin my work. I wrote out the newly ordered alphabet, corresponding letters, and flipped back to the beginning of the ledger.

The accounts lined up how I'd predicted with two columns of names and dates along the right side of the page. As I worked throughout the evening, I realized the names in the first column appeared to be prominent men within society. I recognized parliament members, many titled gentlemen, wealthy businessmen, and landowners as well. The editor for *The Times* and *The Daily Telegraph* was among the many names repeated in the column. My pen skidded over the parchment when I decoded quite unexpectedly: Earl Fairbanks.

What was John doing listed in this ledger from Piker House? Was he in debt? But there were no monies or transactions listed in this particular record. It was unlike all the others.

With renewed suspicion and a general sense of doom, I jumped to the middle column and translated the name beside John's: Juniper. The date was six years prior. I continued my search, looking only for the group of letters that translated to Earl Fairbanks. And I found them. Often.

Based on the dates therein, it seemed as if John had some sort of recurring arrangement with this "Juniper." Always during the season. Sometimes weekly. Other times more or less often. The transactions, whatever they were, happened less frequently in the prior two seasons, but they still occurred at least monthly.

I attempted to think back on the dates in question, but it was nearly impossible to pick out random days and times during my courtship with John. Were we attending a ball, the theatre, the opera? I couldn't recall. But I was getting an unpleasant feeling in the pit of my stomach.

After isolating all of John's interactions, I went back to decoding the notebook in full. By now it was late evening. My neck had an odd crick and my shoulders were tight with tension from remaining in the same position for hours. I'd deduced the initial column on each page identified the client list, full of London's elite. The far column listed dates, of what I called service, going back nearly ten years and concluding when Quinton had taken over Piker House. And the middle column specified a smaller circle of recurring names that likely indicated they were the ones providing the service.

Jezebel, Scarlet, Juniper, Isobel, Kitty, Ginger, Veronica, and several others.

And not to be a Presumptuous Posey, but I'm pretty sure they had been running a brothel.

I was compartmentalizing at the moment. Taking the evidence of John's infidelity and locking it away in the trunk of unpleasantness in my mind. I tried not to focus on his relationship with Juniper. Based on time and frequency, she had more of a claim on Lord Fairbanks than I ever did.

And I suppose it's socially acceptable for a gentleman, married and unmarried, to frequent brothels and pay for intimacies. It's just not what I want for my gentleman.

I was somewhat ashamed to admit that my heartbeat was far more erratic while searching for Quinton's name on the list of clients than when I uncovered the depths of John's deception. And the relief I felt at Q's absence from the notebook made no sense to the rational part of my brain. We'd only known each other for a matter of weeks. Realistically, it mattered not what Lord Sullivan did with his time and with whom, past or present. I had no right to judge and even less of a claim on Quinton. But there we were.

I was easily able to ignore over a year of betrayal from the man I'd hoped to marry. That likely said more about me than it did about John. More surprised than anything, I realized that the scandal I feared was just as probable with a companion such as Lord Fairbanks… One that I'd deemed safe and innocuous. Here I was assuming that a life with Quinton would be fraught with endless gossip, when I'd been so wrong, so mistaken about everything else. Marriage to John would not have been the placid, comfortable one I'd assumed awaited me. I felt even more foolish for misjudging him so completely.

Quickly gathering the ledger and the papers containing my translation, I knew what I had to do. With the mystery partially solved, I wouldn't be able to rest until I compared the cipher I'd discovered to the other account records. I didn't know if the code would work to decipher the transactions and patrons indebted to the gambling establishment. But if I was right and they were linked, did that mean Piker House was connected to the brothel I'd uncovered? Did Quinton own more than just the gaming hell?

I had to find out.

~

In an effort to maintain secrecy, a quick hackney ride later found me knocking at the kitchen door of Piker House. St. James's Street was bustling with revelers coming and going from the gaming hell. From my vantage point, I'd seen Mr. Stanley guarding the front entrance with another large gentleman. But Daniel and Quinton were nowhere to be found. I hadn't expected them to be on guard duty, but just knowing we were occupying the same space was… electrifying and troublesome.

I donned my cloak and slipped through to the side gardens and service entrance undetected. Mrs. Hooper took in my manic expression and overwhelming explanation with wide eyes and a concerned pucker between her brows. But she'd allowed me entrance and cautioned me to stay in the offices on the third floor. Her gentle scolding reminded me that Piker House was in full swing tonight.

I hurried above stairs to find the offices and my desk just as I'd left it. There was no fire in the grate, but the oil lamps from the hallway allowed me to find my way around the room. I lit the lamp on the desk.

Quickly removing the ledger from the drawer, I compared my decoded alphabet to the pages within. I don't know how long I sat there translating the text, uncovering names of gentlemen who were indebted to the gaming hell for tens of thousands of pounds.

I'd gotten to the bottom of one of the pages when the name I'd decoded stopped me in my tracks.

Lord Samuel Morrison, the Marquess Middleton

My father.

My father was indebted to Piker House. My father was one of the men Q wished to ruin. I quickly scanned just one of the ledgers from dates over four years past. I found Lord Samuel Morrison listed many times and nearly always at a loss. My family owed Piker House a staggering sum of money, based on this one record book alone.

No wonder Quinton was interested in collecting on these debts. He could ruin many a peer with the notes held within. With his distaste for London high society coupled with his vengeance for his fallen brother, Q would be able to accomplish his plans and damage many reputations thanks to the knowledge I had uncovered.

I wasn't sure how I felt about that.

On the one hand, I tended to agree that these lords should be held accountable and pay their due. However, their debts weren't always their own. Many of these lords were spending their daughters' dowries, their wives' fortunes, and mismanaging the income from their tenants. More people would be affected than just the gentlemen on these pages. Lives would be ruined.

My father's life would be ruined.

I would need to search further to determine the damage such debt would mean to my family's already nonexistent fortune. And I would need to compartmentalize this latest discovery until I could deal with it.

There were years' worth of transactions for me to wade through. Now that I'd confirmed the connection between the brothel ledger and past Piker House records, some of the urgency began to wane. I could come back on Monday morning and continue my work. This would take me some time yet.

I was desperate, however, to speak to Q. I needed answers regarding the brothel, as well as the plans for the debtors I planned to reveal.

I felt strongly that Q needed to come to terms with his brother's death without drowning himself in guilt as well as revenge. But that wouldn't stop me from sharing what I'd discovered. He deserved to know.

I was contemplating the intelligence of seeking Q out on the floor of the gaming hell. He would likely be very angry. Truthfully, it was dangerous, and I didn't need to be spotted and draw more scandal unto myself. Perhaps I could find Mr. O'Connor or another guard and have them relay a message to Q.

Turning toward the window to mull over my options, I started at the sight before me. The rear portion of the gardens was alight. Beyond the path and the pond, the flat expanse of shorn grass had been roped and sectioned off into what appeared to be a boxing ring. Rough and rudimentary at best, the area was lit with torches. Evenly spaced, the light threw large shadows and cast an orange glow upon the many bodies surrounding the circle of onlookers.

It was hard to imagine I'd ignored these sights in my haste to get to the ledgers in the office. But the rear of the gardens was quite far from the entrance to the kitchens. And if I failed to notice the torchlight, I wasn't surprised. When fixating on a task, I was often difficult to deter. The noise from the street was loud despite the late hour. I'd likely heard carriage wheels, hoof beats, and raised voices enough to drown out the sounds of the gathered crowd in the gardens beyond.

And it was quite the crowd. They surrounded the ring as two fighters, stripped to the waist, circled one another. I jolted in my chair as a punch was thrown and landed with deft precision. The audience cheered, their voices barely discernable through the window. With applause and triumphant hands raised, well-dressed gentleman—aristocrats most likely—watched the two men continue their boxing match. At the conclusion, when one man was counted down after having received a devastating blow, money deftly changed hands between livered servants stationed around the crowd. Did Piker House provide this sort of gambling and entertainment? Was this just one more part of Quinton's world that I was discovering this evening?

As if conjured by my unanswered questions, I spotted Q in the crowd. He was along the perimeter of those assembled and… he… he wasn't wearing a shirt. I'd risen from my chair at some point, and with fingertips pressed lightly to the windowpane, I leaned forward to see Quinton standing in front of Mr. O'Connor.

His friend and employee seemed to be wrapping one of Q's hands with strips of cloth. Was he going to fight?

My breath expelled in a rush and fogged the glass.

With a squeak, I rubbed my fingers back and forth across the pane to dispel the moisture and resume my clandestine voyeurism.

Q was here. It would be much easier to gain his attention in the gardens than trying to track him down on the gaming floor. I needed to tell him what I'd uncovered.

And I needed to find out how much he knew about the brothel.

The hedges along the border would provide excellent cover. I was confident I could flag down either Q or Daniel. This could work.

I quickly grabbed my cloak from the armchair and pulled it on as I made my way back down the servants' stairs. Raising the hood to shield my identity, I proceeded slowly out into the garden. I was relieved to have avoided a run-in with Mrs. Hooper.

Creeping past the pond on the graveled path, I skirted the edge of the property and stayed close to the hedgerow as I proceeded toward the glowing torches in the distance. As I moved closer, Daniel and Q came into view. He was wrapping Quinton's other hand with a long strip of linen. They weren't talking at the moment, and Daniel seemed focused on his task while Q watched the assembled audience.

I wasn't quite ashamed, but something close to it, as I peered at Q from behind the hedges. The torchlight painted his form golden and I couldn't look away. He was facing away from me and wasn't wearing a shirt. His britches were quite snug across his posterior. The planes of muscles across his back were smooth and tight. They seemed to ripple beneath his skin with every minute movement. Light from the glowing fire emphasized the shadows and definition of Quinton's shoulder blades and torso. I squinted in an effort to take in more details. What would his skin feel like? Contrasting hard muscle and soft skin? I had the sudden urge to judge the texture with my lips, my fingers, my nails.

I slouched in my stance as the men finally stepped apart. Daniel tucked the last of the linen within the wrapping. "That feel all right?"

A short nod was Quinton's only reply.

"Yer going to get yer arse kicked if ye don't focus," his friend cautioned.

I could imagine Q's baleful glare.

Hands raised in surrender, Daniel tried again. "I'm just saying. Yer preoccupied. I get it. Women are distracting. I just don't want ye to be in an even worse mood once yer flat on yer back in the ring."

My face pinched in confusion and concern.

If Q gave a verbal reaction, I didn't hear it.

But before I could ponder over Daniel's statements, Q turned minutely, curled his hands into fists and pushed them out in front of his body, testing the resistance of the wrappings. His triceps and shoulders flexed beautifully with the movement. I must've made a sound in response because Mr. O'Connor's head came up, eyes narrowed in my direction. Quickly lowering myself behind the boxwoods, I cursed my lustful confusion. I should have just waved and then I would have had their attention. I could have proceeded with my plan and told Q about the ledgers and asked him about the status of the brothel. But everything about this situation felt illicit, as if I should be hiding my presence.

Determined to get my ridiculousness under control, I raised my head, intent on gaining their attention, and found both men looking in my direction. Oh, good. I smiled and offered a jaunty salute. I don't know why. That was weird.

Quinton's eyes widened incredulously, and he immediately stormed my way. Daniel stayed put but gave me a salute and a wink in return. I thought he may have mouthed "good luck," but I couldn't be certain because Quinton was almost directly in front of me by this point.

It was difficult to meet his gaze, not precisely because I was embarrassed by the situation but mostly because the front of a shirtless Q was greater than or equal to the back of a shirtless Q. His chest was magnificent, broad and defined with a light dusting of dark hair. My stare quickly traveled lower to his stomach, tight and paved with little bricks of muscle until the vee of his hips angled sharply into his trousers.

I shook myself and straightened at Quinton's approach, offering a bright smile. But before I could speak, Q continued advancing and pushed through the hedgerow. Grabbing my arm, he towed us behind the foliage.

Emitting an outraged squawk, I turned my confused stare to meet his incredulous expression. Before I could protest being hauled behind the bushes, Q asked in exasperation, "What are you doing here?"

"I came to tell you that I cracked the code on the ledgers." I was surprised that my words didn't elicit a reaction from Quinton. Apparently he wished to remain unmoved by my good news.

"You could have told me that during daylight hours. It isn't safe for you here or anywhere so late in London. Did you come alone?"

"Yes, but it was important. I needed to further research my findings and the records were here in the offices."

Quinton swiped a taped hand through his hair in frustration. "Jane, you could have been accosted on the street. You could have been seen and recognized. Ruined."

He brought up very good points. Yet, I'd weighed the risks and decided I could hide my appearance and therefore preserve my anonymity. I was loathe to also admit that my overall fixation on testing the code against the ledgers in the offices had driven me to distraction. I'd ignored the dangers of traveling alone at night in London as well as risked my reputation at a known gaming establishment. But it felt worth it in the moment. With supporting evidence and Q's stern admonition staring me in the face, I admittedly now felt a bit foolish.

My reply likely came out small and cowed. "I was just focused on my work. I needed to talk to you. I didn't consider… I was foolish."

Q's hand moved down my arm. No longer grasping and holding me to him, but softer. Fingers trailed until he clasped my hand within his own, palm to palm. "I'm glad you're okay. I was worried. And I know how devastated you'd be if you'd been seen by anyone besides Daniel and myself."

He was right. All my worries about scandal and gossip and I'd overlooked and ignored every precaution this evening in my pursuit of answers. Simply being spotted near Piker House would land my reputation in boiling water.

As if sensing my withdrawal, Quinton tugged on my hand and began leading us out of the gardens and back toward the building. We remained stooped as we moved behind the hedgerow, out of sight of the fighters and assembled audience.

We entered the kitchens and ascended the servants' stairs to the third floor. Instead of stopping at the library where I generally conducted my work, Q led me along the hallway to a wing I hadn't visited. I'd been aware of living quarters on this floor, but only vaguely. Apparently Quinton was leading me to his private rooms.

We entered a lavishly appointed drawing room. The carpets were thick under my feet and the wall hangings a deep red and filled with decorative but comfortable looking furniture. A deep armchair by the fire caught my eye and I could imagine sitting there curled up with a book. An open doorway allowed me a glimpse of a large bed, and I decidedly turned away. Best not to entertain any ideas or test the boundaries of our familiarity. This space was obviously very private, and I'd forced my way in with no invitation.

Quinton dropped my hand and disappeared into the bedroom. He returned momentarily with a shirt and began shrugging it on. I allowed myself a brief moment to mourn the loss of his skin. I was being unladylike, I knew this. Yet men were often ungentlemanly and you didn't hear them feeling bad about it.

I was still lamenting the appearance of the fine lawn shirt when Q finally spoke, "Come. We should talk, and it'll be easier to keep you from being seen if you're in my quarters."

I nodded my agreement. Settling into the chair by the fire, Q occupied the settee across from me. His shirt remained loose and unfastened, and I could see the luminous skin of his neck and collarbones.

As if understanding my sudden paralysis at being alone in his quarters with him, Quinton offered me a small smile. "Do you want to tell me what you discovered?"

So I did. I told him about uncovering the hidden page in the small notebook and decoding the names within. I explained my subsequent hypothesis that the same code would uncover Piker House debtors, and the confirmation as well. I wasn't ready to address finding my father's name in the account ledgers nor John's in the small record book. I would deal with those issues later. But there was something I needed to know.

"Did you know about the brothel? That is what those women's names mean, correct? Do you own that as well?"

I brief pause. "No, I don't own it." His gaze was steady, but he seemed prepared for an outburst or accusation. When none came, Quinton continued, "The previous owner of Piker House was a scoundrel. I already told you that he didn't protect his patrons and left them to fend off the cutthroats in the alleys. He used to take a huge portion of the brothel's profits, hence the small ledger that was in your possession. He had a deal with the madame who runs things below the gaming hell. I don't know what it entailed, but he helped her start the business but continued skimming large sums of her revenue. When I took over, I wanted to ruin the entire establishment, destroy everything and everyone associated with Piker House. But didn't realize so many livelihoods were tied up in this place. I couldn't simply shut everything down without impacting so many people… women, children. The brothel runs out of the first floor, and yes, some of their business does overlap with the gaming floor. But I'm basically a landlord at this point. The madame below stairs takes care of her girls and my men make sure they are protected. That is all."

I considered his explanation and marveled at his inability to see himself clearly. Quinton had his demons. Didn't we all? But while he was determined to punish himself for his brother's death, he seemed unable to find any redeeming qualities within himself. Q was no longer the gallivanting lord, the worry-free second son. He'd reclaimed his place in society and was now successfully managing a business that provided support and impacted the lives of his employees. He may have acquired the gaming hell in an attempt to ruin all those involved, but it hadn't turned out that way at all.

Making my expression very even, I replied, "I see. And what will you do with the names I uncover? All those aristocrats indebted to your establishment."

"I'll see that they pay their dues."

"How? With your men? With violence?"

"That's not my aim, but they need to be held accountable for their actions. Once word has spread and Piker House has the reputation for making sure even the nobility pay their debts… Well, then perhaps they'll be more careful with their investments. Aristocrats are not exempt from justice, Jane."

My smile was slow but gratified. I liked that I could predict his motives and responses. I wanted to know him. Know more. Know everything. "Ah, there you are. The vigilante once again. You're absorbing these responsibilities. Taking on more than you bargained for. You hate these nobles, but you'll protect them on the streets. You wouldn't see what happened to your brother happen to them."

"No one deserves that."

We were quiet for a time. Q staring into the fire, remembering the past. Me watching Q, hoping for a future.

With no preamble, Quinton asked, "When's the last time you saw your sister June?"

I jolted in obvious surprise, unable to imagine where this line of questioning was going nor why it had evolved from our discussion. My brows furrowed in thought. "I… don't know. She left after our mother died. I was thirteen, maybe fourteen when she left. Why?"

Quinton turned away from the fire then, meeting my gaze. His expression was careful, gauging. "June is the madame of the brothel, Jane."

The shock undoubtedly registered on my face. I recalled the scarlet woman I'd seen on the stairs. The one I'd chased. She'd seemed familiar at the time and if I was honest with myself, it was because she'd reminded me of June. If Q was looking for truth in my countenance, I assume he found it because he kept going, answering my unspoken questions. "Do you remember the man who met us on the street? With the bowler hat?"

He was changing course and I wasn't following, but I nodded. I could easily recall that moment and those following. Quinton chose to distance himself from me as a result of that encounter and I still didn't understand why.

Q angled my way and took my hands. "That man works for Seamus. He runs a gang in Whitechapel, and I used to supply him with guards and extra men for whatever he needed. We had a contract and—and I didn't ask questions. If the men had problems with what Seamus asked them to do, they didn't let on. But I know, I *knew* they were hired muscle for theft, smuggling, loading and unloading ships, whatever Seamus needed the manpower for."

My brows crinkled in concern. I attempted to keep the judgement out of my tone and asked, "Why are you telling me this?"

"I want to explain, but I also want to be honest. I'm not… I wasn't a good person, Jane. But I stopped. I broke the contract and told Seamus we were done. I didn't want my men used for that. I couldn't be responsible anymore and I wanted no part of hurting anyone else. Seamus was angry. He's not used to taking no for an answer. He had his man following me that day in Mayfair. And when he saw you… He thought you were June. He misread our relationship and assumed June and I were linked in more than just business." Quinton took a deep breath. "That's why I stayed away. I didn't want you to be a target. The more I was seen with you, the greater the chance they would realize you weren't your sister. I needed Seamus and his men to stay in Whitechapel and never approach you again. I knew they'd use you as leverage, threaten you so I'd agree to come back and provide manpower for his enterprise once more."

After everything, after all I'd learned as Quinton divulged these truths, I was having trouble focusing on any fact but one. "Did you—" I cleared my throat and looked down at our clasped hands before I continued, "Did you think I was June as well?"

It was ludicrous to receive this influx of information and focus on the most juvenile of points. I wanted Quinton to want me for me. The idea that he could have mistaken me for June during our first encounter settled cold into my veins.

"Jane." At the sound of my name on Quinton's lips, I looked up. "At first, I did. Briefly at the ball with your ripped gown in hand, I entertained the idea that you were June." At his reluctant admission, I attempted to extricate my hands from his grasp, but he tightened his hold and hurried on. "But I realized pretty quickly that you were not. One only has to speak to you, to know that you are uniquely your own person. I was intrigued and enchanted. Confused, yes. But completely captivated."

Thinking back to that night, it was hard to parse our chance meeting. I had been too much in my own head, first fretting over my gown and worried about furthering the gossips of the *ton*. And then I was distracted by Q's presence. His voice. His face. His very existence did ridiculous things to my focus. The mystery of him in those moments far outweighed my ability to discern if he had mistaken me for my sister.

For some reason, Quinton's assessment of that night and how he described me felt… flattering. I could feel my cheeks heating under his praise. While I'd been labeled unique and somewhat *other* my entire life, this was the first time it didn't feel like a deficiency. I was odd and spoke out of turn. Standing out, when the aim of society was to fit in, made being my own person a shortcoming. But when Quinton found me captivating and my friends cherished my opinions and valued my peculiarities, I didn't feel like being different was such a terrible thing.

"June and I don't have much interaction. I'm essentially her landlord. I oversee Piker House and she controls the brothel. The gaming hell is my purview, but my men provide security for the women in her employ. June's identity is admittedly rather mysterious, but I didn't honestly think to find her in a ballroom in Mayfair. I was curious after meeting you at Benton House. You and your sister look similar but not the same." He looked down before continuing. "Vincent told me where he'd taken you, so I went to the Finley residence and waited. I saw you that morning bustling from house to house and being turned away at each. I honestly didn't know what to make of it. So when I saw you again at Foxworth's masquerade, I realized I wanted to know you."

There was much to think about and work through. The ramifications of the ledgers, Quinton's past, my sister's involvement, and still I longed to force it all away. The trunk in my mind holding life's unpleasantness was likely to explode soon.

I reached tentatively for Q. Sliding my gloveless hand along his stubble-roughened cheek, I turned his downcast face up toward mine. It felt as natural as breathing to rest my forehead against his and occupy his space. To be this close felt like a necessity, like an eventuality.

We were quiet for a long while, but Quinton eventually broke the silence. "Are you still angry with me?"

I didn't know how to answer that. Accepting that Q hadn't withheld his title in an effort to hurt me went a long way toward easing the path for my pride.

When I didn't respond, he asked, "Do you trust that I'd never hurt you?"

"I know that."

"Give me a chance, Jane. I'd still like to court you. It would be different knowing I'm the Earl Sullivan, I know that. But I'd do all in my power to shield you from scandal. I've met with Seamus and we've reached an understanding, I believe. I wouldn't put you in danger. I just want to know you, and for you to know me as well."

I considered his proposal. Sitting back a bit, I released his wrapped hands but kept them in my possession. I reached for the tucked end of the linen and began the process of removing the fabric from about his knuckles, relishing the intimacy of the action. I liked the idea of uncovering his skin little bits at a time. This felt like trust. Like familiarity and tenderness from a man who was difficult to know.

No longer my mysterious Lord Dashing, Quinton was becoming something more.

Focusing on my task, I set to unwrapping the linen. "How would that work exactly? Our courtship. Would I still work for you?"

"Only if you wanted to," came his measured response. "It's a fair assumption that your former clients might register our association and ask you to come back and preform your previous duties. If that would make you happy, that's all I want. You have no obligation to me or Piker House. I don't want you to leave, but you should only stay if it's right for you."

As I uncovered Quinton's hands, I registered callouses and work-roughened palms. He didn't have the hands of an aristocrat. I wondered how often he joined in these fights. Something to discuss later. "Letting our relationship re-open doors for me wouldn't sit right. If they didn't want me then, they don't deserve me now. I would never use you like that."

Q watched as I began on his second set of wrappings, our skin brushing with every movement. Could he feel it, too? This intensity building simply by sharing the same space.

"Of course I know you wouldn't, Jane. You're too good. You'd never use someone." His lips twitched. "Besides, it's not as if you knew you were secretly courting a future duke."

I gaped at his cheekiness. "That isn't funny yet!"

"When might it be funny, do you think? When we are married?"

I abruptly stopped what I was doing and turned my incredulous expression toward him. I had but a moment to read the mirth and surprising sincerity in his features before he kissed me.

The press of his lips started out teasing, like our conversation. Small nips and exploration. Quinton moved to kiss the corner of my mouth and then the cupid's bow. His warm hand moved to the side of my neck as he gently guided my lips to meet his own. Our kiss progressed from teasing to something far more serious. Slow and deep, I was consumed. Quinton's tongue invaded, but his retreat encouraged me to move with him. I did some exploring of my own. My hands grew brave and pressed against his muscled chest. Through the thin fabric, I could feel how warm and solid he was. I'd never much considered a man's body beyond function and form, but that tantalizing glimpse of Q by torchlight this evening made me appreciate his appearance in an entirely new way.

Quinton abruptly turned his head to the side, breaking our kiss. Foreheads touching, we were both surprisingly breathless. "Let me prove myself to you, Jane."

My throat felt tight all of a sudden. "What if this is a disaster and every gossip rag in town prints our misfortune for all of England to dissect and discuss?"

"I may curse the very establishment that makes it so, but my standing in society and my reputation grants me the power to withstand much in that regard. I will do everything I can to help you avoid scandal." He huffed out a small laugh. "Well, after this moment right now… when you're an unchaperoned woman in a room alone with me."

My eye roll was legendary.

Smiling, Quinton said with earnest conviction, "I want you."

More than his declaration, even more than his warm body pressed so close to mine, it was the certainty in his tone that impacted me the most. As if he'd reached this conclusion: that we were inevitable. And he hadn't come to such a realization lightly, or even reluctantly. But he had gathered his nerve, reasoned through his doubts, and actively decided to want me. As if it was worth something. As if *I* was worth something.

It was time for me to be brave as well.

"I want you, too."

Eighteen

This time I took the lead, kissing Quinton with every ounce of pent-up frustration from weeks of indecision and denial. I felt overwhelmed by all that I wanted to touch, to taste.

As if sensing my directionless urgency, Q gently guided me onto his lap. I settled myself astride and resumed kissing his eager mouth. Hands wandered and lips tasted. After a time, I was squirming in my seat needing… something.

While I was a virgin, I was an avid reader. Dr. Finley's library was full of medical texts. I knew what happened between a man and woman, and I knew what I was feeling was arousal. My body was preparing me for intimacies. I could detect dampness between my thighs and an empty, aching feeling as well. My body was impatient for release, something that had only happened in the darkness of my own bedroom, searching clumsy fingers between my legs. My breasts felt full and heavy. Why wasn't Quinton touching them? I thought that would help. Grabbing his hand from where it rested sedately on my waist, I moved it to my bodice. The material cut across the tops of my breasts, but I figured Q was resourceful enough to provide the touch I needed.

His hand stilled. Perhaps not.

"I'm trying to be a gentleman, Jane. Is this really what you want? To be with me… like this."

My reply was breathless and slightly impatient, "Yes. Yes, please."

Those icy blue eyes searched my face. "Are you sure?" Quinton whispered.

In answer, I rose as elegantly as possible from my straddled position, trailing my hand down his arm. I grasped the remaining linen wrapper still circling his right hand and tugged him to his feet. Pulling the last bit of fabric free, I linked my hand with Q's and guided him through the open doorway into his bed chamber.

Heels lifting, I rose and kissed him gently on the mouth. "I'm ready."

And with that, I laid myself upon the coverlet and awaited his ministrations. My bravado from moments before was still with me. Well, perhaps it had faded just a bit. Keeping my eyes trained on the ceiling seemed the best course of action. I assumed any moment now I'd feel Quinton's weight on the mattress. Perhaps I should have removed my stockings and my shoes. Surely that wasn't required to perform the act. I'd witnessed sexual congress between a myriad of animals during my summers in the country. It would likely be over very soon, shoes or not.

Eyes heavenward, I felt the bed depress at my side. I braced for Quinton's touch. It wasn't that I didn't enjoy his touch, because I did. I just didn't know what to expect in this moment and yes, my previous bravado had completely abandoned me.

Risking a glance to my side, I saw Quinton sitting near my hip, chin resting in his palm. His eyes were bright and fond, but he was just staring at me as if he had no idea what to do with me. This wasn't an unusual expression. Most of my acquaintances exhibited similar reactions in my company. But perhaps I was wrong to assume that due to the nature of Q's relationships—the mistresses and trollopera singers—that his experience in the bedchamber would translate to a successful first attempt together.

"Jane." Q's voice brought my attention back to his amused faced.

I frowned. "Are you laughing at me?"

"No." He sobered immediately, amusement vanishing. "I'm just trying to figure out what you are doing."

Cheeks burning, I said, "Well, I said I was ready, so I assumed you would… just…" I waved my left hand in a vague get-on-with-it motion.

Smiling down at me, Quinton said, "Let's try something different. Sit up for me."

I did as he asked as he removed himself from the bed. This seemed counterproductive. I didn't imagine we could conduct sexual congress while five feet apart.

Quinton began by removing his shirt. Having never tied the strings, he simply reached an arm behind his back and smoothly lifted the shirt over his head. My expression was undoubtedly confused. I still didn't understand what we were doing, but I was easily distracted by the sight of his naked chest. There was a fire lit in the hearth and the gas lamps provided adequate lighting with which to see his lean and muscular form.

He leaned over to unstrap and remove his boots quickly and efficiently. When he returned to stand, his hands went to the placket on his trousers before pausing. "I'm not going to mount you like an animal, Jane. I want our pleasure to be shared. Not mine alone, and not over before it's even begun. Perhaps you can become acquainted with my body and get comfortable. I thought you might like to do a little exploring. Will you touch me?"

I nodded. And with painstaking deliberateness, Q removed his pants.

I could feel my eyes widen. Seeing a beautiful naked man in the flesh was very different than seeing a diagram in a medical text or a sculpture in a museum. Quinton was a marvel.

Raising onto my knees, I made my way to the edge of the bed. I was drawn by the sights and the honesty and openness before me. Reacquainting myself with Q's chest seemed a safe place to start. So, I smoothed my hands along the planes, tracing the lines of his collarbones and over the rounded tops of his shoulders. My eyes followed the path of my hands. Quinton was all power and heat beneath my fingertips.

Unsure where to venture next, I skimmed down his sides, hitting a ticklish spot and making him jump. His grin was quick and devastating, but he remained in my possession. I felt the hard lines of his stomach and the trail of hair, so coarse and dark, arrowing toward his manhood. He sucked in a ragged breath as I ventured lower. Blind curiosity propelled my movements. I was eager to feel him… that part of him. But I was also impatient to learn what he liked. I wanted him to crave my touch, demand it.

Circling the base, his erection jumped in my hand. Quinton whooshed out a breath and dropped his forehead to my shoulder. "Is this okay?" I asked.

He kissed my collarbone in response.

I continued my exploration, noting the contrasting textures. He was hard beneath my grip but smooth, lavishly so. My movements grew unsure. I didn't know how to please a man, how Quinton liked to be touched. "Show me what to do," I begged.

Q wrapped his right hand around my own, his left grasping my hip. His head remained on my shoulder and I noted, with perverse satisfaction, he was watching as our hands moved in tandem. He showed me how firmly to grip and how fast to move. And when his breath became labored and his right hand fell away to cling to my hip, I felt a heady satisfaction. Those little growls and grunts of pleasure were caused by my touch. Owning someone's desire felt powerful. And I liked it.

In one swift motion, Quinton surged forward and kissed me. It was in no way tentative and I savored the deep stroke of his tongue against my own. He distracted me soundly and my hand paused in my ministrations. He used the break in my concentration to remove his lower body from my grasp before saying, "Any more of that and it'll be over before it has begun." Quinton's breathing was heavy and uneven, but he graced me with a mischievous grin. "Besides, I haven't had my turn to explore yet."

I considered that. Would he want to strip my clothes and examine every inch of my skin? To touch and taste and learn all the ways to elicit gasps and moans as I had done? Did I want that?

Yes. Yes, I did.

Thinking of Q's hungry gaze gave me courage when before I might have been shy. His body's response to my eager hands bolstered my nerve when my instinct was to lean toward self-consciousness. And his words and encouragement gave me the final push to step away and begin removing my garments. Q's clever fingers assisted, loosening my stays. Eventually I stood before him in nothing but my nearly transparent shift.

"Is this still what you want?" he murmured, kissing the spot beneath my ear. The pins had been removed from my hair and my wild curls spilled down my back.

He carefully gathered the rebellious auburn locks and continued kissing down my neck.

"Yes," I breathed at last.

And with permission granted, he reached down and pulled the fine material up and over my head. Standing naked before Quinton, I noted my alabaster skin next to his warm sun-kissed hue. His eyes drank me in and those blue orbs burned with desire. This felt like a dream.

He stepped closer, grasping my hand and pulling it to his lips. With a kiss to my inner wrist, he whispered against my skin, "Still okay?"

I nodded and moved to lie back on the bed. But this time, I pulled Quinton down with me. He lay at my side and began an exploration of his own. Making his way along my body, I was awash in sensation. His stubbled cheek gently rasping. Hands stroking and caressing. His midnight hair grazing my skin, soft as a raven's wing. The pressure from his lips, the lave of his tongue, the suction from his mouth. I was breathing hard from his attentions and clinging to the back of his head as his mouth found my nipple. The sensation was unreal, and I was surprised to realize how sensitive I was there.

I was too consumed to feel embarrassed or ashamed or any other expected emotion from a woman of my station. Society would call me a fallen woman, yet Q would be praised for his sexual prowess. If that disconnect didn't alert me to the disparity and social injustice of the situation, nothing would. Yet I knew Quinton cared for me. I was making this decision for myself and no one else. Not for my family and not for parliament. My body was my own, and Quinton was worshiping it.

Q's lips began their descent while his hands took their place on my breasts, kneading and plumping. I was squirming on the sheets as his mouth did something I had never imagined. Warm breath met my slippery, overheated flesh before Quinton licked the seam of my sex. I jolted at the sensation. Q's hand moved to my hips to hold me in place as he continued his assault.

My breath whooshed out as I absorbed the feeling of his mouth on me *there*. So slick and warm. Positively indecent. My nerve endings were electrified, buzzing sensation from my womanhood throughout my body.

"Jane," Quinton murmured, lips pressed to my sex. My eyes came open at his address and I looked down to meet his amused gaze. "Watch me. Don't close your eyes." I hadn't even realized I'd done so but, oh my, they were open now. There was something about watching his head, framed by my breasts, move between my legs. Suddenly I couldn't look away.

Between the visual stimulation, the utter decadence of Quinton's mouth, and the obscene sounds our bodies were making together, I started feeling tight all over. I knew my body was reaching and straining toward crisis, but it felt unbearably strong. The intensity was staggering. A warning bell inside my body, blaring.

"Quinton," I breathed, overwhelmed and searching.

His hands tightened on my hips as he continued to lick and suck at the entrance to my body. I moved shamelessly against his mouth, chasing the friction that was drawing me ever closer to the brink.

"So close," I said on a harsh gasp before that tightness in my body pulled as taut as a bowstring. And then all at once, it snapped. Relief and warmth flooded. My release washed over me in a rush of sensation and Quinton saw me through it. His lips coaxed me through the finest orgasm of my life.

I felt languid and loose, utterly comfortable in my skin. Raising my arms above my head and stretching along the sheets, I told Quinton, "Come up here with me."

He pushed up onto his elbows and the way his muscled shoulders moved and bunched made my core tighten in response. Q kept eye contact as he raised his hand and very deliberately wiped the moisture away from his mouth. It was strangely erotic, and from his expression, he could tell I thought so. Quinton stalked up my body, pressing kisses along the way, until he settled his weight atop mine.

"That was…" I was unsure how to finish. How to adequately describe the pleasure I'd felt not only at his touch, but from his care and attention. So I kissed him instead. Planting both hands on his cheeks, I poured every ounce of my desire and joy and freedom into that kiss. He groaned into my mouth, and I remembered that he was still in a state of turmoil. Quinton had not yet found his release as I'd so blissfully done, and I wanted that more than anything.

Breaking our kiss, I whispered against his lips, "Will you make love to me?"

He searched my eyes for a moment before gifting me a small smile and a kiss to each of my cheeks. "If you're sure?"

It could feel him hard against my thigh. Impossibly hard. And I knew what would come next. I nodded my assent.

Q swallowed audibly and his amusement bled away. "I'm afraid it will hurt, this first time." I knew this. Every young woman had been reminded of their virtue often enough. And something about him saying *this first time* gave my chest a hopeful ache at the thought of more times to come. Before I could offer any reassurance, Quinton continued, "But I vow to make it up to you."

And he did. Several times.

~

In the predawn hours, I startled awake. One of those jerking movements that seemed inexplicable and refused any attempt to return to sleep.

The sun wasn't close to rising and the fire had dwindled to embers offering just enough light to see by in the darkened bedroom. Despite my abrupt transition from sleep to wakefulness, I knew where I was. I could hear Quinton's deep breaths at my side. Feel his warmth as his legs remained tangled with mine. I longed to turn into his body and lock away the outside world. But I knew how fruitless that effort would be. Servants would be rising shortly to begin their day. I could not be discovered here.

Sleep would be elusive now, I knew. And while my heart rate had slowed following my jolt into consciousness, it was climbing once again with my restless thoughts and doubts.

What was I thinking? What had I done?

My mind was spinning with desires, consequences, foolishness, and above all… self-serving recklessness.

I needed to leave at once. Like a cornered animal, self-preservation became my driving force.

Carefully and quietly, I extracted my limbs and felt equal parts relief and nausea as I succeeded in my efforts. Quinton remained asleep in the quiet darkness of early morning, his breaths slow and even.

Gripped with overwhelming panic, I dressed as quickly and quietly as possible. Foregoing my undergarments, I settled a cloak about my person in an effort to conceal my state of dishabille. The movements of my body made the ache and soreness between my legs more pronounced. It *had* hurt that first time. But Quinton had been gentle and considerate. He'd more than made up for the pinch of discomfort caused by initial penetration with his further attentions. Figuring it out more quickly than I ever had by my own hand, he'd brought me to orgasm twice more before I settled in his embrace and we'd slept. I'd been too replete to consider leaving, and perhaps I'd been selfish in my desires.

But I knew the cost of indulging self-serving cravings. That was why it was imperative I make the difficult decision now. To avoid ruination and the consequences of my actions.

Finally, nose burning with ridiculous emotion, I took one last look at Quinton.

Then, I took my foolish heart from the room before it could do something unforgiveable… like stay.

Nineteen

I hadn't slept upon my return very early this morning, merely sneaked in through the kitchens upon arrival. Quinton's driver, Vincent, had once again delivered me to Dr. Finley's in my hour of need. He'd been on watch outside of Piker House as I'd attempted to hustle from the property. Witnessing my escape and in such a state, he'd bid me wait while he retrieved the carriage to escort me home. *It's what my lord would want*, Vincent had said. I couldn't argue with him even though I knew what Quinton would have actually wanted was to throttle me for leaving unaccompanied before the sun was up. Vincent, bless him, didn't offer any judgements nor recriminations for finding me the way he had. Perhaps he often encountered frazzled women with clothing askew leaving Lord Sullivan's quarters. I'd decided I didn't want to consider that.

Now, in my borrowed room, I had to consider the gravity of my actions from my early morning escape. Raised voices from the first floor drew my attention. I watched my locked door with a wary eye in case Quinton decided to force his way past Botstein to the family wing and my guest suite beyond.

Breathing a sigh of relief when the commotion settled a short while later, I picked up my ridiculous embroidery hoop and resumed my state of dithering by the fire. Reflecting on my actions from the previous night—and early hours of the morning—did little to settle my nerves.

That was the problem. I'd wanted to stay and so I had, jolting awake by accident before three in the morning. I'd only considered my wants and cravings. Selfishness rearing its ugly head.

Like mother, like daughter.

Ignoring the consequences and impending disaster, I'd behaved just as my mother always had. Acting on her baser instincts, uncaring of the lives impacted by her brazen behavior. I was inviting scandal and gossip. What if I'd been seen leaving Piker House? What if the servants registered my stay last night? Ruination and dishonor would follow in my wake. Could Eliza and her burgeoning career be tarnished by her association with me? The consequences of my actions had the capacity to be far-reaching in their devastation.

In my heart, I knew what I'd done with Quinton was not wrong. I didn't regret it so much as resign myself to the knowledge that my actions didn't align with society's mandate. And the results would be disastrous. I was once again putting my future at risk. And for what? A moment's pleasure with a lord so far out of my league, it was laughable. *I* was laughable.

Running had been cowardly and so was the hiding I was doing now in Eliza's guest suite. I knew I'd have to speak to Quinton. He was the kind of man to pursue, facing a problem head on. An alpha predator who wouldn't be stopped for long by pompous butlers and locked doors.

I, however, sought time to recover and regroup. I knew I was letting my fear rule me. I was alarmed by my feelings for Quinton. The intensity of which could leave me ruined in more ways than one. I was scared of being abandoned like my father and my ruined sister. My fear was driving this carriage, but there was nothing to be done for it. Last night's events and the potential scandal were forcibly wrestled into the trunk in my mind. I'd deal with it later after I'd gained some perspective. I needed to consider my future—with or without Quinton.

With a deep sigh, I laid my embroidery aside and decided to venture out for sustenance now that the coast was clear. It was now early afternoon and I was starving. I'd stayed in my rooms to avoid Quinton's inevitable visit, as well as the potential questioning I'd be sure to face from Eliza.

Making my way now toward the kitchens, Botstein descended upon me as soon as my slipper reached the bottom stair. "My lady, Lord Sullivan called upon you earlier and left this note after I explained you were still abed." He thrust the note at my person, frowning disapprovingly before spinning neatly on his butlered heel.

I stared down at the folded correspondence. My ungloved hand smoothed the parchment under my fingers. I was scared to read the words within. Would he scold me for leaving? Dissolve our courtship? Fire me? Reining in my nervousness, I decided I'd behaved enough of a coward today and unfolded the paper. Quinton's note reflected the haste with which it was written, perhaps some frustration bleeding through as well.

Jane,
I won't pretend to know why you fled my home in the middle of the night. I wish you'd stayed. I wish you'd talked to me. I wish you'd take better care of yourself and your safety. And above all else I wish I could have woken with you by my side. I had visions of seeing your perfect body in the early morning light, sharing breakfast with you, and convincing you to have coffee instead of tea.
I wanted you to know I'll be traveling. I received some urgent correspondence from my sister Rochelle and must leave directly. I'll stay away from Piker House. You do not wish to see me and I would never force you to abandon your post. The position will always be yours, even if you no longer wish to have me. I don't want you to go through that again.
Yours,
Q

THE NOTE LEFT me feeling wretched and weak. Quinton wasn't putting pressure on me. He was giving me space. He knew how trapped and isolated I'd felt following my split from John, how my future had been taken and the rejection I'd faced. It said quite a lot that he didn't wish that for me again. Q was putting my wants and needs ahead of his own, and yet I couldn't fully appreciate the gesture due to my self-recrimination.

I wasn't ready to face Quinton following my actions, but I wasn't ready to say goodbye to him either. I needed time to think.

~

Monday morning dawned misty and gray. Autumn finally held London in its grips and seemed to reflect my dour mood. I was wary of the upcoming workday at Piker House. Quinton had said he'd stay away. Rather than providing solace, the knowledge of his absence from the offices left me disappointed. I missed him, and I regretted running away from him and from my feelings in equal measure.

Knocking the rain from my parasol, I shuffled awkwardly into the service entrance of Piker House and bid Mrs. Hooper a good morning. With a promise of a warm pot of tea shortly, she sent me on my way. Despite my inner turmoil and Quinton's absence, I was eager to continue my work. I had plenty to occupy my thoughts, more records to decode and translate.

With a deep breath and a concentrated effort to focus my attention on my work, I entered the library offices and came to a dead stop. Lounging behind the desk… my desk, sat Quinton in a relaxed sprawl. Clearly lying in wait.

"I thought you wouldn't be here." My voice was embarrassingly breathless and my heart was pounding in my chest.

"I lied," came his unrepentant reply. He rose from his position and maneuvered around the furniture in my direction. He wore dark trousers and a white shirt with a patterned cravat. He'd lost his jacket at some point, and his hair was disheveled.

"That wasn't very gentlemanly of you," I accused. Q's approach never slowed.

A wry twist of lips. "I warned you I wasn't a good man." His muscled form crowded me the short distance back to the doorway before he reached beyond and pulled the door to, shutting out the hallway beyond and trapping us inside together. "We need to talk."

"I know. I'm… I'm sorry. I got so scared after what happened. I kept thinking about everything that could go wrong and all the ways I was behaving selfishly. And I didn't know what was happening between us. I couldn't see a future without scandal—"

"Shh, Jane. It's okay." He quieted my frantic rambling and urgent explanations. Placing a warm hand on my cheek and the other around my waist, he continued, "I should have been more definitive with you. I regret not making my intentions known. That is important to you: expectations, the future. I know you don't need me. I know you don't require my name or my station or my assets. In fact, I know those things make a future with me a hindrance more than anything." I squeezed his shoulder, and perhaps he could tell I was attempting to interject so he hurried on, "I know you don't need me, but I can't help but want you to want me. The way I desire you. You're so smart and so capable. You could make your own future. But I think we could make a future together. What happened last night—I don't want a mistress. I want a wife, a partner."

Hearing him discuss our potential marriage didn't elicit quite the same shock as it had previously. Raising my eyebrows expectantly, I teased, "Is that a proposal, my lord?"

"Not yet. I think you need some time to wrestle with the idea." Sobering a bit, he added, "And I wouldn't want to pressure you before you're ready. I don't want you to run again."

"I won't, Q. I'm sorry I panicked. I vow to talk to you in the future. I will endeavor to not let my fear rule me."

He nodded, leaning close. I could feel the hard lines of his body pressed against all my feminine softness. Nose brushing mine, he whispered, "Do you believe me? That I want you? Not just for now and not simply in my bed."

"I do." And I did. While I wasn't entirely sure what qualities he admired in me above all others, I still believed in his sincerity. It wasn't fair that Quinton should be so honest with his heart while I guarded mine so closely. It was time to give him a real chance, one ungoverned by fears from the past and doubts from the future. I was ready to live in the present, and live honestly at that. "I want you, too. So much that it terrifies me."

Quinton breathed a sigh at that, one of relief. Could he really not know how I coveted him? How overwhelmed I was by his nearness?

Emboldened by my admission, Q's lips raised to capture mine. His hold tightened and I felt the door at my back as he eased forward. Quinton wedged a thigh between my own, and despite the layers of fabric I moaned at the contact, the press of hips. Our kiss grew fevered. I was once again pouring my frustration into the mating of mouths. Stripping away my fear and reluctance, I wanted to consume him and be consumed in return.

Breaths heaving, Quinton broke contact to reach down and gather my skirts in his hands. His fingers skimmed my legs until he reached the tops of my lace stockings and then his mouth was back on mine. Quinton stroked my inner thigh and his clever fingers worked their way inside the slit of my drawers. My soft moans played the accompaniment to the gentle pressure on my womanhood. Quinton moved in small circles, my hips seeking the friction he offered.

"Yes," I gasped as two fingers breached my sex. The heel of his hand was rubbing perfectly against my mound as I began to feel the stirrings of release. Hands tightening on his shoulders, my head fell back against the door. A champion multitasker, Quinton's other hand rose to palm my breast as he kissed and tongued the column of my neck.

Feverish and frenzied, I continued to move against his hand as my release broke over me in a wave. Breathing hard, my sex clenched again and again while I did my best to remain standing.

Quinton's mouth returned to mine in an infinitely gentle caress. Such a contrast between the desperate wildness that had just taken place against the door. This intimacy following our lewd act nearly undid me.

This man, this future duke, would be my husband someday.

And I would be ready.

When I came back to myself and straightened my clothes, I stroked the hair at the nape of Quinton's neck and offered to meet his needs as well.

"I'm fine. You're likely still a bit sore, and honestly, I think we should wait until we are married."

"What?" came my squawked reply.

"There is still a risk of pregnancy even with the measures I took last night, and I would not bring that sort of scandal to your doorstep. I've vowed to take the utmost care with your reputation. And I shall endeavor to keep my promise."

Last night Q had withdrawn before completion and spent himself on the sheets. Now I understood why he'd taken such precautions. He'd done so for me. For us. So any future child could enter this world without scandal attached to their name. I valued his commitment. But honestly, no intimacies before our wedding? The horse was rather out of the barn at this point.

"Perhaps we can discuss this later. I'll make a list. We can weigh the positives and negatives."

His eyes narrowed in amusement. "Very well. Can I call upon you tomorrow? Perhaps another picnic if the weather is fine."

"That would be nice—Oh! Tomorrow is Tuesday. I have my embroidery meeting tomorrow with my friends at the Duchess of Compton's home."

"I see. How about Wednesday after work? Would you like to share an early supper here in my quarters?"

I smiled, happy Quinton hadn't asked me to choose him over my friends. I also had every intention of staying the night following our shared meal. I didn't mention any of this and simply replied, "I'd like that."

Perhaps we could use the time to debate the finer points of premarital intercourse before I was declared the winner.

"Janie. Yoo-hoo! Jane!" I started as my friend's voice finally registered.

"Yes! Sorry. Yes, Ashleigh. What was that?"

"I asked if ye could pass the wee cucumber sandwiches."

"Right, sorry. Here you go." Passing over the serving tray closest to me, I realized I might have been slightly distracted. I couldn't recall much of the conversation thus far. Although granted, once the food arrived, the ladies had descended like a pack of wolves.

Making a concentrated effort to be more engaged, I lifted my gaze and met Eliza's scrutinizing one. Whoops, best to look away. I hadn't yet confided in Eliza about Quinton and the progression of our relationship. Since last she'd heard, I'd been misled regarding his true identity. Through a combination of circumstances, I hadn't had time to explain that Lord Sullivan and I were… together. Eliza had been busy with patients, and I had been… well, frankly, hoarding my memories of Quinton. I hadn't felt ready to share the intimacies and emotions passed between us, the plans and the possibilities. Not that the feelings were tenuous, but everything felt new and precious. And I'd wanted to hold it within myself a bit longer.

Apparently my time was up.

"Jane." My name rang like an accusation. It wasn't a question. My friend knew something was afoot. Damnit.

My eyes snapped back to Eliza guiltily. "Yes, Eliza?"

The other ladies quieted and now only distinct sounds of delicate chewing and scraping china could be heard in the sudden stillness.

My friend's eyes narrowed, taking me in. I could hardly meet her stare. A blush was working its way up from my bosom. Eliza's eyes widened dramatically. "Something happened with Lord Dashing!"

Oh, lord.

The room erupted with the squeals and demands of five ladies. Kathleen was too shy to join in the riotous inquiry, but her eager expression belied her silence.

"Quiet, ladies!" Mary shushed. "Give her room to talk."

"In grave detail," added Ashleigh.

"If she wants to, that is," Fiona interjected with a concerned frown aimed my direction.

I smiled to reassure her, but I didn't know where to start. So much had happened since we'd discovered who Lord Dashing really was. There was nothing for it. I settled in and began to recount the events starting with the musicale I'd attended with Cassandra. I revealed how Daniel had vouched for his friend and that Q was waiting to speak to me in the carriage on the way home, and then I proceeded to relay the discovery of the coded ledgers and my subsequent translation. I explained the brothel: my sister's involvement, Quinton's role as landlord, and John's years' long affair with an employee there. I still hadn't had the capacity to consider John's presence in those pages, so I sought to analyze my feelings with my friends.

"I knew Sir Soggy Britches didn't deserve you," Eliza fumed.

"He'd been with Lady Juniper for years?" Kat quietly confirmed.

I nodded. "Off and on, yes."

"I'm so sorry, Jane." Kathleen was so kind to worry for my feelings. And while I'd been surprised by John's infidelity, I wasn't upset over it. John was my past.

He could do as he pleased. And if I'd married him, well… He would still be doing as he pleased. It was no great loss; I could appreciate that now.

"What a skilamalink, that one. Better off without him, I say, Janie darling." Cassandra offered condolences in her own special way.

"So what happened next? Did you tell Quinton about the ledgers and your decoded translation?" Eliza brought us back to task. I continued describing the events of the evening I sneaked into Piker House and found the men fighting in the courtyard.

Stopping around the part where Quinton escorted me back to his quarters, I blushed furiously and directed my gaze toward my lap. I wasn't ashamed that we'd made love. And I knew my friends wouldn't judge me or shun me for the loss of my virtue, but intimacies were not so openly discussed. Fiona was the only matron present. And… Eliza. Well, that was not my story to tell.

I was prepared for my friends to be very curious about what had taken place between Quinton and myself.

The ladies were waiting. Cassandra crunched loudly on a biscuit. "Oof, sorry," she mumbled. Brushing crumbs from her yellow day dress she continued, "Go on. What happened next? He didn't put a shirt on, did he?" My friends laughed.

Cheeks aflame, I murmured, "Well, he did, but he removed a lot more later." Fingers twisting in my lap, I awaited their responses. Wide, surprised eyes met mine.

"Jane, was… was that what you wanted? He didn't hurt you, did he?" Fiona's worry was palpable.

"No! No, he didn't hurt me. I… I wanted it—him. I initiated everything. He was —" I floundered for the appropriate adjective. "He was glorious."

Fiona was thoughtful but nodded. Cassandra grinned hugely and waggled her eyebrows, making me laugh. Ashleigh looked knowing, a private smile on her lovely face. Perhaps Fiona wasn't the only lady present with knowledge of the marriage bed. Mary and Kathleen wore identical shocked expressions. And dear Eliza looked rather smug. "I knew it!" she all but crowed, wiggling in her seat.

I rolled my eyes but continued my story, admitting how I'd run from Quinton. I recounted our confrontation and conversation yesterday in the offices, glazing over any sordid bits. Now that the facts had been disclosed, it felt good to share my new relationship with them. I wanted our lives to intersect, for my friends to know my intended. And that's what our conversations had indicated. Quinton would be mine and I would be his. I was dazed by the prospect, and I wanted my friends—my chosen family—to be happy for me.

The assembled embroiders were all silent at the completion of my shocking tale. Not even Cassandra was munching despite the presence of her favorite onion spread nearby.

"Are you happy, Jane?" Eliza asked soberly. All eyes focused on me and for once, I didn't mind the attention.

My smile felt radiant as I replied, "Yes, I am."

Six equally delighted grins reflected back at me. Their joy and support emboldened me and gave me strength. The women in this room did not consider my station or my wealth. They cared not about my ruined state. These ladies valued my happiness and safety above anything else. And if Lord Sullivan brought me joy, then they would support our union. And that's all they would ever need to know.

"Go back to the part with the torches and the muscles," Cassandra hooted.

Well, perhaps that wasn't *all* they wanted to know.

Later that evening at the Finley residence, I was gathering my book from the front receiving room where I'd left it earlier in the day. After the excitement with my friends this afternoon, I was eager to retire to my private quarters. Dressed simply in my wrapper and nightgown, I happened to glance out the window. By the light of streetlamps, I could see a plain black carriage was parked in the drive. I didn't imagine that should Quinton decide to visit me at eleven in the evening, he'd knock on the front door.

Regardless, I bustled to the entryway and pulled the door open just in case. My hopeful expression died on my face. "June?"

"Do close your mouth, Janie. You look like a fish." June breezed past.

Closing the door and following in her wake toward the receiving room, I whispered furiously, "What are you doing here?" I cast about for Botstein and thanked my lucky stars he was nowhere to be found. Eliza had been summoned for a house call and Dr. Finley was away on one of his mysterious outings.

"Don't worry. I'll be leaving soon."

"I haven't seen you in over a decade, June." Well, that wasn't technically accurate. My memory conjured the woman in scarlet and my mad chase down the staircase at Piker House. It *had* been her.

My eyes took in the woman before me, the stranger. She was dressed for a night out: ball gown in dusky rose, elaborate coiffure, and jewels sparkling on her neck and wrists.

My sister's face remained closed, my accusation failing to provoke. "What do you think you're doing with Lord Sullivan and Piker House?"

"What does it matter to you?" Pulling my wrapper tighter about myself, I noted how similarly we'd aged. June and I, and Gemini for that matter, shared our mother's auburn curls and brown eyes. June was about my height and build. I could see for myself how we'd been mistaken for one another by Quinton and Seamus's men.

"It doesn't *matter* to me. For one, I don't need you meddling in my business—"

"Oh, your *brothel*," I cut in rudely. I didn't begrudge my sister her establishment, but I also wasn't about to make this easy on her. How bloody dare she? Showing up unannounced after over ten years of nothing; not out of any sisterly bond, but to instead sling accusations at me.

She'd done god knows what to support herself since leaving home. Actually, I could image how she'd supported herself. Brothel madames didn't start at the top, after all. She'd very likely started on her back. I wouldn't shame June or judge her for her choices. Women made decisions for all manner of reasons, usually out of desperate necessity. It wasn't my place to find fault in her lifestyle, but I could damn well take offense to being cornered here and having my motives questioned.

"Yes, my brothel," she confirmed with a sniff. "It's mine, bought and paid for many times over. I finally have a fair shake with that blighter run out of town.

My deal with Sullivan suits me just fine as it is. And I don't need you interfering. Q will use you as leverage against me."

"Or he'll simply allow you to run your business in peace and protect the ladies in your employ," I retorted.

June huffed a humorous laugh. "You always were oblivious. He's an aristocrat, Jane. He has no reason to treat me fairly in business or otherwise. You know how they are. Or are you too busy taking after our mother to care? Like the finer things, do you, Janie darling? Q plying you with expensive trinkets and jewels to keep you happy?"

The comparison to our mother landed like a blow. I struggled to keep the reaction from my face as I replied carefully, "You don't know me anymore, June. Nor the woman I've become."

"I know enough," she spat back. "Landed another earl, have you?"

I didn't manage to hide my surprise at that.

"Yes, I knew about you and Lord Fairbanks as well. Thought you'd wised up. He is a pitiful fool. Good for his money and not much else." Her husky voice had changed in tone as she spoke of John and a knot of suspicion was forming in my throat.

Eyes narrowing, I asked, "I didn't realize you two were so well acquainted."

Her answering smirk was cruel and knowing. "Our paths have crossed a time or two."

And I knew.

Lady Juniper. June.

I made sure my expression was flat and my gaze stony before speaking. "You should go. There is nothing left for us to discuss."

"Do you truly wish to be the wife of a gaming hell owner? Of course, he'll be a duke someday and his reputation can take the hit of being a businessman. But, Jane, you'll be under constant scrutiny. Do you really want gossip and scandal to follow you your entire life? Didn't you learn anything from Mother?"

"Since when do you care? What I want for my future and myself doesn't concern you. You left us. You took what you wanted and didn't trouble yourself with me or father or Gem. Just like Mother."

If my barb found its mark, I'd never know. June was completely unruffled. If she had emotions, they were buried under layers of makeup and cool indifference. "Just stay out of my way. This is my livelihood. I don't need you exposing my clients and causing trouble. It's bad for business."

June tugged her gloves higher on her arms and made her way around me toward the front door. I made no move to escort her out, remaining firmly planted in the doorway of the receiving room instead.

She turned at the last moment and offered her final parting advice. "Do yourself a favor and stay away from Sullivan. He'll hurt you, humiliate you… Just like the lot of them. And when you're a future duchess, everything you do will be news to someone. No playing with your precious numbers then."

June pulled the door shut behind her and I sagged in relief. What did it say about me that I was glad my sister was gone? Who was this person, coming here and threatening me out of utter selfishness? I supposed I had happy memories of our childhood buried somewhere. Yet they remained difficult to recall in the wake of her intrusion.

She was threatened by my proximity to Piker House, my work there. That much was obvious. Warning me away from Q would only serve her purpose. By appealing to my aversion to scandal and gossip, she was attempting to play on my fears. It hurt to know my sister was attempting to manipulate me for her own perceived gain. I felt a little nauseous if I was being honest. It wasn't as if I expected some big reunion with either of my sisters someday. I honestly don't know what would have happened had I caught June in the stairwell that day weeks ago at Piker House. At least with her surprise visit tonight, we were on somewhat equal footing. Thankfully Quinton had revealed her profession and their business arrangement in advance.

And June's relationship with John was so very odd. He'd been her client long before we'd been acquainted, but June had obviously known of our courtship. Perhaps she was resentful. I couldn't actually imagine she had feelings for John. The woman seemed calculating and untouchable. But maybe she didn't like to share. She'd meant to hurt me or provoke me or… something with the mention of him. With that realization, I felt more tired than troubled.

I sighed deeply and went to retrieve my book again before turning down the lamp and ascending the stairs.

As I lay in bed that night, I considered how fortunate I was to be in the Finley home. Eliza had welcomed me as a sister. It made the disconnect between myself and my own family that much more glaring. Nevertheless, I was lucky to have Eliza and my other friends in my life. June was my blood, but that didn't mean anything to her. I didn't know what it meant to me anymore either. What good was claiming family if the only path between you had washed away long ago?

Dear Jane,
Looking forward to our dinner together. I'm afraid business meetings will keep me away much of the day, but I will see you this afternoon.
Yours,
Q

"What's that face for?"

I glanced up from the note I was holding to Mr. Stevens. "Oh, nothing of consequence. Just…" I hesitated, unsure if I should divulge the personal nature of Quinton's letter. Mr. Stevens and I were friends. I was being silly. And yet I wasn't sure if he would look at me the same. I didn't know if having a romantic relationship with our shared employer would reflect poorly in the solicitor's eyes. "Quinton was letting me know he'd be busy today and we were unlikely to cross paths until later." I'd found the letter on my chair shortly after my arrival moments ago.

A small smile quirked my officemate's lips. "Ah, I see." He offered nothing more and returned to the papers in front of him. Hmm, that was odd. I felt certain Mr.

Stevens was secure enough in our friendship to tease me. Perhaps he was very busy.

"I'd make that face too if I were you."

Ah, there it was.

I tossed him a smirk, knowing I was being baited. "And what face is that, sir?"

"Like a little girl denied the pony she wanted for her birthday."

I gasped in righteous indignation. "I do not look like a spoiled child, and furthermore, Q is not a pony."

Mr. Stevens's lips compressed, fighting a smile before it escaped entirely. "You're right. He's definitely a stallion."

Our laughter rang out in the quiet library. It was quite a while before we settled, quieted, and got to work.

A stallion indeed.

~

Mr. Stevens and I worked well into the evening before Quinton appeared to escort me to dinner in his rooms. My coworker and I had enjoyed a long day but stopped around four o'clock for afternoon tea and a lengthy chat. I confided that Q and I were courting. He gasped dramatically in jest, but expressed his support for our new relationship. Mr. Stevens went on to discuss a recent charitable dinner he'd attended for St. Bartholomew's where he'd met an interesting and frankly arrogant physician. I told him the next time Dr. Finley hosted his fellow medical colleagues in lecture or in leisure, I'd inquire after a Dr. K. Miles. Mr. Stevens's cheeks had pinkened a bit but he didn't protest. I was happy he trusted me enough to discuss this mystery doctor who'd caught his fancy. Hopefully he'd come up in conversation again.

Mr. Stevens was packing away his paperwork and gathering his overcoat and hat when Quinton walked in and greeted us both. My friend cast me an amused glance before bidding us both a good evening and made himself scarce.

"And how was your day?" Quinton inquired as I stood from my chair behind the desk.

He made his way around the furniture to my side and pressed a gentle kiss to my cheek. "It was productive, thank you. I hope you had a good day as well."

"I did." He seemed to hesitate and consider his words carefully before continuing. "I toured some properties in Mayfair. I'm thinking of purchasing one in the coming months."

My eyebrows raised at his admission. "Is that so?"

"Indeed." We smiled pointlessly at each other. Assisting me in gathering my belongings, Q tucked my satchel under his arm and threaded his fingers through mine. "Shall we?"

I nodded and let him escort me out of the library and down the hall to his living quarters.

"I had dinner brought up, if that's agreeable?"

Again, I nodded. Apparently I'd gotten shy at some point, despite the fact that we were simply sharing a meal together and this man had seen me in my entirety.

Our dinner had been laid in Quinton's sitting room. A couch and several armchairs were arranged near the fire with a dining table and four chairs opposite. He removed his coat and placed my pelisse alongside it on the coatrack. Q led me toward the dining table and settled me in my chair.

"This was kind of Betty and the servants," I noted.

"I typically take my meals here." Q scooted his chair in and draped the linen napkin across his lap.

I looked up in surprise. "You don't frequent Benton House?"

He seemed preoccupied with pouring the wine and uncovering the dishes before he met my curious gaze. Clearing his throat, Quinton finally confirmed, "This is my primary residence. I… don't like Benton House. It reminds me of being in London before." His speech was so stilted and affected, I could hardly believe it was Quinton before me. "It reminds me of when I had a brother… and parents and a family. There are too many ghosts there."

I reached across the table and squeezed his hand. "I understand. Besides, you're likely here so late in the evenings managing the gaming hell that it's more convenient to be in residence at Piker House."

His nod was grateful. "That is true. However, I thought it might be prudent if some time in the future I had a home in Mayfair, something comfortable."

"Oh, yes. The purpose of your meetings today. That's exciting." I spooned some roasted vegetables on my plate. The beef smelled amazing. As I reached for the serving fork, I noticed Quinton's attention was still on my face and he looked curious, assessing. "What?"

"Do you think it would be a good idea for me to acquire a residence? Away from Piker House?"

Oh. *Oh!*

"If that's what you want!" I replied brightly. And felt immediately that my response was the wrong one. Q's face dimmed and he began serving himself again.

This. This is what made relationships so difficult. And not just romantic or intimate relationships, all of them. How were you supposed to know the correct thing to say? I had never been good at reading people or making the expected remarks. Mindreading was not one of my strong suits. Clearly Q was looking for a different reaction from me, and I didn't know why.

"Q, I don't know how to do this," I tried to explain.

He paused and swallowed before dragging his napkin along his mouth. "How to do what?"

"How to say the right thing. I didn't… before. About your housing search. I said the wrong thing and made you… distant." I looked down briefly. "I don't know how to be what you want."

A frown marred Quinton's lovely features. "No, Jane. It's my fault. I don't know how to do this either. I should have just said 'Jane, I want to buy a home for us to share some day. Would you like that?' or simply asked if you'd like to view the homes together. I should not expect you to read my thoughts."

I was stunned. And yet not stunned. I should have realized the blatantly obvious direction of his thoughts regarding a future home. I was embarrassed at misreading the situation, and yet I felt warm at the idea of choosing a home together.

Still frowning, Q released a breath. "I want to be worthy of you, Jane. You know I don't care about my title and all that accompanies it, but for you… I want to be a good man. And if you want me to sell Piker House, I will. I've legitimized my practices and pulled my men away from disreputable jobs—like with Seamus's crew. But if this life, here," he waved his hands to encompass the suite and our surroundings, "isn't what you want, I'll fix it. I don't want this place to damage your reputation. Or associating with me to hurt you."

"No, Q," I rushed to reassure him. "No, I don't want you to sell Piker House. If you're happy and you like your involvement here, then I would never wish to discourage you. I think you're doing good here. And you were right. There are so many livelihoods intertwined within these walls. I would never want you to change that… for me." I thought of my sister and her accusations, how my interference with Piker House and influence with Q would alter her future. "You're a good man, Quinton. And you don't need me to tell you that. It's not my job to change you or judge you or make demands of you."

"What is your job then?"

I smiled at him. "Just to care for you."

Dinner forgotten, Quinton came around the table and pulled me to my feet. Slipping an arm around my waist, he drew me close. "And do you, Jane? Care for me?"

With a shuddering breath I admitted, "So much it frightens me."

His brows creased. "Why?"

"This isn't how relationships work in London. You know that. Marriages are contracts and, if you're very lucky, complacent companionship. What I feel for you is neither lukewarm nor merely content."

"Good. Because I don't want just a companion or a contract. I don't want a dowry or land or a… goat for your hand." I laughed at both the goat and the luxury of having a dowry to offer.

Quinton smiled in response to my obvious mirth before pinning me with his heated stare. "I want to be completely and totally yours. And I want you to be very, very satisfied and all mine."

Our lips met in a kiss rife with meaning, full of want and desire, promise and commitment. With our dinner abandoned, we made our way to the bedchamber. And true to his word, I remained there until very, very satisfied.

THE FIRE WAS BURNING and I was deliciously warm, snuggled against Quinton's side. Remembering our ruined meal and our recent physical exertion, my stomach chose that moment to rudely make itself known.

Quinton chuckled and kissed my shoulder. "I'll get us some food. My apologies for cutting our meal short." He drew back the coverlet and emerged completely nude and utterly glorious. I stared as he marched unclothed from the bedchamber. His confidence alone made him so very admirable, and this angle and his backside didn't hurt either.

I sat up abruptly, clutching the bedclothes to my bosom. Surely he would dress before going downstairs to the kitchens. Mrs. Hooper had likely retired for the evening, but surely there were servants about. I suddenly remembered catching my sister on this floor once before. What had she been doing up here?

Unable to exude the confidence of a nude Quinton, I reached for my shift and drawers from the floor beside the bed. Evidently alerted by the shuffling of blankets and squeaking floorboards, Q poked his head back in.

Clad now in a dressing robe, he made a disgruntled face. "Don't put those on. Stay in bed. Relax. I'll return shortly."

Sliding the shift over my head, his frown deepened and I teased, "Are you trying to keep me trapped in your bedchamber, my lord?"

He padded over before lifting the shift from my body once again. I laughed and smacked his shoulder in mock outrage. Q grabbed my hand and placed a kiss on the center of my palm before spinning me around and swatting my bottom back toward the bed. "Perhaps I should tie you up and keep you here." I laughed at his playfulness. A playful, nearly nude Quinton was quite irresistible.

He ushered me under the covers and tugged the coverlet around my shoulders for warmth before dropping a tender kiss on my nose. "I'll be right back. Don't go anywhere, and do not put clothes back on. If you're undressed, you cannot leave." Another kiss, on my forehead this time. "And I'm not ready for this to be over."

His words triggered a memory of the last time he'd uttered that phrase. Back before I'd known he was Lord Sullivan, heir and future Duke of Benton. I'd asked his name and he hadn't given it because at the time he'd known it would change everything. Q had begged for a little more time. I'd indulged him because I, too, hadn't been ready for whatever secret he'd been unwilling to share.

Secrets. That gave me pause.

I realized I'd been woolgathering far too long when Quinton returned with a plate of fruit and cheese and whatever else he'd pilfered from the kitchens. He removed his dressing gown and joined me under the covers, settling the tray on the bed in front of us.

"There's still wine in the other room if you'd like some," he said before popping a grape in his mouth.

Seemingly out of nowhere, I blurted, "I found my father's name in the Piker House ledgers."

Quinton's eyebrows popped up high on his forehead and his chewing ceased.

"Sorry, I was thinking about something you said before and it reminded me about what I'd recently discovered in the accounts."

Q swallowed carefully before responding, "I don't believe he's been in since I've assumed ownership."

"No, I doubt he has the funds to continue on as he had been. My father—my family—owes you a great deal of money." Nerves fluttered uneasily in my middle as I made this admission.

Quinton rolled another grape between his fingers and replied with steady assurance. "Your family owes me nothing, Jane. Of course I won't pursue your father for his debts. It's unlikely he'll return, as you've said. Have you been in contact with him since you've been residing with Eliza? Does he know of our connection?"

"No," came my slightly embarrassed response. "I haven't heard from him at all. I don't think he even knows where I am. Nor does he seem to care." I sounded like a petulant child and I hated it. With eyes downcast, I said, "Thank you for being generous where my father is concerned. I know he doesn't deserve it."

Grapes abandoned, Q reached over for my wringing hands. "Don't thank me. I've done nothing. I would never attempt to hurt your relationship with your family. Who knows what the future holds for you. For any of you." I knew what he was implying, but I didn't anticipate a reunion of any sort. My sisters and my father felt so far beyond my reach. Quinton continued, "Families are difficult, Jane. Sometimes intentions and wishes don't matter. But it's never too late… until it is."

Taking in his somber expression and serious tone, I thought perhaps he wasn't only referring to my familial relationships. Maybe there was hope for Quinton and his parents after all. I couldn't envision suddenly having a good relationship with my father. We'd never had that. But Q had good memories of the Duke and Duchess of Benton. Perhaps he could have that again.

I nodded in agreement, more for him than my own circumstances. "You're right. One never knows what the future holds."

Squeezing his hand in understanding, I considered broaching another secret revealed within the coded ledgers.

"Did you know about John's patronage at the brothel?"

Likely growing used to my quick change of subjects, Quinton barely paused before nodding.

"I found his name in the brothel's records. Many times, over many years," I clarified.

Q's gaze was assessing as he responded, "Yes, I did know John frequented the establishment. That's where I recognized him—coming and going from St. James's. But I didn't think it was my place to tell you, especially while harboring my own secret. It wasn't right to try to earn your favor by belittling John when I had my own sins. I felt he owed you the truth. Much as I did myself."

I nodded, lost in thought. I could definitely see Q's point of view. Even if he had revealed John's indiscretions, I would have likely blamed the messenger.

"And I didn't want to hurt you—in case you decided to go back to Fairbanks," Q added quietly. "Of course, I thought you deserved better than that imbecile. I hoped you were done with him. But I wanted you to be sure, for yourself, not because of a secret I dropped on your doorstep."

"He was with June all those times," I admitted in a small voice. I wasn't broken-hearted over John's betrayal. I was mostly remembering my disheartening conversation with my sister.

Quinton looked over at me sharply. I met his gaze briefly before nodding and reaching for a grape. "She as much admitted to me that she goes by Lady Juniper now."

Q turned on the bed to face me. "When did you see her?"

I relayed June's visit from the evening prior, trying to minimize the damage she'd done to my emotions.

Immediately upon concluding my tale, Quinton demanded, "Did she threaten you?"

I thought for a moment before responding. "No, not explicitly. She merely warned me away from Piker House, her business affairs, and you," I finished lamely.

Q appeared thoughtful and conflicted. "I'll have Stanley accompany you from now on. I'd feel better if you had a guard with you just in case. And we'll look for a home in Mayfair. I don't want you coming here to be with me if June is dangerous."

"Wait, wait, Q. She wouldn't hurt me, I don't think. Let's not get ahead of ourselves and overreact. She just didn't want our relationship—mine and yours—to affect her business. And it won't. There's no reason for anything to change. You can return the ledger for the brothel. I have no need of it. She can manage her own accounts. See, nothing really needs to change because of me. Except for the housing situation. If you're amenable, I'd love to accompany you to look for a home." I'd grown self-conscious by the end of my speech and focused my stare on the serving tray before us.

I felt Quinton grasp my hand and draw my attention to his lovely face. "I want that. A home with you. A future. A marriage." My heart accelerated in my chest, but I made no outward sign of discouragement should Quinton change his mind and stop speaking such lovely things.

He toyed with the fingers of my hand, but his gaze remained steady and true. "I know you've had a poor experience with Fairbanks and society, and I know the kind of marriage you don't want. But would you consider one that was a partnership? Instead of being bound, it meant being free. Would you want that with me?"

Heart racing and unwavering in my resolve, I spread my fingers wide and linked our hands together. "Yes, Q. I think I would."

There in the night, staring at the man who would be mine, I refused to let the fear come. And focused instead on our future, together.

Twenty-Two

"Jane, what's going on over there?" Eliza fluttered her hand, attempting to garner my attention. I was in a fog, a Quinton-induced fog that made doing nearly anything a challenge. I'd just been reminiscing on the morning's events when Eliza reminded me we were in the middle of post-luncheon tea and I was behaving atrociously.

"I'm sorry! I'm having some… trouble concentrating," I replied sheepishly.

Eliza's grin was knowing. "I bet you'd be able to focus on our conversation if I was tall, dark, and ridiculously broody with intimidating eyebrows."

Q's eyebrows were rather judgmental.

"I'm being a bad friend. What were we discussing? I shall do better," I vowed.

"Why don't you tell me what has you so distracted?" my friend inquired, looking very knowing and smug.

I thought back to waking up with Quinton this morning following our evening spent together in his rooms at Piker House. It had been surprisingly easy to plead my case regarding premarital relations. What a fine way to greet the day. Quinton's front snuggled up tightly to my back, his lips kissing my neck, my shoulders. His hands had worked their way around my body, massaging my breasts as he continued his assault with lips and tongue. I'd moved mindlessly against him, seeking friction until his strong fingers had skimmed down my body to where I needed his touch the most. After teasing and torturing, Q had finally guided my leg up as he'd slid inside. So leisurely he'd moved within me until we were both breathless and—

"There it is! There's that face again," Eliza accused.

"What face?" I said, flushing wildly. I should not be replaying those events in the Finley family room.

"You're all dreamy-eyed and swoony. I feel I must send for Botstein and the smelling salts."

With an aggrieved sniff, I replied, "You know I'd never swoon. It's undignified."

Smile firmly in place, Eliza scrutinized me, undeterred. "So you love him then?"

"I—" I broke off, eyes wide with shock at Eliza's casual questioning. She took an unhurried sip of Earl Grey.

Did I love Quinton?

"I can see I surprised you. Perhaps you weren't ready to examine your feelings for Lord Dashing." Eliza's smile lost its smugness and transformed into something gentle and patient. "Think about how you feel when you're apart, and how you feel when you're finally together."

I considered her suggestion and thought back to all the times he was out of the office and I grew frustrated and distracted at work, missing him. Missing his presence and our discussions and that lightning strike of attraction that seemed to concentrate all the energy in the room. And then I considered those moments when we were alone together.

"I can't think when he's in the room. He absorbs all of my attention. I don't get distracted by numbers or thoughts or ideas or an article I read about something or another. My eyes seek him. My mind is always eager to know his thoughts. And my body seems to vibrate with wanting him." I looked down at my hands, somewhat ashamed of my obsession with Quinton.

He was taking me apart, piece by piece. Everything that made me Jane. Examining it, studying it, and simply putting it back in place without asking for anything in return. Like a library of myself, Quinton was borrowing the books from my shelves to learn and grow and for no other reason than to read and enjoy them. He simply wanted to know me. But without ever meaning to, he was changing everything. Every line of text, every volume on the shelf. Everything I knew about love and affection was changing because of this man and his presence in my life. I was remade. Fulfilled, strong, and content, all because he sought to know me without ever asking me to be anyone other than myself.

"Jane, don't be embarrassed because you're brave enough to love someone. I know relationships in our society are seldom based on affection, but that says more about society than it does about us. It's okay to want more, and to be gratified when you find it." Eliza was resolute in her opinion, but the underlying sadness in her eyes reminded me once again that my friend's experience with relationships wasn't a pleasant one. I felt certain her story wasn't over. Despite her assertions about love and matrimony, there had to be future happiness for her as well.

I smiled in response to my wise and thoughtful friend.

Realization dawned and Eliza squeezed her hands together in obvious delight. "You *do* love him!"

I grinned at her reaction but didn't speak.

She turned thoughtful. "Think of it this way. If I put you in a library full of books, old and new, floor-to-ceiling bookcases, just overflowing with volume after volume. And I placed Quinton in that library. Where might your attention stray?"

Icy blue eyes unseen in nature, raven black hair, lips quirking, and an expectant eyebrow.

I laughed. Of course my wonderful friend who knew me so well and wished so fervently for my happiness would devise a scenario to help me realize what my heart already knew.

When a bluestocking picks a man over a room full of books… It must be love.

~

LATER THAT AFTERNOON, Eliza bustled off to see patients in clinic with her father who'd returned from his latest mystery outing. I donned my reading spectacles and made my way to the front receiving room, book in hand. One never knew who might call during receiving hours in the afternoon. Well, hopefully no one. Besides, I preferred the armchair in this particular room and the light was fair for reading.

Engrossed in my book, I lost track of the time. Suddenly, Botstein entered and announced, "The Countess of Bexley." And in walked Lady Lydia Ellsworth in a lavender day dress that complemented her fair hair and complexion rather nicely.

I rose to greet her despite my confusion. "My lady." I offered a shallow curtsey. "How do you do?"

"I'm well, Jane. Do call me Lydia," my guest replied. Lady Bexley had asked me to call her Lydia once upon a time, but since I was no longer welcome in her home, I had assumed I should address her formally.

I nodded my agreement and motioned for her to sit if she desired. With a small smile, she selected my recently vacated armchair. Sigh.

"What can I help you with, my la—Lydia?" I inquired, not unkindly but rather with intention. I didn't know why the countess was here and I wasn't a fan of surprises. The last time Lydia and I had spoken was when I'd reviewed the Bexley household accounts some time ago. I'd tabulated her husband's recent spending and offered a plan to offset the excessive amount the Earl of Bexley had recently lost gambling. I'd been gentle in manner and positive in tone. Her troubles were not insurmountable and I was happy I could help her and her household. Lydia had been embarrassed but determined. But that was over two months prior. Last month, I'd been turned away at her door when I'd attempted to conduct our standing appointment. I could only imagine the damage her wastrel husband had conducted since then. Except it wasn't really my concern anymore. I'd been dismissed as a result of my broken courtship with Lord Fairbanks.

With no small amount of chagrin, Lydia met my inquisitive gaze. "I want to apologize, Jane. It was not well done of me to reject you at my home some weeks past. I've always liked you and appreciated how smart and capable you are. And you've always treated my situation with the utmost discretion. I'm sorry for dismissing you the way I did."

"I see."

Color high, the countess continued, "It's just that Lord Fairbanks thought it would be best if we didn't trouble you during such a difficult time."

My head snapped up at the mention of John. "Lord Fairbanks?"

Something in my tone, no longer docile and accommodating as befitting an employee, must have signaled a shift in my mood because Lydia replied warily, "Why yes, Lord Fairbanks. He had his mother write to me and others, I would imagine. I know you had somewhat of a business with many ladies of the *ton*. Anyway, the Duchess explained you were likely overcome during your separation from John, you poor dear."

"So, at John's request, his mother told you not to receive me at your home because I was overwrought. Have I understood this correctly?"

"Yes, exactly. But I realized when you were seen with Lord Sullivan that you must be feeling better. I hope you don't mind me gossiping, but good for you. Sullivan is quite the catch. Don't tell Her Grace, the Duchess I said so."

I didn't know the Countess of Bexley well enough to know if she was too dim to realize she had been manipulated, or if she really thought I was unable to function without John in my life. I was under the false assumption that his mother had acted alone in ostracizing me from my livelihood and source of income among my peers. Apparently I'd been just as naïve as poor Lydia.

John had been hiding more from me than I realized.

Utterly lost in thought, I didn't realize the countess was prattling on. "Jane," she said, finally gaining my attention. "I did wonder if you might consider returning to our arrangement. I value your expertise and with the season underway…" She trailed off, but I could infer her meaning. Now that the season was underway, her profligate husband would find himself in even more trouble with so many lords in London and the resulting society gatherings.

I briefly considered my options. Lydia likely didn't realize she'd be going against the wishes of the Holesome family, but that didn't concern me. I had time in my schedule to resume our monthly meetings. And it would allow me a measure of independence. I enjoyed the work I was doing at Piker House and didn't feel compelled, at this point in time, to give that up. Yet, I was concerned about Quinton acting as my employer. It made things messy as our relationship progressed and our futures became more intertwined. I liked things to be neat and tidy. Yet I wasn't ready to make a drastic change. Perhaps adding back a personal client in the Countess of Bexley was a smart move.

In a way I could understand her position. Even a countess was limited by her sex. A woman's reputation was everything in London. If she'd gone against John's mother, the wife of a duke, in those early weeks following her explicit instructions, the countess would have taken a social hit. Lydia was undermining the Duchess of Archford even now, but she didn't realize it. Or perhaps she saw my association with Lord Sullivan as more advantageous and wished to gain our favor. I didn't know. That was the problem with the *ton*. Everyone held an ulterior motive, no one was sincere, and actions were seldom made without consequences. Living in London meant living a chess game.

One thing I could recognize in the countess was desperation: the tenuous smile, the tightness about the eyes, her forced cheerfulness. I may not be an expert at reading people, but even I could see the strain in Lydia's features. Money troubles with a spendthrift in residence were stressful. It was the most likely reason she'd sought me out. I knew she despaired over her husband's negligent spending, and she knew I could help.

And so, I would. "Shall I come by Tuesday morning next week?"

Lydia's relief was palpable. "That's perfect. Although I'm sure I'll see you at the Huffleton ball on Saturday. You and Lady Mary are quite friendly, are you not?"

Oh, blast. That's right. Mary's mother was hosting a soiree in the coming days. "Yes, you are correct. I will be there."

"Do come over and say hello while you're there!" Lydia insisted. Perhaps in my cynical musings, I'd judged the countess too harshly. Including her among the nosy members of society was unfair of me. "And bring Lord Sullivan with you. I'd love to make his acquaintance."

Ah, there it was.

WITH A PROMISE TO say hello at the upcoming ball and our appointment for Tuesday next confirmed, Lady Bexley finally left.

I'd barely settled in my favorite chair when Botstein entered, announcing, "Lord John Holesome, the Earl Fairbanks."

Blast.

John stepped smoothly through the arched doorway, tugging and straightening his sleeves as he moved in my direction. A nervous gesture I'd noticed during our time together.

I heaved a sigh and got to my feet to greet this intrusion. I knew John was unwilling to see reason and accept the end of our relationship. Unsure how he would continue pressing his suit, I'd expected a confrontation, but that didn't mean I was prepared for it, especially so soon after learning of his continued deceit. I wasn't equipped for this conversation, so my arguments would likely be underdeveloped and lacking sound reasoning. Oh well, I'd wing it. And whatever I couldn't make up for in sound reasoning, I'd follow through with hysterical accusation. John had asked for it, showing up uninvited. And I was about to provide.

"Jane! You're looking lovely as always," he said. When he got a good look at my face, his steps faltered. Wisely rethinking his forward advance to likely clasp my hands or simply move into my space, John offered, "Shall we sit?"

"Of course," I replied. "We have much to discuss." Hope flared in his green eyes for a brief moment, but my next words would extinguish the tiny blaze. "About Lady Juniper, for one."

An already pale John turned the shade of the recently deceased. His mouth opened but no words emerged.

"Were you aware that I was her sister all along? Were you hoping to gain some advantage by hoarding that knowledge? Or did you think it would be a fun story to share at the club in the future? Married to one sister and tupping the other whenever you felt like it."

Finally regaining his voice, John rushed to assure me, "No! God, no. I mean, yes, I knew fairly early on that you were sisters. But it was obvious you didn't know about June's employment. As I got to know you, I realized you had no idea what had become of June after you confided in me about your sisters. I wasn't going to tell anyone. It wasn't like that, Jane. You know I care for you."

"If you cared so much for me, why did you continue visiting my sister?"

John blinked, clearly taken aback at my question. Good little ladies weren't supposed to question acceptable indiscretions committed by men. "Well… I—I," he stumbled over his words, at a loss.

"Did you care about June, too? Is that why she was the only lady of the night you visited?"

He flinched at my language and crass demeanor. I'm sure he expected tears and delicate feminine emotions to accompany my questions. But I didn't feel like crying. I felt tired. I didn't even care about his answers, nor did I care about his relationship with June. I was ready to move on to a different subject altogether.

But before I could shift focus, he answered, "Yes, I care about her." His voice was small, ashamed. "I've known her for years, and… And she's always viewed our relationship as a transaction. June didn't care about me at all. I was just another lord to her. And then I met you, and you were kind and smart and funny in your own way. You looked like her, but you didn't hate me for being an earl. I don't know why I kept returning to her. I thought… I thought she would care that I'd met someone, that I'd met you. But she didn't. She didn't react at all."

I stared at John and felt even more exhausted by his admission. He'd picked me because I was an amenable June. A different version of the woman he really wanted. One who didn't hate him for buying her body and asking her to thank him for it.

The impact of his confession must have shown on my face because he hurried to add, "No, Jane. It wasn't like that. I honestly care for you. I love you. I… still want to marry you. We could be happy. We *were* happy," he insisted, grabbing my hands.

I shook him off and stood. "No, John. I don't want to marry you."

He stood as well. "I know you were out with Sullivan. I heard about your stroll in the park. But we can just ignore that and go back to the way things were."

"Back to before?" I tapped my fingers to my lips thoughtfully. "When we were courting and I counseled your mother and her friends. 'My little hobby' as you'd called it. Could I have that back, do you think?"

"Yes. Yes, of course. I'll speak to Mother." He seemed desperate to grasp onto my perceived agreement. Either John was too hopeful to realize the mockery in my tone, or he thought his involvement had gone unrecognized.

"Would you have her write letters to all of her friends? Explaining I'd recovered from my nervous ailment at our prior separation. And now that I was again your betrothed, they'd be free to associate with me instead of cutting me at every society function. Is that how you'd do it?" My tone, which had started out as calm yet condescending, regretfully spiraled into outraged somewhere toward the end.

Thankfully, John realized I was aware of the role he'd played in the manipulation of my life. He could no longer meet me gaze, instead staring at the floral carpets, hands on hips.

"How could you, John? You *knew* it was important to me. How dare you go behind my back and alienate me and force your agenda—"

"I'm sorry!" he exploded. "I just wanted you to come back. I thought… I thought if you needed me, you'd return, and we'd marry."

"I see." And I did. I saw John for what he was. Sad and fraught. Perhaps a little lonely. And not above using two sisters to reach his desired outcome. He was a spoiled aristocrat, a product of his environment. And despite what he said, he didn't love me. That wasn't love.

Love wasn't about control or expectations. It didn't have an agenda. One shouldn't have to plot and scheme to validate their love.

Quinton was not above fighting dirty to get what he wanted, of that I had no doubt. But the difference between Q and John was that Quinton would never force his hand at my own expense. I knew that. He wouldn't bring me down to build himself up. John, on the other hand, needed to minimize me in the eyes of society to achieve his own ends, when I was already diminished just by breathing. Keeping me dependent made sense to him in his limited capacity to understand love. John wanted to bind me to him. Quinton wanted our marriage to be a partnership and a means of freedom.

In his effort to find passion and companionship with someone who resembled June, John had settled for me. I hadn't followed my initial instincts where John was concerned. He'd called me endearing and refreshing, and I'd foolishly believed him and thought him sincere in his words and his suit. Perhaps that was why I'd been so skeptical of Quinton initially. I didn't trust that a man could really want me in all my oddities. Maybe I'd always question the motivations of others.

Apparently my sister only wanted John's money, and I had only wanted a comfortable life. John used me to fill a role, and in a way, I'd done the same to him. With that in mind, I turned to the crestfallen man at my side and gentled my voice but said with conviction, "I wish you happiness in the future with whomever that might be… but it won't be me."

The following morning broke bright and hopeful. After the awkward and enlightening conversation with Lady Bexley yesterday, followed by the slightly more awkward and enlightening conversation with John, I felt a sense of closure. John finally understood and accepted my position. I wouldn't insult him in public, but being polite didn't mean I had to be friendly. With so much between us, I didn't think friendship would be appropriate any longer.

My exchange with John made me even more resolute in my decision to marry Quinton. The thought of marrying for love made my stomach give a hopeful swoop. I could still have a future and make it my own. But it could be even better if we made it together. Having a partner who not only valued but sought out my opinions made the prospect of marriage all the more enticing.

My discussion with Lady Bexley also made me optimistic that my other former clients would return as well. And even if they never materialized, the possibility gave me confidence nonetheless. There was nothing quite like feeling competent in your abilities. I couldn't wait to tell Quinton. I was ready to focus my attention on the future. Our future.

It felt like even the weather was on my side as the sun shone through the curtains.

I dressed with care, selecting a lovely ensemble in shimmering emerald green. The matching slippers were rather extravagant for a day at the Piker House office, but I didn't care. I wanted my inner optimism for the unknown future to be reflected in my outward appearance today. And nothing says hopeful naïveté like a woman in gorgeous but uncomfortable shoes.

Mr. Stevens was waiting for me as I entered the library midmorning. "Good morning, Jane."

"Good morning, Mr. Stevens. How do you do?"

"Quite well, thank you. I have your new contract. It's ready for your signature."

Brows wrinkling in confusion, I asked, "My new contract?"

"Yes," confirmed the solicitor. "Q had me draw it up yesterday in all possible haste. It outlines your duties moving forward and ensures your position as accountant for Piker House. The contract safeguards your position should the gaming hell ever change ownership, additionally it will never alter based on your marital status. All funds procured through your employment shall remain your own in the designated account. Basically, should you desire it, and as long as Piker House has paying customers, you shall have gainful employment overseeing income, debts, patron accounts, and so forth."

Why my brain fixated on one particular topic, I didn't know. "Is Q planning on selling Piker House?"

Mr. Stevens's gray eyes looked at me with concern, and he answered slowly, "Not to my knowledge." He guided me to our shared desk and we both sat before he continued speaking, "This is a good thing, Jane. It ensures your place here is protected should anything ever change." He speared me with a meaningful look.

Oh.

"Oh," I echoed my thoughts aloud. "You mean if my relationship with Quinton doesn't work out," I confirmed.

My officemate's eyes softened and he smiled. "No, Jane. I meant for when you and Q decide to marry. Your position will be protected and nothing would have to change. You wouldn't be expected to be merely the wife of the Earl Sullivan. You could still be yourself."

Oh.

Q had had a contract drawn up to solidify my place at Piker House, to preserve my independence separate from him. Because he knew how important it was to me. He understood. He took my worries and tried to create a solution to ease my anxiety. When had someone ever sought to do that for me? I couldn't remember a time.

Throat unexpectedly tight, I swallowed hard before speaking. "Where do I sign?"

~

LATER THAT AFTERNOON, the weather had turned. Dark clouds gathered menacingly and forced the sun away. We'd had to light the lamps due to the darkness brought on by the approaching storms.

I still hadn't seen Quinton. I was eager to talk to him, to thank him for his gesture. I wanted to confide in him regarding Lady Bexley's visit and our renewed agreement as well. So it was a stroke of luck when Daniel entered the library with a smile and a greeting for myself and Mr. Stevens. I hoped that meant Q was nearby as Daniel seemed to generally accompany Q or at least be aware of his friend's whereabouts.

Removing his hat and smoothing his brown hair, Daniel turned to the solicitor. "Q would like to see you at five o'clock. He has a meeting in his rooms shortly, but should be free by five to speak with you"—with a sly glance in my direction, he finished his statement—"about the matter you discussed yesterday."

Mr. Stevens nodded in agreement and Daniel bid us good day and quit the room, heading in the direction of the stairs. If Q had a few minutes before his next meeting, perhaps I could catch him quickly and thank him for the contract. Maybe steal a kiss.

I hopped up and swiftly made my way to the door. "I'll be back shortly, Mr. Stevens." He waved me off with a knowing grin.

Moving quickly down the hallway, the plush carpets cushioned my steps and muffled the sounds of my approach. I heard voices coming from the direction of Quinton's personal rooms. Slowing my pace, Q's voice made its way to my ears. I couldn't determine the words, but his tone was bored, apathetic. I could imagine the unaffected face he wore.

It seemed I'd missed my opportunity and his next meeting had already begun. I started to turn back to the library when a woman's voice floated down the hallway. Frozen by the familiar sound, I listened for a moment before resuming my path to Quinton's rooms. Pace slow and measured, I listened to my sister say something about clients. Her voice was similar to my own, but whereas I could occasionally sound robotic in my cadence, her delivery was all husky seductress. Tools of the trade, I would imagine.

Without conscious intent, my feet carried me to the open doorway and found Quinton seated in an armchair with his back to me. June was lit by the muted gray light from the unadorned window and stalked toward Q with a tumbler in her hand. I knew it was wrong to eavesdrop, but I didn't trust my sister.

"I think a collaboration would be quite beneficial for both of us, Lord Sullivan," she purred as she stood directly in front of Quinton's sprawled form. Unease worked itself into the pit of my stomach.

"I'm content with our current arrangement, Lady Morrison," came his indifferent reply.

June smiled slyly and tsked. "Now, now, Q. You know I prefer Lady Juniper." And with practiced ease, she slipped one leg between Quinton's spread thighs and straddled the other before lowering herself to his lap. My sister raised the glass of amber liquid to her lips and looked directly at me before smiling and taking a drink. I stumbled back a step, my heart hammering in my chest.

Quinton's posture was no longer relaxed. He'd straightened as she'd eased so smoothly into his space. But I couldn't stay to see what happened next, to bear witness to whatever was happening between them. I felt sick. Disgusted by what I'd seen.

Even knowing I'd vowed to face my problems, muscle memory and my protective instincts instructed my feet to carry me out of danger, to defend my fragile heart, and escape the pain before me. I heard raised voices from behind me but couldn't acknowledge them over my thundering pulse, nor could I focus on the implications of the scene I'd fled. I could only move forward. Time collapsed as I hurried toward the stairs. The hallway narrowed in my field of vision and I was vaguely aware of passing Mr. O'Connor and another gentleman. I evaded the newcomers in the hallway and kept moving.

In my turmoil, all my actions and emotions became simplified. Down the stairs, heart pounding. Out the door, breath sawing in and out. Around the garden, eyes blurry. Along the cobblestones, cheeks wet.

I didn't know how long I'd been walking, unaware of my surroundings in a trance-like state. But when thunder cracked overhead and the skies opened up, I stopped and turned my face upward. Rain pelted down from the heavens in cold, heavy droplets. The clouds gathered and darkness descended.

How strange that just this morning everything had been different. I'd been so optimistic, so ready for this new chapter of my life to begin. And now look at me. Shivering in a rainstorm, panicked and confused, green slippers covered in god knows what.

Considering the scene I'd just witnessed, I reflected on the idea of Q and June. Yes, they worked together, in a way. And I had caught June on the third floor once before. Had she been there for a liaison? I'd never found Quinton's name in the brothel's ledgers, but perhaps all of his appointments had been off the books. I'd known all along Quinton was a rake. But, god, why did it have to be my sister? But, no. Surely he would have told me. It would have been too easy for me to find out. June would have taken great pleasure is throwing a relationship with Q in my face.

My mind was battling with itself, considering and discounting theories at maximum speed.

Everything changed because of one moment involving my sister.

My sister.

June.

Perhaps I didn't know Q as well as I should, but I did know my sister. June was aggressive and selfish. And she'd seen me in the hallway outside Quinton's rooms. Looked right in my eyes when she'd made her move. June had known I was watching, and she had manipulated me. I'd failed to see what her visit to the Finley residence actually was… A warning. And the scene before me today was the consequence.

What was I doing? I knew better than to run from my problems, and yet I was behaving like a fool. I'd run once before and nearly been killed by cutthroats because of my oblivious negligence. I was not doing that again. Refusing to put myself in harm's way and terrify my friends, I looked at my surroundings. I wasn't as far from St. James's and Piker House as I'd thought. Spinning on my ruined green heel, I turned back in the direction of the gaming hell and hardened my resolve. I wouldn't make a rash decision that could change my entire life because of one person.

The rain was coming harder now as I slogged through the flooded sidewalk, cursing myself and my stupidity. I would confront Quinton and my sister. I would figure this out. I would be a logical, rational human, dammit.

I just had to make it back.

The rain was blinding and my clothes were drenched, but I was determined.

Swiping my hair out of my eyes, I continued on. Nearly there now.

I hurried toward the intersection, arranging my thoughts and my plan of attack, when an arm snaked out from the alleyway and pulled me within.

Twenty-Four

"Can ye be a good girl now? I'll uncover yer mouth, but ye have to promise not to scream." The voice was coaxing and a little grating, like the speaker strove for charming but his aim wasn't quite true. Like charming's older oafish brother: impetuous.

I nodded jerkily, rainwater running into my eyes. I wanted to scream for help; it was instinctual. Knowing I wasn't so terribly far from Piker House gave me the illusion my voice alone would send help running my way. But logically I knew we were still some distance from the gaming hell, the storm was muffling all sound, and at this time of day there wasn't likely to be a guard on duty to hear my call for help. So I kept my mouth shut.

The large man who'd carted me into the alley was somewhere between twenty-five and forty-five. It was often difficult to tell with men who'd lived a hard life. The signs of drink and vice reflected on his skin and teeth, and his eyes were predatory and assessing. I could tell from the man's clothes that he'd attempted to emulate the appearance of a gentleman but fell short once more. He looked like a businessman or proprietor of some sort at first glance, but upon examination, one could see the cut and fit of his clothing did not lend itself to the higher quality typically possessed by men of that station.

Nevertheless, he was large and dangerous and held me at knifepoint.

"Imagine me surprise when one of me boys here reported Madame Juniper leaving her lair." He indicated his man with a thumb over his shoulder. "I thought to meself, that's a stroke of luck, innit. We were following ye to have a chat about our mutual friends when low and behold, ye came right back to us." As the leader spoke, he pulled me under a balcony in the narrow alley. Here the rain lessened and I was no longer swimming in the deluge.

I spotted the man he'd indicated at his back as well as two other men farther down the alley, blocking the rear exit. I pressed my back to the bricks in an effort to appear smaller and escape the continued rain.

"I'm not Madame Juniper. I'm afraid you've made a m-m-mistake." My teeth were chattering with cold and made speaking a challenge. I could hear the waver in my own voice from fear. If these men thought I was June, god knew what they'd do with me.

The leader laughed in good humor and looked to the man closest to him. Prompted by his employer's notice, he joined in and chuckled along with his boss. "That her, Eddie?" he asked the laughing man who I now recognized as the man from Mayfair, the bald bowler-hat-wearing gang member. If that man was here, then the leader in front of me must be…

Seamus.

"That's her. She was wif Q for a little stroll in Mayfair last week," confirmed Eddie.

"Mayfair," chortled Seamus. "That's a bit out of your jurisdiction, innit? Those toffs don't usually want their whores in the same neighborhood as their wives."

"That's because I am not June—Juniper. And I live in Mayfair, hence my presence there. My name is Jane. I am not who you think I am," I attempted to explain again.

Seamus scrutinized me, but before he could refute my claim, we heard footsteps rapidly approaching at a fast clip. My captor moved swiftly and wrapped an arm around my waist, pulling my body flush to his. With my back plastered to his front, he brought the knife up to my throat.

And that was how Quinton found me when he entered the alley with both Daniel and Mr. Stanley at his heels. My chin trembled as they quickly took in the scene.

Q's eyes snapped back to mine and I could so easily read the banked fury in his features.

"Just the man I hoped to see," Seamus called out.

"Oh, feck me," came Daniel's muttered curse.

"Shut up, Danny. Take Stan and get the feck out. I need to talk to Q." Seamus tightened his hold on my waist. "Seems we have a mutual friend here. Juniper can help the negotiations go more smoothly."

"Seamus, you feckwit, that's not Madame Juniper. That's Jane," Daniel said.

Seamus turned me to presumably get a better look, but he didn't withdraw the knife. I squeaked a little at his manhandling and he glanced over his shoulder to Eddie in the alleyway beyond. "Yeah, well Eddie says he saw this here bird with Q up in Mayfair. And then here she is right outside Piker House. I think I'll take me chances. I don't really care what J name she's got. From the look on Q's face, she means something, and that's good enough for me. She can get me what I want."

"What do you want, Seamus?" Fists clenching at his side, Quinton's hard tone and manner promised violence.

"There's a ship coming tonight. I need yer men to offload the shipment to me warehouse. There's too much for just me boys. The bobbies have been coming 'round more and I need this job done fast and quiet. So I'm going to take this fine lady here with me down to the docks as a little insurance. Ye bring yer men tonight to do the job and she'll go free back to her brothel or back to Mayfair or wherever. I don't really care as long as I get that shipment."

Quinton's stare was calculating. I knew he and his men were reluctant to attempt a rescue due to the knife held firmly at my throat. I was trying not to swallow or move, but I could feel the panic in my limbs. I was shaking all over.

"Seamus, you feckin' eejit. Find someone else to steal your shite. We don't want part of that anymore. We already told ye," Daniel said from the mouth of the alley.

"Q, does me brother speak for you now? Should I slit her pretty throat or are we going to do this the easy way?" Seamus asked.

"Fine," Q's voice was low and dangerous. "I'll get my men and we'll meet you at the docks."

"See? Was that so hard?" Seamus smiled and flung his hand out to the side. As the knife moved away from my neck, I deflated and a large breath rushed out of me. My muscles ached from the tension of trying to hold perfectly still. I thought I might collapse.

I looked to Quinton, grateful for his acquiesce. He'd agreed to Seamus's terms for me. He was putting his men at risk to save my life. When I focused on Quinton, some twenty feet away, flanked on either side by foul-mouthed Daniel and the stoic and reliable Stanley, he wasn't looking at me. In fact, all three men were staring slack-jawed beyond me to the far side of the narrow passage.

Seamus and I turned in tandem to see what had drawn their attention.

I blinked. Then I blinked again.

At the rear exit to the alley, one of Seamus's men inexplicably lay face down on the cobblestones. As we watched, an attacker dressed solely in black took a running leap toward the brick surface of the wall, rebounded, and pushed away to land a devastating kick to the head of the other henchmen. Eddie, who had been positioned between Seamus and the two cutthroats guarding the rear exit, began moving toward the black-clad figure.

Seamus and I, and presumably Quinton, Daniel, and Stanley as well, stood in astonishment as the fighter faced off with Eddie. In the space of a moment, the mysterious vanquisher had felled Seamus's other employee. The individual moved so quickly and fluidly, I felt like I was watching a performance. The unknown fighter danced to and fro before delivering violence with their slight form. The figure wore close-fitting dark trousers, a slim-cut black shirt and a black rain-soaked scarf wrapped around their face, obscuring all but their dark eyes. A boy's flat cap completed the mysterious ensemble.

The skilled fighter was much smaller than Eddie, but he or she—it was impossible to tell which—circled the large man with confidence. Finally, after a series of whirlwind moves, likely some form of acrobatic combat style from the East, Eddie collapsed in a heap.

This small savior straightened from the three men littering the alleyway before looking directly at me and nodding. I didn't know who and I didn't know why, but this person had come to my aid. Those brown eyes… I squinted and took a step closer. My rescuer backed away at once before turning and sprinting for the narrow alley wall. They took one, two, three steps up the brick before reversing in midair and grasping the balcony overhang. Quickly and effortlessly, they pulled themselves up and over the side before disappearing through the window and into the building.

I stared after them for a moment longer before remembering the villain at my side. I spun toward Seamus. He gaped up at the balcony with the knife still in his right hand. I reared back and kicked Seamus in the knee as hard as I could with my pointy green slipper before dashing toward Quinton. Q was already moving, catching me up and wrapping his arms around me. Daniel and Stanley moved swiftly to subdue Seamus. Before I could even process or worry about the incapacitated men in the lane behind me, Quinton had scooped me up and moved determinedly toward Piker House.

The rain had finally let up I noticed as we splashed through puddles along the cobblestones. I felt so very tired all of the sudden as the energy from the encounter with Seamus threatened to flee my body all at once. I wrapped my arm around Quinton's neck and sagged against him. His hold around my shoulder and under my knees tightened in alarm before he whispered, "Jane, are you all right? Are you injured anywhere?"

I shook my head, unable to find my voice. Teeth still chattering from the cold and rain, I snuggled closer to the warmth emanating from Quinton's form.

"Come. Let's get you inside and warm you up." He looked down at me then as if finally giving himself permission. The worry and tension on his face nearly broke my heart. He smacked a desperate kiss on my forehead before pulling back, his stride closing in on the gardens outside Piker House. "And then I'm never letting you go."

"My fingers look like raisins. I think it's safe to get out now," I insisted.

"Your lips are still tinged blue. Five more minutes," Quinton countered.

I sighed but relaxed back into the copper tub, steam rising from the surface as the fire blazed nearby. My long legs were bent but the tub in Quinton's washroom was surprisingly roomy and allowed me to recline my upper body along the back edge where Q had thoughtfully placed a towel to cushion me.

Quinton had entered the kitchens with me in his arms and immediately started issuing orders. Servants had drawn a bath to warm my chilled body in which I had remained in Quinton's quarters for the last twenty minutes under his lordship's watchful eye.

He was seated in a chair, chin resting on his fist as he examined the dried fruit-like texture of my fingers. Gently cradling my hand as he smoothed the tender skin of my palm, Quinton's gaze cut to mine. "Are you sure you are well? You're remarkably calm for someone who was kidnapped and held at knifepoint."

I raised a brow in his direction. "I told you before. I'm exceptionally good at compartmentalizing. Did you expect me to swoon? You know I find it undignified."

Quinton squeezed my hand in warning. "You know what I mean. You could have been hurt or killed. Because of me. Because of who I am."

"No, because of who you *were*," I corrected. "You've changed and your business has changed. It's not your fault Seamus can't take no for an answer. And after the London police raid his shipment tonight on the docks, we won't have to worry about him for quite some time."

Q was visibly frustrated. "It's not enough. I want—I need to be worthy of you, Jane. I need to be safe so I can keep you safe. If that means I sell Piker House and we relocate to the country, then I think it's something to consider."

"Now wait a minute. I don't want to live in the country. Well, not all the time. I have a life in London, as do you," I argued.

Q finally nodded but did not drop his intense gaze from my own. "And what you saw before… Jane, you must know I would never touch your sister."

I looked down at the swirling soapy water, shame tightening my throat. I hadn't forgotten about the scene in Quinton's sitting room in all the commotion and attempted kidnapping, but I figured we'd get around to the incident with June eventually. Not that I was terribly eager to do so.

Q put a finger under my chin and tilted my gaze up to his. "She barged in and said she had an urgent matter to discuss regarding her clients. June made up some nonsense about working more closely together before she climbed into my lap. I imagine that's what you saw before you raced down the hallway past Daniel. He was escorting Mr. Jephram, my afternoon appointment and the man I've hired to manage Piker House in the evenings. Anyway, Danny realized something was wrong with you and hurried to get me. He found me covered in whiskey after I pushed your sister off my lap." I looked to his cravat and white shirt. Both were soaked through from the rain but were also stained a brownish amber.

With a small voice, I replied, "I know you wouldn't touch her. I was on my way back to talk to you and figure out what June was up to. I'm sorry I ran, but I was coming back."

Quinton nodded at my admission. "Do you trust me, Jane? I would never hurt you. I swear it."

"I know. I do trust you. I should not have fled the way I did. I knew my sister wanted to keep me away from you and Piker House. I feel so foolish for falling into the trap she laid. And if I'd remained, Seamus wouldn't have been able to grab me. None of this would have happened." My voice had grown very small and emotion threatened. I sniffed rather indelicately.

Quinton released my hand and leaned up from the edge of the tub to cup my face in his hands. "Shhh, it's okay. You're not to blame. You were manipulated. I want you to know, I could never want a marriage like those among the *ton*. I have no desire for a mistress. I just want you, living your life freely. No golden cages. You should continue your work, if that's what you want. We could raise a family together, if you'd like that." He paused to stroke my cheeks before sliding his hands through my wet hair. "I know I'm not perfect. I'm bossy and controlling. Demanding and stubborn. But I know I could very well be perfect for you." I smiled at the sweetness of his statement. "And I know you're not perfect either."

Well. That, I was not expecting.

Quinton's lips twitched, undeterred by my sudden frown. "You find trouble at every turn. You're truly terrible at embroidery, and this mouth." He brushed his thumb gently over the profanity-spewing body part in question before pressing on. "But you're perfect for me as well. I know at one time you sought companionship and complacency, but, Jane, we could never be merely content together."

He leaned close and kissed the corner of my mouth before saying, "We could be everything."

I smiled against his lips and used my wet hands to pull him closer before whispering, "I love you, Q."

He pressed his mouth to mine once before drawing back. "I love you, too."

Quinton reached in the now tepid water and soaked his sleeves to the shoulder as he hauled me out against him. Placing me gently before the fire, he attempted to dry my body with a linen towel as my hands and lips roamed before finally succumbing to distraction. I removed his ruined shirt and the remainder of his rain-soaked clothing, and we spent the next hour warming each other.

Much later, as I lay in Quinton's arms, I thought about the uncertainty we'd face. I could ask myself a thousand questions about where life would take us, but as long as we faced it together, our future seemed a manageable thing. I didn't have a plan for being the wife of a future duke, but I had the love of one. I had faith everything else would fall into place.

Epilogue

One Month Later

"Jane, do you or Lord Sullivan have a preference for the wedding breakfast?" Mary inquired before listing off a large number of food options.

I began shaking my head almost immediately. "No, Mary," I said, gently interrupting her recitation of breakfast meats. "Truly, you can pick whatever you think is best. Q wants me to be happy and I'd be happier if I wasn't planning this wedding."

The assembled ladies laughed. Mary smiled warmly before making a note on her list. My lovely and formidable friend was happy to jump in on the wedding preparations once I'd made it known the planning brought me nothing but misery. I wanted to *be* married to Quinton, not suffer through the process. I'd known Mary was exceptionally organized with unrivaled tastes. Truthfully, I'd felt nothing but relief when she'd offered her assistance.

Having no mother available to assume the responsibility of planning our nuptials, Quinton and I had been rather at a loss. Neither of us had strong feelings one way or the other regarding anything: flowers, location, garb, guests, and, most recently, the breakfast. When two people in decision-making positions have little to no opinion on any of the topics at hand… Well, nothing gets done. I'd finally conceded at a Tuesday meeting several weeks prior that I was overwhelmed and cranky as a result of our inability to move forward in our wedding planning progress. I didn't want to elope to Gretna Green. Ashleigh and Cassandra both contributed *that* helpful alternative to planning a large *ton* event. But I believed Mary would be able to strike a lovely balance. I was actually getting quite excited for the big reveal. I couldn't wait to experience the wedding she'd planned for us.

Currently, it was a dreary Tuesday afternoon in early December at Fiona's London home. We were entertaining several topics and many biscuits. My upcoming wedding just before the holidays was merely one of the items on the agenda. All the ladies would be in attendance, and I was so grateful for the support.

When news of my engagement to Lord Sullivan reached the scandal sheets, I'd felt overwhelmed, but I'd come to learn the only opinion that mattered was my own. I didn't owe strangers or acquaintances anything, much less my worry over their eager eyes and whispered conversations.

Most of the nosy busybodies were keen for gossip, their intentions clear. We received a large number of invitations to society events, and four more of my former clients had called or written requesting my services once more. Each request had come with a barrage of questions regarding the mysterious Earl Sullivan and, at times, genuine well-wishes for our future happiness. I'd been able to resume my role as a consultant for these women as well as maintain my position at Piker House. In truth, my duties were less strenuous now with the ledgers fully translated, and all known debts and clients identified. My current task of maintaining the accounts moving forward didn't require nearly as much time. However, I still enjoyed sharing the library office space with Mr. Stevens. And the occasional long luncheon with Quinton made the workday rather agreeable.

Cassandra grasped the newspaper with surprising aggression before smoothing the pages. "Did you ladies see the recent theft from Umberland House? There are few details, but apparently the robbery occurred during Lady Vega's ball last month."

Fiona shifted forward on her chair, peering across the low table laden with refreshments toward the inked parchment in Cassandra's grasp. "Does it say what was stolen?"

"Not at all. Merely… Let me find it," Cassandra said, before quoting from the article. "'Valuables which are irreplaceable to the countess and earl in residence.'"

"Odd," was Fiona's only reply. Her brown eyes narrowed on the newsprint before her.

Ashleigh reached over and plucked the paper from Cassandra's outstretched hands. Focusing her attention on the side opposite, she then held up the print in my direction. "Isn't this the theatre yer Lord Dashing is taking ye to this evening?"

I squinted at the black and gray picture. The words above them did indeed reflect the name of the theatre Quinton and I would be attending tonight. "Yes, that's it," I confirmed. The image itself must be an artist's rendering of the lead in the play. I wasn't familiar with the actors, but I enjoyed the theatre. Quinton was due shortly to join us for a cup of tea before whisking me off to our event.

I felt Eliza stiffen next to me and suck in a startled breath. Immediately, I turned and saw her staring at the newspaper held aloft by Ashleigh. We were squished together on the small couch near the fire, so it was unlikely anyone else noted her strange behavior.

"Eliza, what is it?" I asked quietly as the conversation resumed and none of the other ladies were looking in our direction. She didn't answer, merely continued gazing at the space where the paper had been. Ashleigh had already tossed it aside, losing interest. "Are you well?" I attempted to draw Eliza's attention once more with my whispered words. In truth, she looked suddenly very *un*well. Her distant stare was glossy and her face had gone utterly white. She looked as if she'd seen a ghost.

Finally registering my words, Eliza's attention snapped to mine. "Yes. Yes, I'm sorry. I'm fine." Her fingers trembled as they rose to pat a loose blond curl along her collarbone.

I frowned at my friend's obvious distress, but if she didn't wish to discuss it, I wouldn't force the issue, especially in a room full of people. Eliza loved and valued the friendships of all of those assembled, yet she was a woman with a seemingly untouchable history at times. I often felt like we only saw the Eliza she wanted us to see. Perhaps she'd tell me when she was ready.

Before I could ruminate on Eliza's odd reaction, Quinton walked into the room with a nod and greeting for the ladies present. Fiona rarely stood on ceremony and seldom had her guests announced, especially on Tuesday when so many of us were in attendance. Q was able to sneak in with little fanfare which rarely happened when he was a visitor in someone else's home. He was still getting used to the ladies, my friends and chosen family. He'd confessed that they were so different from the only other feminine influence in his life up to this point. Quinton's sister Rochelle Jameson was undoubtedly more reserved in her displays. I couldn't imagine anyone being as honest and amusingly forthright as Ashleigh Winstead. Nor did I anticipate the daughter of the Duke of Benton to be as outspoken and outrageous as Cassandra Fields. Quinton required time to adjust to the unique personalities of my friends.

Perhaps one day they would go easy on him.

"Lord Dashing! You made a wise decision in escorting our dear Janie to the theatre. I know most nobles prefer the opera, but Jane is too good for those trol-lopera singers," Cassandra finished with a wink in my direction.

Today would not be that day.

Quinton's frown was confused, but he nodded at Cassandra. He glanced down at me questioningly as he reached the armchair at my side. I smiled and shook my head as he leaned over to kiss my cheek. "Don't ask."

Q's lips quirked before turning back to Cassandra. "You know, you can call me Q. All of you," he said to my friends. "Or Quinton if you prefer."

Mischievous and knowing grins were the only answer he received until Fiona took pity on him. "Of course, Q. You're well, I hope?"

My betrothed seemed relieved that the duchess was addressing him. Fiona was the most compassionate among us. And normal. She was the least outspoken and Quinton seemed to appreciate that about her. "I am well, thank you. Has Compton returned to town?"

Fiona looked a bit dejected when she responded, "No, I'm afraid Gregory's business in the country is keeping him longer than expected." She straightened from her seat and smoothed the peach muslin of her day dress. "If you'll excuse me, I'm going to check on Grace. She was giving the nurse some difficulties this morning." With that, she moved toward the door. There was a small hitch in her step, but she seemed to catch herself and moved as smoothly as possible from the room. That was odd. I wondered if there had been some sort of accident or fall to cause my friend to be so unsteady on her normally graceful feet.

I turned to Quinton who had scrutinized Fiona with a thoughtful frown as she exited the room. Before I could speak, Eliza poked her head around my side and examined Q. Seemingly recovered from her earlier stricken behavior, she asked rather flippantly, "So have you decided where you're taking Jane after the wedding?"

I opened my mouth to answer but Quinton beat me to it. "Jane and I have decided," he said pointedly, "to travel the continent for a month following the wedding."

Eliza waited a beat. "And upon your return? Do you expect Jane to reside in rooms above a gaming hell?"

"Eliza," I admonished. She widened her eyes innocently as if this inquisition was not meant to find Quinton lacking in some way. Attempting to provoke him and chide him in front of our friends was not going to end well. As if he were dragging me away on a honeymoon of his choosing with no input from me. And to insinuate that living above stairs at Piker House was somehow unseemly. Eliza's protective instincts were manifesting in odd and mysterious ways.

Quinton took my hand and gave it a squeeze before replying to my friend. "We've actually been touring homes available for sale in Mayfair." With a glance in my direction, he continued, "And I think we've found the perfect one."

Straightening in my seat, I turned my full attention to Quinton. "How did the meeting go?"

With Eliza's demands forgotten, Q gifted me a small smile. "Stevens is finishing up all the paperwork. The Randolph estate is ours."

My joy was overwhelming. I faced my friends, happy to share the details of the home that would be ours.

After some time, Ashleigh cut in, "Jane, yer giving us the dimensions of every room. Tell us what ye love about it."

I shook myself from my exuberant descriptions, noticing a small visual standoff between Eliza and Quinton. Each assessed the other with eyes narrowed.

Sigh.

I could see we'd have to work out some sort of arrangement. I wanted my two favorite people in the world to be on good terms with one another, not constantly in battle for my time and attention. Because between Eliza and Quinton… I didn't know who would win. Both could be incredibly resourceful in getting what they wanted.

I rolled my eyes at their dramatics before turning back to Ashleigh. "I guess… I suppose what I love about it is that I can see myself there. I can envision the home it will be for Quinton and myself. I look at the hearth in the family room and see us gathered for Tuesday embroidery. I picture the dining room at Christmas filled to bursting." Facing Q, I continued, "And I can see us there. Partners in marriage and happy in life." Quinton squeezed my hand once more.

The world quieted and the murmurs of my friends fell away as they continued discussing perfect homes and abundant gardens.

I smiled at my betrothed, noticing the line of his jaw, his masculine beauty that stole my breath and stopped my heart. How lucky was I? To have found love, a partner, and a future after all.

He leaned close then and whispered, "What are you smiling about?"

My smile grew. "Just thinking how lucky I am. How happy you make me."

Quinton gave me a curious look before replying, "Jane, I'm the lucky one. From the moment you stumbled, quite literally, into my life with your ruined dress and foul language." I released his hand to whack his shoulder.

He smiled wide and grabbed my hand again. "I mean it. I'm the luckiest bastard in London to have your love." Quinton turned over my palm and kissed the center before hauling me to my feet. "Do you believe me?"

I nodded. Because I did.

I may not have grown up knowing what love looked and sounded like. But I knew it now in so many different ways. It was being surrounded by the people in this room. The admiration in Quinton's gaze that made me feel utterly seen. His touch on my skin and the resulting swoop in my stomach. And the whisper in my heart that said *you belong to each other and together you belong.*

Acknowledgments

To Emily: thank you for being the voice in my head when all my doubts get in the way.

To Nicole: thank you for giving me confidence that I didn't know how to claim for myself. And for the best reaction email…ever.

To Shan: thank you for fostering the story in my heart and listening to ridiculous VMs about where that story was going.

To Penny and Fiona: thank you for not killing me after that Maury Povich paternity reveal phone call.

To my husband: thank you for facilitating and enabling late nights reading and writing, supporting something that probably still surprises you, and for showing me every fucking day what happily ever after looks like…laundry and all. I love you. I love you.

About the Author

Laney Hatcher is a firm believer that there is a spreadsheet for every occasion and pie is always the answer. She is an author of stories that have a past, in a language of love that's universal. Often too practical for her own good, Laney enjoys her life in the southern United States with her husband, children, and incredibly entitled cat.

Find Laney Hatcher online:
Facebook: https://bit.ly/3s6KnuY
Newsletter: https://bit.ly/3sUGwAk
Amazon: https://amzn.to/3IaOwU7
Instagram: https://bit.ly/3s4IRcS
Website: https://laneyhatcher.com/
Goodreads: https://bit.ly/3BD0Gme

Find Smartypants Romance online:
Website: www.smartypantsromance.com
Facebook: https://www.facebook.com/smartypantsromance
Twitter: @smartypantsrom
Instagram: @smartypantsromance
Newsletter: https://smartypantsromance.com/newsletter/

Also by Smartypants Romance

Green Valley Chronicles

The Love at First Sight Series

Baking Me Crazy by Karla Sorensen (#1)

Batter of Wits by Karla Sorensen (#2)

Steal My Magnolia by Karla Sorensen(#3)

Fighting For Love Series

Stud Muffin by Jiffy Kate (#1)

Beef Cake by Jiffy Kate (#2)

Eye Candy by Jiffy Kate (#3)

The Donner Bakery Series

No Whisk, No Reward by Ellie Kay (#1)

The Green Valley Library Series

Love in Due Time by L.B. Dunbar (#1)

Crime and Periodicals by Nora Everly (#2)

Prose Before Bros by Cathy Yardley (#3)

Shelf Awareness by Katie Ashley (#4)

Carpentry and Cocktails by Nora Everly (#5)

Love in Deed by L.B. Dunbar (#6)

Dewey Belong Together by Ann Whynot (#7)

Hotshot and Hospitality by Nora Everly (#8)

Love in a Pickle by L.B. Dunbar (#9)

Checking You Out by Ann Whynot (#10)

Scorned Women's Society Series

My Bare Lady by Piper Sheldon (#1)

The Treble with Men by Piper Sheldon (#2)

The One That I Want by Piper Sheldon (#3)

Hopelessly Devoted by Piper Sheldon (#3.5)

It Takes a Woman by Piper Sheldon (#4)

Park Ranger Series

Happy Trail by Daisy Prescott (#1)

Stranger Ranger by Daisy Prescott (#2)

The Leffersbee Series

Been There Done That by Hope Ellis (#1)

Before and After You by Hope Ellis (#2)

The Higher Learning Series

Upsy Daisy by Chelsie Edwards (#1)

Green Valley Heroes Series

Forrest for the Trees by Kilby Blades (#1)

Parks and Provocation by Juliette Cross (#2)

Story of Us Collection

My Story of Us: Zach by Chris Brinkley (#1)

Seduction in the City

Cipher Security Series

Code of Conduct by April White (#1)

Code of Honor by April White (#2)

Code of Matrimony by April White (#2.5)

Code of Ethics by April White (#3)

Cipher Office Series

Weight Expectations by M.E. Carter (#1)

Sticking to the Script by Stella Weaver (#2)

Cutie and the Beast by M.E. Carter (#3)

Weights of Wrath by M.E. Carter (#4)

Common Threads Series

Mad About Ewe by Susannah Nix (#1)

Give Love a Chai by Nanxi Wen (#2)

Key Change by Heidi Hutchinson (#3)

Educated Romance

Work For It Series

Street Smart by Aly Stiles (#1)

Heart Smart by Emma Lee Jayne (#2)

Book Smart by Amanda Pennington (#3)

Smart Mouth by Emma Lee Jayne (#4)

Lessons Learned Series

Under Pressure by Allie Winters (#1)

Not Fooling Anyone by Allie Winters (#2)

Out of this World

London Ladies Embroidery Series

Neanderthal Seeks Duchess (#1)

www.ingramcontent.com/pod-product-compliance
Lightning Source LLC
Chambersburg PA
CBHW030621310726
48979CB00003B/819

* 9 7 8 1 9 5 9 0 9 7 4 7 1 *